CW00872105

Seven Plates at the Table

by Denise Waldron

All of the characters in this book are fictitious, and any resemblance to actual persons, living or dead, is purely coincidental. The names, incidents, dialogue and opinions expressed are the products of the author's imagination and are not to be constructed as real. The events in this book are entirely fiction and by no means should anyone attempt to live out the actions that are portrayed in the book.

www.californiatimespublishing.com

Prologue

THE WAITING ROOM is tired, its furniture ill-fitted and worn, its overhead lights dimmed in spots, its tiled floor spotted with well-scrubbed but still visible stains. The fluorescent lights emit their characteristic buzz. A television silently displays its tedious cycle of round-the-clock news to the room; they muted its sound hours ago. There is a faint smell of bitter coffee from the cups, not quite finished, that have accumulated in the trash bin. The seats are comprised of hard-edged dark wood and tightly upholstered cushion; no one remains in the same position for long. An almost-empty tissue box sits on the low coffee table among the month-old magazines chirping “The 6 Sex Moves He Likes Best,” and “The Best Chocolate Mousse Cake Ever.” No one reads them. Rarely, a nurse or doctor scurries by, but it is in the hours before dawn and the hospital is quiet. This is not a city hospital where a constant stream of barroom brawlers, drug addicts, and gunshot victims come through at all hours. When they first arrived they saw people come and go, but now it has been hours since they’ve seen anyone. One of them wonders if it’s wrong to wish for company in a hospital waiting room.

They hear a door open. Seconds go by and they hear the door close quietly, pulled shut by a hydraulic arm. Faint footsteps approach, slow deliberate footsteps. The family unknowingly holds its collective breath. They want the footsteps to walk on by, if the news is bad. They desperately hope the footsteps will stop, and tell them the news is good. A man with sallow skin, brown eyes, and deep lines around his mouth stops at the entrance to the waiting room. He is still wearing the blue surgical cap from the operating room. His white doctor's coat hangs fresh on him, but it is the only thing about him that isn't tired. He sees the intense hope and fear in all of their eyes. He hates this part of his job. He takes a deep breath, exhales, and shakes his head, saying, "I'm so sorry."

Chapter 1

GRETA ASCENDED THE wide stone stairway leading to her son's capacious front porch, knocking snow onto the carefully swept steps. Large columns flanked the staircase, two lonely wicker chairs stood sentry to one side, and a small table set just so between them bore a bowl of gourds and a spray of dried grasses. Even the porch, she thought, looked ready for a magazine.

George stomped up beside her and banged the large brass knocker on the grey front door. They waited, their breath fogging little pockets of air as they exhaled. It was below freezing, and she wished they could just walk in. It was Thanksgiving, after all, and they were expected.

Greta glanced at her husband, his left arm holding the heavy red casserole dish full of sweet potatoes, a bag of her homemade potato rolls clutched in his right hand. Shivering suddenly, she said, "George, just open the door." She worried the cold air would wilt the expensive bouquet of flowers she was holding for her daughter-in-law. She'd made a special trip to the florist for the small but elegant bunch of calla lilies and roses.

"Isabel has made it clear that we're to knock," George replied, shaking his head, rapping the door with the knocker again.

George let out a frustrated breath and banged his fist against the door a few times. Greta sighed and pulled her fleece scarf tighter around her neck. Her sturdy black wool coat usually kept her warm but there was a chill wind today and she was grateful for the scarf, as garish as it was. George, who didn't usually notice anything she wore, had made a face when he saw the lime green and yellow fabric with harsh streaks of red, but Isabel had given it to her and she wanted to show her appreciation. It was an unusually cold Thanksgiving Day and she considered pulling the scarf over her head, which she had foolishly left uncovered. She hoped she wouldn't be receiving a matching hat for Christmas. Pressing gently against George both for companionship and warmth, she said, "Remember you promised to be nice today."

"I'm always nice," he said.

"I mean you're going to spend time with everybody, not find excuses to fix everything in sight."

"All my tools are at home, which is where we should be," George said.

This was the first Thanksgiving they'd had since they'd been married that wasn't in their own home, and Greta was as sad about it as George was, although he'd been expressively grumpy all week, whereas she'd pretended to be happy about it.

"They really wanted to christen their new house with a holiday meal this year," she said, trying to comfort herself as much as George. She felt like she was saying goodbye to something but she didn't want this day to be a sad one for herself or anyone else. She inhaled briskly and said, "They deserve to do that, just like we did at their age. They certainly have a big enough kitchen for it," she added, thinking of her own modest kitchen and how crowded it usually was on Thanksgiving. She would miss the camaraderie of the close quarters but she continued hopefully, "At least we won't be stepping on each other's toes."

George grunted. "I'm going to spend the day with Henry. He's easy to get along with, unlike the rest of them."

"George," Greta warned, "comments like that aren't going to help."

When George didn't respond, Greta asked, "Why don't I ring the bell?"

George shrugged and said, "I'll do it." He lifted the bag of rolls and punched the doorbell with his thumb. It made no noise, only a strange buzzing sound that seemed to be coming from the outside wall rather than from inside the house. He shook his head and muttered, "Damn thing's still broken," pounding the door again with his fist, adding a few bangs with the knocker for good measure. "If you can't hear someone knocking on your front door, your house is too big."

"Didn't you fix the doorbell last month?"

"I told Alan how to do it. He should remember; how many years did that kid spend in the workshop with me? Shouldn't take more than twenty minutes."

"Just because he watched you work when he was a child doesn't mean he's as good an electrician as you are."

"Flattery will get you nowhere," he said. "Where the hell are they? It's colder than a witch's tit out here."

Greta winced; her husband only used that phrase when he was irritated, and she wanted today to be special, a day when they were all happy together. "Really, George, what if Henry's on the other side of the door?"

"If he is he should be opening the damn thing."

Greta could hear movement, finally, inside the house. "How do you know how cold a witch's tit is, anyway?" It was her response every time he said it, designed to cheer him up.

"You really want me to answer that?" George said, a half-smile on his face, as they heard the deadbolt unlatch.

The door swung open and George saw Isabel, one arm behind her like a game show hostess, rattling a jumble of bracelets as she waved her hand. He thought the jewelry looked like rejects from a metal factory, but Greta said most of Isabel's things were made by her arty friends and that he shouldn't criticize.

"George! Greta! Please, come in! Isn't it cold out?" Isabel asked with a pretend shiver. "I really had to bundle up for my run this morning." She practically pulled George, who had stopped to inspect the hinge of their front door, into the house with one nail-polished hand, and relieved Greta of her bouquet. "How nice. What pretty fall colors," she said, adding, "Let me hang up your coats." George spied the wrought iron side table across the cavernous foyer, looked down at his overshoes covered in snow, and opted to lower the casserole dish and the rolls onto the Italian slate floor that had taken some fancy contractor three weeks to install, when he could have done it in one. He handed his coat to Isabel just as Boo, their black Labrador, came loping into view, his bottom half wriggling so much that it was slowing him down. George swept up the casserole and rolls before Boo could get to them, and stood helplessly as his crotch was enthusiastically greeted by the damn dog. "Boo, no!" Isabel commanded, which the dog ignored completely. Greta, having extricated herself from her coat and switched from boots to shoes, reached down and dragged Boo away by his collar seconds before George was going to knee it in the ribs.

"Al!" Isabel called sharply. "Get Boo out of here!"

George felt a wave of irritation wash over him, but clamped his mouth shut. He didn't like the way she talked to Alan, like she was his boss, or worse, his mother. He felt a bit of satisfaction that his son did not immediately do her bidding, although he would have been relieved to see Alan. He never knew what to say to Isabel; he was always afraid he'd put his foot in it. He glanced at her hanging up the coats, chatting with Greta, who was still wrestling the crazy hound. Putting down the casserole and rolls once again, he grabbed Boo from Greta and marched the dog to the front door. The dog's official name was Bruiser but like everything else in this house, he was emasculated to Boo.

"That electric fence still working?" he asked, hand on the doorknob.

"Yes, but—" Isabel started, but he interrupted her with "This dog needs to run around, not be stuck in a box," and opened the door. Boo flung himself onto the porch and skittered down the stairs, tearing around the front yard like a greyhound at the track. Satisfied, George closed the door and turned to Isabel, who was looking at him with a concerned expression on her face.

"He'll be all right," George said. "Dogs are meant to be outside running around."

"Yes, I know, it's just that we're still crating him, and … well, it doesn't matter," she finished, shrugging and putting a smile on her face. "Why don't we all go into the kitchen?" She nudged their overshoes aside with a pointy-toed boot, knelt down and picked up the casserole dish and rolls before George could get them, and headed for the kitchen. George followed Isabel, staring at her high-heeled black boots as she clipped across the floor. He didn't know how women could walk in those things. She was wearing a short tight skirt and some crazy shirt with weird colors and shapes all over it; she had one earring down to her shoulder and a bunch of little ones on the other ear. Remembering Alan's neat, pretty, normal college girlfriend with a sigh, he squinted as he entered the kitchen.

The room was blazing with sunlight owing to the enormous window overlooking the back yard. George had warned them about heat loss but they'd said it wasn't a problem what with the new windows on the market, and they'd also installed radiant heat in the floor. His son had put a lot of money into this big fancy house, money he got as a financial manager, whatever that was. Alan had tried to explain it to him more than once; apparently a financial manager could make quite a bit if he managed the right people's finances. Good thing, because even though Isabel put in a full week's work as a fundraiser, she didn't make much money off it. George thought she should be home with Henry anyway instead of having Greta run over here all the time. Still, he couldn't quite believe this house belonged to a relation, much less his own child.

"Thanks so much for these flowers, Greta," Isabel said, opening a glass-fronted cabinet to retrieve a vase, "they're beautiful." She filled it with water and plunked the flowers into it, then began spreading them around and fluffing them up. When she was satisfied with the way they looked she placed it on the giant slab of granite countertop that housed her kitchen sink. George noticed she had a tremendous bunch of flowers already sitting on her kitchen island. He knew Greta would be disappointed; she had specifically asked Isabel if she could bring flowers, even dragging him along to the flower shop instead of picking them up at the grocery store, and now she'd probably be feeling snubbed. Sometimes she was too sensitive about Isabel, but he couldn't tell her that or she'd just get more upset.

"So where's our favorite grandson?" he asked. Henry was his pride and joy, a respectful five-year-old who was fascinated by all things mechanical. He loved watching his grandpa work, whether it was on a lamp, a clogged sink, or a car tire. George figured if he lived long enough he could give his business to Henry.

"Hankie is upstairs putting on his special Thanksgiving clothes," Isabel said.

George opened his mouth to speak, but Greta elbowed him in the ribs. Every time he heard "Hankie" he thought of a woman fluttering a handkerchief, and it wasn't right. But he'd promised Greta, so he cleared his throat and asked, "What kind of clothes is he getting into?"

"Oh, you'll see. It's a surprise! But make sure to tell him you like it, because he picked it out himself. Let me see if they're ready," Isabel said, and headed for the back stairs off the kitchen.

"Think he'll be dressed in a bunch of hankies?" George asked Greta, turning to look at her and leaning back against the counter.

She smiled and then shook her head. "I don't care if he's wearing a dress, you be nice. You don't want to hurt his feelings."

"No, ma'am. Although at a certain point you have to toughen a boy up. And if he ever wore a dress I'd take it off him in a heartbeat."

"He's not going to be in a dress, for God's sake," Greta said testily, and George knew he better behave himself. Greta rarely snapped at him.

"I was just joking," he said contritely, and she rewarded him with a smile as they both heard excited little footsteps skittering down the stairs.

"Grandma! Grandpa!" Henry yelled as he crashed through the doorway and ran headlong toward Greta. George saw a blur of bright blue and yellow before Henry disappeared into Greta's open arms. He sure stood out against Greta's beige and brown outfit.

"Hi, sweet pea!" Greta said, holding him to her

and kissing the top of his little blond head.

Henry pulled away and plunged into George, who thumped the boy's back a few times and allowed him to cling for a moment. He'd tried shaking his grandson's hand once when the boy turned four and Isabel had scolded him, telling him you were never too old for a hug. True if you were hugging a woman, but men didn't hug. Still, the boy was only five, and he didn't mind waiting a few more years before laying down that law.

"Come see my Lego's!" Henry said, pulling back, grabbing his hand and tugging on him. "I built a house with them, and it has a door and two windows."

"Hankie!" Isabel said disapprovingly, having just appeared in the doorway. "Grandma and Grandpa just got here. Let them visit with us for a little while. And show them your Thanksgiving clothes, honey."

Henry's little shoulders had sagged when Isabel first spoke, but the offer to show off his clothes seemed to cheer up him and he stepped into the middle of the kitchen and twirled around. He was wearing dress pants, dress shoes, a button-down shirt, and a vest, which was already a little much for George, but he was also wearing a bow tie. A flowery knitted bow tie.

Greta broke the silence with, "Well, those are nice bright colors, Henry. It looks homemade."

Homemade like a kindergarten project, thought

George.

"It is!" said Isabel. Everyone turned to look at her, and she continued, "One of the clients at the women's shelter I've been working with made them for me as a thank-you. She made four, so George, we have an extra one for you," she added, picking up a small carefully wrapped box from the kitchen counter.

George accepted the box reflexively. He sure as hell didn't want to wear a bow tie like Henry's, but he'd promised to be nice. He stood staring at the box for an uncomfortable moment until Greta rescued him.

"Isabel, that's so thoughtful of you. And I'm sure Grandpa will love to have a bow tie like yours," she said to Henry. "But Grandpa doesn't have the right shirt on for a tie, so he's not going to wear his right now." She looked at Isabel again. "But thank you, dear, we really appreciate it." Removing the lid from the box that George was still holding, she peered inside and said, "Make sure to thank the woman who made them, too."

At that moment Alan appeared behind Isabel. Relieved to see his son, George said, "Those are some nice clothes, Henry," and patted his grandson's head as he walked past him to shake hands with his son.

"Son, how are you?" he asked, extending his hand. As Alan stepped out from behind Isabel,

George noticed for the first time that his son, who resembled him physically, barrel chest and all, was dressed identically to his grandson, right down to the same silly bow tie. He stifled a laugh into a throat clearing. Alan took his hand and shook it firmly but met his eyes only briefly.

"Nice to see you, Dad. How are you?"

"Can't complain." And suddenly George had had enough. The bow ties had tipped him over the edge; Greta would surely understand. He bent over, clapped his hands on his thighs, and said, "Well, champ, you have some Lego's to show me?"

Henry's eyes lit up and he ran out of the kitchen, calling behind him, "Come on, Grandpa!"

With an apologetic smile George said, "My boss is calling," and hustled out of the kitchen. With any luck he could stay in Henry's gigantic playroom until the turkey was ready. The big screen TV in there was just begging for a football game.

Greta accepted a kiss on the cheek from her son as she watched her husband scurry out of the kitchen. George was not a man who believed in doing women's work but Henry had brought out a tender side of George she'd never seen before, and although she knew he'd have that giant television on, she also knew he'd be playing with Henry's Lego's and whatever else Henry dragged out onto the floor. Henry was their first and only grandchild and he was growing up just fine, already like a little adult owing to the fact that he didn't interact with other children much. He took piano lessons and attended art and yoga classes during the week, and he played occasionally with a little girl in the neighborhood, but she thought Henry would benefit from having a little brother or sister.

Greta wondered often if Alan and Isabel planned to have more children but never wanted to ask; she didn't want Isabel to think of her as nosy or interfering. She wished Isabel would talk to her more, but her daughter-in-law seemed to appreciate her most when she was babysitting Henry. Greta had hopes for this Thanksgiving, though. Alan had promised not to work for even a minute that day, George had sworn off any home repairs while they were there, Isabel had gotten her exercise in early, and Emily was scheduled to arrive midday. They would finally have a chance to spend a nice bit of time together.

"When is Emily supposed to arrive?" Isabel asked, interrupting her own thoughts.

"She said she'd be here by noon," Greta replied.

Alan laughed. "If she said noon, she'll be here by two."

"She promised she'd be on time."

"Two hours late is on time for her," he said.

"Now, Alan, that only happened once and it was out of her control," Greta said, purposely smiling. She knew Alan was trying to get a rise out of her.

"She got a flat tire."

"Yeah, and normal people call AAA. But who's she going to call, the American Bike Association? What are they going to do, send out a tow bike, and she'll jog alongside until they find some eco-friendly fix-it shop that trades repairs for fresh eggs?" Alan shook his head. "She doesn't even have a cell phone, for God's sake, and we were two hours late to my own company party."

Greta quickly put a stop to his complaining. "Alan, I don't want to hear a peep out of you about Emily today. You're both adults—"

"One of us," Alan muttered.

"—adults, and I expect you both to behave that way. Understood?"

Alan glanced at Isabel briefly and then bowed his head towards Greta and said lightly, "Yes, Mother dear. I promise not to say anything mean to my little sister."

"Thank you."

"And having made that promise, I must select some wines for dinner," he said, raising a finger and giving her his best conciliatory smile. "I'll be in the cellar." He turned abruptly and disappeared down the basement stairs.

When Alan left the room, Greta felt a small tension creep into the kitchen. Isabel always seemed guarded around her. Greta couldn't imagine why; she went out of her way to be nice to the girl, babysitting

Henry all the time, cooking for them, picking up around the house. Isabel had the equivalent of a full-time job with her work fundraising for various needy groups. Isabel told Greta that all she did was ask rich people for money, but it was admirable, and Greta had told her so many times. At any rate, Isabel spent a lot of time talking to people on the telephone and meeting them for lunch or dinner, and Greta was happy to fill in for the times Isabel wasn't at home; it made her feel that somehow she was helping those unfortunate souls as well. But whenever she and Isabel found themselves alone in a room, which was rare, there was a strain to their relationship, and it bothered Greta.

Hoping to fix that today, too, she kept her tone light and asked, "Is there anything I can do to help you?"

"No. The turkey's in the oven, and the stuffing and broccoli casserole are ready to go in. You brought the sweet potatoes and rolls, and Emily said she's bringing a pie," Isabel replied, tapping off the items on her fingers. "I think we're ready."

"Could I help you set the table?"

"Oh, no, I did that last night."

"My goodness, you've done a lot of work already. Why not let us help you when we're all together?" Greta felt like she was at a restaurant.

"I didn't want to be stuck in the kitchen cooking. This way we can relax and not have to work so hard,"

Isabel finished with a shrug and half a smile.

They stared at each other for a moment. If there were no chores to do and Henry was occupied, Greta wondered what Isabel had planned. Was it possible that she felt like Greta did, that they should get to know each other better?

"Would you like a cup of tea?" Isabel offered.

"Yes, thanks, I'd love one," Greta smiled, pulling out a stool from the counter.

She watched as Isabel took a mug from the cabinet and opened a beautiful wooden box that she kept on the counter. "What kind would you like?" she asked.

"Anything's fine."

"Earl Grey, English Breakfast, Irish Breakfast, lots of herbal varieties, green, white," Isabel said, fingering through the packets.

"Really, I'll take anything," Greta said, but seeing the look of expectation on Isabel's face, she said, "Do you have any Red Rose?"

"Is that black tea?" Isabel asked, furrowing her brow. When Greta nodded, Isabel said, "I think Organic Black is the closest," plucking a tea bag and dropping it into Greta's mug. She pressed a spigot at the sink and water steamed into the mug, which she presented to Greta with a spoon and a small plate for the tea bag. Greta wondered if Isabel was having coffee instead.

"Well, I really should help Alan pick out the

wine. He's good with the reds but at a complete loss with the whites."

"Oh," Greta said. "I like white wine."

"I'll make sure to pick out a nice bottle, then," Isabel said. "Why don't you go visit with Henry for a little while? He's been talking about you all morning."

"All right," Greta said. She loved her grandson but she saw him several times a week. Still, she had plenty of time later to visit with Alan and Isabel, and she probably should check in on George. Greta steeped her tea bag for some time before discarding it and heading upstairs.

***

Their basement was finished and as elegant as any other room in their house, but as Isabel opened the door into the climate-controlled wine cellar she was struck once again by its beauty. She had grown up solidly middle-class, and although she had occasionally seen the inside of a rich kid's house, she had never seen a wine cellar until she had one of her own. The door clicked behind her as she ran her hand along the smooth dark mahogany racks glowing under the recessed lights; one rack was constructed like a staircase to showcase certain labels. An arrangement of crystal decanters sparkled beneath a small spotlight. There was a tasting table in the center of the room, and that's where Alan was now, already almost finished with a glass of red wine. She frowned slightly, but he didn't see; he was pouring her a glass as well. Rearranging her face into what she hoped was a neutral expression, she accepted it and they clinked.

"Cheers," he said, smiling. "Let me know what you think."

She swirled the glass, smelled the bouquet, sipped and tasted the wine carefully, just like he'd taught her. "It's lovely," she said. "Balanced." Repeating the process, she asked, "Blackberry?"

"Yes!" he said, and she was pleased she'd guessed it right. Years ago they'd learned a lot about wine, attending tastings, reading wine magazines, but she'd stopped when she was pregnant with Henry. Now her interest in it was disappearing as much as Alan's was growing.

"Is this what we'll be drinking with the bird?" she asked.

"Mm-hm. I have a dessert wine too, and I picked up a port the other day that my dad will love with a cigar."

"Isn't he supposed to be cutting those out?"

Alan made a face. "Mom's already got him eating rabbit food twenty-four/seven and walking every night after dinner. A little fun isn't going to kill him."

Isabel shrugged and twirled the stem of her

glass. She thought Alan sounded a little too flip, but he sounded that way a lot these days, and when she criticized him he descended to the wine cellar and stayed there. With Greta and George in the house she knew Alan would be on his best behavior, but she didn't want to push it. Looking around the room, she saw a wine that Alan had brought home a few weeks ago; she remembered the abstract blue, red and green painting on the label. She thought he'd bought a case of it, but she only saw six bottles; he must have gotten a mixed case. She couldn't keep up with all the wine he bought; he did it online now, and spent hours researching before he made his purchases.

"My personal wine expert," she smiled, tipping her glass towards him and bowing her head.

"Always here to help," Alan replied, pouring himself another glass, the lighting casting a downward shadow from his long lashes.

Isabel was careful not to react to the second glass of the afternoon. Quietly she set her wine down and said, "Shouldn't we be entertaining our guests?"

"I need a minute down here," Alan said. "They drive me crazy."

"I really don't understand why, Alan. They're always nice. You know they love you."

"Yeah, I know." He sighed and drank some wine. "They just don't like me."

"That's crazy! Of course they like you!"

"I don't mean they dislike me, they just … I'm

not the same as them. Any of them." He took another gulp of wine and set his glass down.

"I don't understand," Isabel said. "In what way?"

Alan shrugged. "I don't know. I guess I've always felt a little left out, you know? My dad works with his hands, my mom was always artsy-crafty, and now Emily's got a farm. When I was a kid they used to call me The Math Geek, and they never understood what I was into, the Dungeons and Dragons, the computer games. And now they talk about me like I have three heads. So how can they really get me if they don't know what I do for a living?"

Isabel was silent for a moment. Finally she said, "They may not understand what you do for work, but that doesn't mean they don't like who you are as a person."

"Okay, maybe I overstated it a little. But I do feel like I was adopted or something. I just don't fit in."

"I'm so sorry you feel that way," Isabel said. She picked up her wine glass and took a healthy swallow. She felt awful for Alan, but she wasn't quite sure what to do about it. Meanwhile his family was two floors up and they were hiding in the cellar.

The dutiful hostess kicked in. "I really should check on Henry."

"He's with the most doting grandparents in the world," Alan said. "Stay with me a bit." He grabbed the bottle of wine and topped off her glass.

Isabel smiled. It was true; Greta and George hung on Henry's every word, captivated by his every move. She wouldn't mind a few quiet moments with Alan. She realized with a small sadness that it wasn't often anymore that Alan requested her company, unless he needed her appearance at a work function. "Sure," she said, accepting the glass again.

Today she could probably use a few drinks anyway. Isabel thought Alan and his sister Emily had never outgrown a ferocious sibling rivalry, George rarely said a word, and Greta was always watching her like she was a rare species at the zoo. It was all Isabel could do to keep everyone entertained and she couldn't escape to the wine cellar like Alan. She was in charge of this family gathering and she desperately wanted it to end well for once.

"Why are you frowning?" Alan asked. "Things are going well, don't you think?" She knew he was trying to reassure her; she'd kept him up last night obsessing about Thanksgiving Day.

"Yes. So far. Your mother was giving me funny looks again in the kitchen. Why doesn't she like me? She hates that I work, doesn't she?"

"God, Isabel, no, my mother doesn't hate you. I'm pretty sure she thinks you dislike her. Personally I think you're both insane. I can see why my father stays out of everything," Alan said, a small smile softening the impatience of his comment.

"I'm sorry. It's just that I don't want anyone

going home with hurt feelings this year."

"I know, babe." Alan drained the rest of his wine, put the glass on the tasting table and stared at her for a moment. "You look great in that skirt," he said, his eyes traveling to her thighs. "Come here."

Pleasantly surprised, Isabel moved toward Alan. He took her wine glass and put it down next to his, pulling her to him and kissing her, once softly and then more forcefully. She could taste the wine and smell his cologne; it had been a long time since they'd spontaneously kissed each other. Alan's breath quickened and the response excited her; sometimes she wasn't sure if he still found her sexy. She felt such a tug of desire at the thought that she ground her hips into his, and discovered that he was as excited as she was. They remained locked together until Isabel, who normally insisted they wait until Henry was asleep before having sex, shocked herself by unzipping Alan's fly. He pulled back and looked at her, a question on his face which she answered by stroking him. He groaned and reached under her skirt. With practiced moves they caressed each other until after several frenzied minutes they slumped against each other, breathing hard. Isabel felt warm, utterly relaxed, and for a blessed short time she'd forgotten about everything except Alan's body. He kissed her forehead and she looked up at him. His eyes looked sleepy like they always did after sex, his long lashes shading his lower lids, and his thick black hair uncharacteristically out of place as if he'd just gotten out of bed, but there was something else there too, a spark of playfulness she hadn't seen in a long time.

"Can you believe we just did that?" Isabel whispered.

"Happy Thanksgiving," he answered softly with a smile, helping her skirt down over her hips and grinding into her once before zipping up his pants. "We should try every room in the house."

"Right now?"

"Yeah, we'll tell my parents to take Henry on a nice long walk."

"Maybe we could use some time alone, Alan. Your mother's offered to take Henry for a long weekend so many times."

Alan grunted. "I can't just take a day off whenever I want."

"What if we tried to plan it for a few months from now?"

"Maybe."

Isabel paused. 'Maybe' was as far as she'd gotten in a while trying to convince Alan to go away with her. He seemed to think that if he took a day off his entire office would collapse, although he had two partners who seemed perfectly competent.

"You know where I've always wanted to go?" Alan asked. "The Poconos."

"The Poconos?" Isabel repeated, not sure if he

was joking.

"Yeah, I want to go there and get a crazy hotel room with a heart-shaped bed and a bathtub shaped like a champagne glass. And I want to get you drunk and take advantage of you all weekend. How does that sound?"

Isabel laughed, as much at Alan's sudden silly mood as at the idea. "Sounds great!" she said.

"Okay, I'll talk to my mother about it today," Alan said, moving to the tasting table, refilling his glass and topping off hers. "Come on, we better go up or they're going to wonder what happened to us."

"I think we both need to tidy up first." Isabel said. "Your shirttail is sticking out of your fly." He grinned at her and her heart lifted; her mind was swimming from the sex, Alan's lighthearted mood, and the wine. She could see why Alan had a few glasses to relax every night; the prospect of Thanksgiving suddenly wasn't so daunting.

***

Isabel and Alan emerged from the basement bathroom refreshed and neat, hair in place, clothing tucked. They carried their wineglasses upstairs and as they stepped onto the first floor Isabel could hear from the second floor the sounds of a football game interspersed with Greta talking and Henry giggling. She didn't want to go up there just yet, though; she wanted to check on the turkey first. “I’m going to go baste,” she said to Alan.

He nodded, saying, “I hear barking. Is Boo outside? Aren’t we supposed to be crating him?”

“Yes, your father threw him out before I could stop him.”

Isabel heard Alan walking down the hall to the front door as she stooped to baste the turkey. It was beginning to brown nicely and the root vegetables she’d strewn around it smelled delicious. She was a little dizzy when she stood up; she wasn’t used to having two glasses of wine in the middle of the afternoon. “Isabel!” she heard Alan call and headed to the front door, where she found him staring out one of the sidelights.

“What are you doing? Is it Boo?”

“No, it’s Emily,” he said. “Look at her.”

Isabel peeked out the other sidelight and saw Emily rolling on the ground, wrestling with Boo. Bits of snow were stuck in her hair and she was laughing loudly, Boo barking and flinging himself on her repeatedly, his tail wagging so forcefully his whole body seemed to wiggle. “What a nut,” Isabel said.

“You’re being kind,” Alan said. “She’s certifiable.”

“I was talking about Boo, actually,” Isabel said, shaking her head. She really didn’t want Alan getting upset with Emily today although lately the mere mention of Emily’s name was enough to set him off.

"My mother asked us to dress up today. Look at me! And what's she wearing? Hemp?"

"Do we need to decant the wine?" Isabel asked, hoping to distract Alan.

It worked. "What? Oh. Yes, I should. Want me to use the crystal?"

"Please. Leave the decanters on the dining room table when you're done, okay? Thanks," she said, playfully giving his behind a swat. The wine was definitely lowering her inhibitions.

As soon as Alan left to get the crystal decanters Isabel grabbed a scarf and slipped outside. She would try to get Emily inside and presentable before Alan reappeared. When Boo heard the door open he looked up, and spying her he broke away from Emily and bounded up to Isabel, who turned away from him and said sternly in a low register, "Off!" She didn't want him soiling her clothes, but more importantly she didn't want him knocking people over with his enthusiasm. He braked, turned, and raced back to Emily, who'd arisen and was busily brushing the snow off her clothes. "Hi, Emily!" Isabel called from the steps, realizing belatedly that boots would have been more practical than the scarf she'd grabbed.

"Hi, Isabel," Emily called. "You're about to kick the dessert."

Isabel looked down at her feet, which were indeed just to the left of a brown box with twine wrapped around it. She picked it up, wondering what it was, as Emily joined her, red-faced, slightly out of breath, and obviously invigorated.

"I left my bike leaning against the garage door. You guys won't be going out, will you?" Emily asked.

"No, of course not! How did you ride here with the snow?"

"I took my mountain bike," Emily said.

Isabel heard a slight impatience in Emily's voice that reminded her of Alan and she urged Emily inside to get her things off. Isabel put the pie on the table in the foyer as Emily unwound two scarves from around her neck and shoved them along with her gloves into a pocket, kicked off her boots, and pulled from another pocket a pair of black ballet slippers, which she tossed on the floor. She dragged her fingers through her curly brown hair, the same color as her mother's minus the grey, flicking the remaining bits of snow onto the ground and settling it back down on her head. Emily was lucky, Isabel thought, that her hair was curly enough to withstand the complete lack of styling. The woman even cut it herself when it started to hang in her eyes, but somehow it always looked fine.

"What kind of dessert is it?" Isabel asked.

"Vegan cheesecake," Emily said.

"Oh. Well, that's interesting. Does it come with fruit?"

Emily laughed as though Isabel had made a joke;

Isabel chose to ignore the misunderstanding and merely watched as Emily unzipped and de-Velcroed two jackets. It appeared that Emily was wearing sweatpants of some sort, and she dearly hoped that Emily had brought something to change into, although none of her myriad coat pockets seemed big enough to hold another set of clothes. Perhaps she could lend Emily something, although Emily was shorter and stockier than Isabel. Isabel took Emily's coats and turned to put them in the closet, and when she turned back Emily was standing holding her sweatpants. She was wearing black cotton tights, an ankle-length shapeless brown skirt, and a black t-shirt under an equally unfortunate brown cardigan. Isabel, who had never worn clothing like that even in her hippie phase in college, tried to make a flattering comment: "The color of that cardigan really brings out your eyes."

"Shit brown?" asked Emily sarcastically, and when Isabel wasn't quick enough to hide a wince, she added, "Sorry. Thanks."

"Your parents are upstairs with Henry," said Isabel, "if you'd like to go say hi."

"How is the little dude?" asked Emily. "Still an uptight brainiac like his dad?"

"Emily," Isabel started, angered, but then faltered.

"Sorry again. He's a good kid. It's his dad that's fuc—you know, I think I'm going to go upstairs and say hello now."

Isabel didn't even care that she hadn't been able to mask her anger. She could handle criticism of a grown man but certainly not a five-year-old child. She was still standing in the foyer a few minutes later when Alan emerged from the basement carrying two decanters, the crystal shimmering in the light and glowing from the deep red wine inside. He lifted them to her in greeting and stepped into the dining room briefly to put them on the table. Coming back he looked at her quizzically and asked, "Why are you just standing there?"

Isabel shrugged her shoulders. "Lost in thought. Your sister's upstairs with everyone."

"How is she?"

"Bitter and sarcastic."

"Finally you're agreeing with me?" Alan said, surprised.

"No, I shouldn't have said that." It was the wine talking, Isabel knew. "She's fine; she biked here, played with Boo, brought a dessert, and now she's upstairs saying hello." Seeing the scornful look on Alan's face, she added, "Her mountain bike rides fine in the snow, she's dressed as nicely as she's capable of, and she brought vegan cheesecake."

"Jesus. What do you suppose that'll taste like?"

"Henry and Greta made brownies just in case."

"You've got everything covered, don't you?" he said.

"Let's hope so. Shall we go upstairs and mingle?"

"Could we go downstairs and have another romp in the cellar?"

Isabel blushed slightly and shook her head. "I think it's time to say hi to your family," she said, taking his hand in hers and pulling him along behind her. He dragged his feet like Henry did sometimes, letting the toes scrape the floor and then flopping the soles back hard on the ground, making Isabel laugh as they headed upstairs.

***

"Hi, kiddo!" Emily said, sauntering into the room and scooping Henry from his puzzle table into a bear hug, swinging him airborne for good measure. He was still giggling when Emily deposited him back on his feet and went over to her father, giving him a kiss on the cheek and a squeeze on the shoulder. "How's it going, Dad?" she asked, settling into the spot between George and Greta that her mother had opened up for her.

"Bears are up 10-7," George said.

"How's it going with Dad, Mom?" Emily asked, smiling at her mother. Her mother smiled back and Emily was struck for the first time with the thought that her mother looked older somehow. Maybe it was just a little more grey woven into her wavy light brown hair, pulled back into a ponytail that Greta called a "poor woman's face lift."

"He's fine, much better now that he's on his new diet."

"Does he have regular bowel movements?"

"Jesus, Emily!" George exclaimed, "What kind of a question is that?"

"It's designed to get your attention, Dad. I asked you how you were doing, not how the football team was doing."

"Sorry, Em. You know how I get focused on the TV."

"Yeah, especially when you're visiting Alan," Emily said, and after receiving an elbow from Greta she added for Henry's sake, "and his big-screen TV." She turned to give her mother an apologetic smile but Greta's green eyes were not reciprocating.

"Little ones have big ears," Greta whispered, shooting a glance at Henry.

Emily remembered what her mother had asked, that she be civil this Thanksgiving. "Sorry," she muttered under her breath.

Greta nodded. "How are the goats, honey?" she asked Emily, and Henry's ears were in fine working order because he immediately raised his head and asked, "Did Belle have her baby yet?"

"No, it's going to be a while yet. In the spring. If you're not busy when she delivers, Henry, would you like to come over and watch?"

"Yes yes yes yes yes!" Henry yelled, jumping out of his chair so energetically that some of his puzzle pieces fell off the table. "Oh, no!" he said, immobilized by the spill.

"No biggie, Henry," Emily said, extracting herself with effort from the oversized couch. "We can pick these up in no time." She proved her point and then glanced at the table, asking, "What is this supposed to be anyway? It looks like a lot of pieces."

"It's going to be this when it's done," Henry said, holding up the cover to the puzzle box.

"Two kittens and a ball of yarn, huh? That's cute … wait, five hundred pieces? Isn't that a lot?" She looked to her mother for confirmation but Greta just shook her head.

"It's hard," Henry said earnestly, "because a lot of the pieces are the same color and because they're small, but Mommy says my fingers need to be good motors."

Greta translated, "Isabel believes he should try to improve his fine motor skills. For kindergarten." Her tone of voice let Emily know that further comments were not welcome, so Emily shrugged and squeezed into one of the plastic chairs next to Henry and said, "Let's see what we can do here, Hen. Looks like there's a ball of pink and a ball of blue yarn. You want to try to find all the pink pieces?"

***

How Em could fit into one of those little plastic chairs, much less how Henry's parents expected him to complete a puzzle like that in the first place, George didn't know. Earlier Greta had insisted George try to help but the pieces were too damn small, so he was relieved when Em settled herself into the chair that had previously been occupied by George's left buttock. Em was so easy to deal with, an uncomplicated girl. She was as straight-to-the-point as a man and that was a high compliment as far as George was concerned. Then there was Isabel, just walking in behind Alan, and he never knew what the hell she was really thinking. His wife somehow managed to keep track of what was said, what was meant, and what was understood by all parties at all times. Based on past experience, this was going to be one of those days when Greta would have to explain it all to him on the way home.

"George?" Greta said quietly, interrupting his thoughts. "Could you turn down the sound a little, please?"

That was her way of telling him to pay attention. The remote was still in his hand and he moved his thumb over the volume control and obliged.

"Who's winning?" Alan asked.

"Bears," George said.

Alan nodded. "So, Em, thanks for getting here on time," he said, unsuccessfully hiding his sarcasm.

"I'm always on time unless something comes up, but you're welcome," Em replied, but that's not what her tone of voice was saying. Alan was giving Isabel a what-did-I-say? look; maybe he'd just gotten a kick in the shin.

George was glad Em didn't rise to the bait; ever since that incident a few years ago Alan never missed a chance to ride her about being late. Alan was a little too particular about time, George thought. Never stopped to relax, that boy.

Greta clapped her hands onto her legs and said loudly, "I'm so glad we're all here! Why don't you two have a seat?" She scooted over close to George, making room for them on the couch.

Alan quickly plopped down in his fancy leather armchair, the one given to him by Isabel last Christmas, the one that had its own remote control. It could recline, hold your cup, give you a massage, do everything but wipe your ass. George secretly coveted that chair but after finding out how much it cost he'd never buy one, even though he could afford it. Some things just shouldn't cost two thousand dollars, and a chair was one of them.

Isabel looked at Alan for a moment and then sat next to Greta, crossing her legs at the knee and bouncing that little boot up and down. George thought she must be relieved to get off her feet.

"So, Alan, I see you and Henry are in matching bow ties," Em said, nodding her chin at him. "Is it father-son dress-up day?" Her voice was sincere but there was a definite gleam in her eye.

"It's a handmade thank-you gift from a friend of Isabel's." Alan's teeth were clenched a bit, it seemed to George.

"Hmm. What kind of wool is it?" Em asked.

"Kind?" Isabel repeated.

"Yeah, from what sheep? Do you know? Is it local? Organic? Factory-processed? Made overseas?"

George could see where Em was going but he sure wasn't going to stop her. Not that he'd ever admit it to Greta, who liked things smoothed over and quiet, but he enjoyed the occasional lively argument; it made him feel energetic. He also knew Em was actually trying to pick a fight with Alan; it seemed like their sibling rivalry would continue forever.

"I really don't know, Emily," Isabel said carefully, "but I can find out if you'd like."

"No, thanks. I was just wondering. The origin of goods is always an interesting question, don't you think?" Receiving blank stares from everyone except George, who fixed his eyes on the football game, she continued, "I mean, let's take apples."

"Are we apple-picking?" said Henry.

"No, kiddo, we're talking about apples and where they come from."

"They come from trees," Henry said emphatically.

"Yes, but how do they get from the tree to your grocery store?"

"Trucks."

"Okay, but some apples have a short truck ride and some have a long truck ride. Which do you think is better for the apple?"

Henry considered this thoughtfully for a few moments and then said, "If the apple likes to ride in trucks it should take a long ride. If it doesn't, then a short one." Satisfied with his Solomon-like answer, he turned back to his puzzle.

George smiled a little at that one as Alan, with a smirk on his face, said, "Yes, Em, let's leave it up to the individual apple. Apples should have the right to choose."

Em glared at him and put a hand softly on Henry's head. "Your kid has a good head on his shoulders, Alan. Someday maybe you'll catch up to him."

George could feel Greta stiffening next to him; this was not the type of conversation she wanted.

Alan made a face at Emily. "There's no reason to get mean. Oh, wait, I forgot who I was talking to. I know the point you're trying to make. The apple that gets trucked here from across the country has hidden costs associated with it. Shop local. I get it. Unfortunately that's not the way business works. When the gas gets too expensive, the long-distance apples will get more expensive, and people will buy the local ones, problem solved. By the market, not by you legislating what people can and can't eat."

"I'm not saying people shouldn't eat apples, for God's sake, Alan. I'm just saying people should make smart choices about what they consume, whether it's—"

"Speaking of apples," Greta interrupted, "Henry, did you enjoy apple-picking with Grandpa?"

Henry gave George a sweet shy smile, then nodded. "He's old."

Everyone laughed, and Greta asked Henry more about the orchard and the apples. This led Henry to recount how he and his grandmother had made applesauce, apple pie, and roast chicken with apples. George thought it went on a little long but everyone indulged, and once again he marveled at how his wife had managed to divert the conversation from going over a cliff. When Alan and Emily got started on economics you could pretty much predict one of them would leave the room in a huff. Meanwhile George kept a careful ear on Henry's words, making sure he wouldn't spill their little secret, which was that Grandpa had had a little spill of his own at the orchard. What did he expect, really; he was an old man traipsing up and down uneven hillsides littered with rotting apples that spun your foot if you stepped on them funny. But Greta would have had him into a doctor faster than he could blink, and there was no sense spending money on that when he felt just fine.

Henry had been bribed with a Snickers bar, something his mother didn't allow in the house. George let the conversation wash over him, felt his body sink deeper into the leather couch, and allowed his tired eyes to close. He would rest them for five minutes.

***

Greta sensed George drifting off; his body relaxed slightly against hers and his breathing deepened. Lately he'd been dozing a lot, which was perfectly normal for a man his age but she knew he didn't like to admit that he was getting older. She glanced at him. He still had the strong nose and formidable chin that made him look like he was cut out of stone, and he kept his hair cut close to his head to hide, she suspected, the grey that was rapidly encroaching. Vanity, thy name is not only woman, she thought. George still did fifty sit-ups and fifty push-ups every day and watched what he ate more than she did, and she'd caught him more than once examining his biceps in the bathroom mirror. She was a lucky woman, really; a lot of her friends weren't even interested in their husbands anymore, but she had a definite and frequent yearning for that old body and he was always happy to oblige.

Greta had tried explaining this to Emily once, that physical contact was a necessary part of life, but

Emily had grimaced and said she had plenty of contact with her goats. Goats! They provided Emily with a nice living, selling her goat cheese to fancy restaurants, places with waiters in tuxedos and real crystal glasses. Emily said that local organic food was "the wave of the future" in gourmet cooking, and Greta had joked that she must have been gourmet cooking her whole life because she'd always bought most of her groceries at the farm stand down the street. Emily had surprised her by agreeing, telling her that her cooking was always top-notch, and that she was part of the reason Emily had decided to purchase that goat farm. It had certainly been a surprise when Emily had quit her day job in computer sales, taken most of her savings out of the bank, and bought the little farm way out in the middle of nowhere, with goats, an old pickup, and a complete change of life included at no extra charge.

But where was Emily going to meet a man now? At least in her sales job she'd been traveling a lot, going to conferences, making sales calls. She'd introduced quite a few young men to the family, polite and successful, good-looking and energetic. They'd all been nice enough but Emily had never seemed to click with any of them, and now she was married to that farm, milking goats twice a day and coaxing her cheeses along. It was true she'd met some single male farmers but they all seemed to be more interested in manure than marriage. Greta had tried to fix up Emily with some of her friends' sons but no matter how much her friends talked up Emily, their sons never got past the fact that she was a goat farmer. She couldn't blame them for picturing a wild-haired woman in dirty jeans and mud boots because that was exactly what Emily looked like most of the time, although she could clean up all right, as evidenced by her current outfit. If only she'd put on a spot of makeup, Greta mused, and something a bit more form-fitting, she'd be turning heads.

Emily must have read her mind because she looked at Greta and said, "Mom, do you recognize this t-shirt?"

"No, not really. Is it new?"

"I got it out of the bag you asked me to drop at Goodwill. It fits fine, and there's nothing wrong with it. I also took a few sweaters. Next time let me look at what you're about to throw away, okay?"

"I'm not throwing them away, Em, I'm recycling," Greta said, always sensitive to Emily's comments about wastefulness. "And I know there's nothing physically wrong with those clothes, but they really are out of date," she couldn't help adding helpfully.

"Emily doesn't care what she wears, obviously," Alan said. "I mean, no one's going to see her but the goats. If Dad ever parted with his clothes she could wear dorky jeans and plaid shirts and be just like him. Unfortunately he still keeps clothes from the

Eisenhower era."

"We're not quite that old," Greta said, patting George's thigh fondly; he stirred a little but his eyes remained closed.

"Dad's certainly doing a good impression of an old man right now," Alan said.

"Watch it, Alan," George said suddenly, surprising them all. Opening his eyes and squeezing Greta's thigh, he winked, "You don't know what your mother and I were doing last night."

Alan and Emily groaned loudly in protest, jokingly covering their ears, Isabel and Greta laughed, and Henry wanted to know what was so funny although despite his best efforts nobody ever answered his question. The smell of roasting turkey was beginning to permeate the upstairs. George and Alan turned their attention to the football game and the women talked about a range of topics, none of which set off another argument. Henry seemed to be enjoying his puzzle although he was probably listening to every word the adults were saying, and Greta was the happiest she'd been in a long time.

***

"Pass the gravy, please," Henry said, having shaped his mashed potatoes into an empty crater ready to receive a brown lake. Isabel, sitting to Emily's left at the head of the table, scooted her chair back and said, “I’ll do it, honey bunny,” but Emily said, “I’ve got it, Isabel,” and handed it to Henry, who was seated on her right. He took it with both hands and carefully poured a puddle of gravy into the little crater, and Emily said, “That looks great, Henry,” but she heard Isabel’s intake of breath when Henry handed the gravy boat back to Emily and it dripped onto the white tablecloth. The few times Henry had been allowed to stay at the farm she gave him free rein, and he loved independently doing some of the easier chores. Pouring the gravy was nothing compared to feeding the goats, but of course Emily didn’t care if some of the feed spilled.

“Where did you get this lovely centerpiece?” Greta asked, fingering the collection of autumn fruits and dried grasses tucked in among small candles scattered along the center of the table, and effectively distracting Isabel from the stained tablecloth. Greta was sitting directly across from Emily and gave her a don’t-rock-the-boat look that Emily chose to ignore. A boat that wasn’t moving wasn’t getting anywhere, either.

“We made it, actually,” Isabel said, obviously pleased that Greta had noticed. “I read how to do it in the paper, and Henry and I put it together yesterday.” She looked at Henry encouragingly.

“I stuck a wire in my finger,” Henry said proudly. “It didn’t bleed much, though,” he added, obviously disappointed.

"But you learned the names of all the plants we used, didn't you?" Isabel prodded.

Henry nodded his head as he dredged cranberries from the sauce and inserted them around his gravy lake. "I like those hiccup berries," he said.

"Hypericum," Isabel corrected.

"It's a nice assortment," Emily said. "I've got some of those berries on my farm. Or something like them. And those straw flowers—one of my friends grows those for florist shops. I could give you a bunch of stuff next time."

"Really? That would be great. Thanks." Isabel gave her a tentative smile.

Emily was somewhat surprised that Isabel was accepting her offer. She seemed unusually mellow today. "Check with me before Christmas; I have loads of holly along the drive and pine trees galore out back. My crafty friends are always 'dropping by' with garden clippers in December." Now Emily was surprising herself, making another gesture of goodwill toward Isabel. She'd stopped doing that a few years back after about the fiftieth rejection.

"Thanks," said Isabel, "I will." She picked up the decanter and offered, "More wine?" to Emily, who lifted her glass with a nod. Isabel refilled Alan's glass and topped off Greta's and George's, then disappeared momentarily into the kitchen to get more grape juice for Henry. When she returned she remained standing and said, "I thought we could go around the table today and each say something we're thankful for."

Emily looked at her with curiosity. What was getting into this woman? Last year Isabel had given an impromptu lecture on teaching kids to read phonetically; this year she was asking them to be a Hallmark family? Interested, Emily took another sip of wine and settled back in her chair.

Isabel shifted on her feet and then said, "I'd like to thank you all for coming today."

Emily thought it sounded like the beginning of a staff meeting, and she probably wasn't the only one because Isabel glanced around the table and then started again. "I mean, I'm really glad we're all together … and healthy … and happy. And … I want to thank Hankie for being the sweetest boy ever," she rushed out, smiling at Henry and sitting down abruptly.

"Yeah, ditto," said Emily. She ruffled the hair on Henry's head and lifted her glass. "Cheers." Say what you would about Alan, the guy sure knew his wine.

Greta frowned at Emily and said, "I would like to thank Isabel for welcoming us into her home, for setting this lovely table, for putting so much time and effort into dinner, and for making such a wonderful family memory for us all. We really do appreciate it, dear." She smiled warmly at Isabel who seemed to blush a little, not that Emily had ever seen her blush before.

“Roger that,” George said through a mouthful of potato roll, winking at Emily.

Alan stood up with his wine glass raised. “I’d like to make a toast. To my father, my mother, my wife, my sister, and my son,” he said, nodding at each of them as he looked around the table. “Happy Thanksgiving.”

They all raised their glasses and then Alan slipped down to the basement for another bottle. When he returned Henry said, “I didn’t go.”

“Go where?” Alan asked.

“To say thank you.”

“Where do you have to go to say thank you?”

“No, Alan, he means he didn’t get a turn,” Isabel said.

“Oh, sorry, little man. Let’s hear it then, what are you thankful for?”

Henry slipped off his chair and stood, his shoulders barely above the table, holding up his little glass of grape juice. “I want to say thank you to Santa for when he brings me my Christmas presents. Especially the purple bicycle.” He drank some juice and climbed into his seat again.

“Purple bicycle?” Alan asked.

Henry nodded. “It’s on my list.”

“But why purple?”

“Because it’s my favorite color.”

Emily saw the look on Alan’s face, one of confusion with a hint of distaste as well. She knew what he was thinking, and she waited with anticipation for him to put his big foot into his bigger mouth. But he didn't say anything, he just looked at Isabel, who shrugged, and they raised their wine glasses to their lips in unison, still staring at each other over the rims. Emily hadn't seen them make eye contact of that duration in years. Something was definitely up, and she wondered if Belle wasn't the only pregnant one around.

Chapter 2

THE SHARP WINTER air highlighted Emily's breath as she stamped along the hard dirt road that comprised her driveway. Her sturdy metal wheelbarrow held a good amount of pine boughs and holly already, but she was attempting to reach a bittersweet vine covered with red-orange berries to add to her collection. Bittersweet was invasive, she knew, and she'd been trying to eradicate it since she purchased the land. Now Isabel was drooling over the stuff, so at least her hard work removing it would be appreciated. Isabel was arriving shortly to make wreaths out of Emily's cuttings.

Emily was somewhat mystified that she'd agreed to this wreath-making event. She was not the flower-arranging type, but she had to admit Isabel's house always had a bit of nature in it and in the winter that was important. The weather had been bitter cold but there was still no snow, so plants were drying up. Her goats spent all their time in the barn, rarely venturing outside. She missed the warmer days when she would take long walks around her property accompanied by whichever goats were in the mood for company. She knew them all by name and they certainly knew her, and they didn't mind the occasional chat either.

Suddenly aware that her phone was ringing, Emily jogged back up the driveway to answer it. She got it on the tenth ring.

“Hello?”

“Emily? Hi, it’s Sharon. Is this a good time?”

“Yeah, fine. I’m just out of breath from running in. What’s up?”

“Out with your goats again or were you experiencing actual human contact?”

“Cutting branches to make wreaths, if you must know.”

“I couldn’t even get you to put up a string of lights in our dorm room,” Sharon said accusingly.

“It’s for my sister-in-law,” Emily said. “She’s coming over to make wreaths and swags and God knows what else.”

“Isabel? The practically perfect sister-in-law?”

Emily laughed at the confusion in Sharon’s voice. “There’s nothing a lot of wine won’t fix. We got drunk together on Thanksgiving and she’s really not a bad person when she’s inebriated. I plan to offer her some wine with dinner.”

“You’re making her dinner and then assembling wreaths? You really need a boyfriend, you know.”

“The goats are my priority right now. I’ve got to settle in first.”

“Emily, you’re settled. Fences up, manure problem handled, grain source identified. Certified organic, fantastic cheese sought out by all the best restaurants. You need to rejoin the human race now.”

“Do you have a cheese-related question?” Emily

asked, annoyed because as usual Sharon was right.

"Okay, I'll stop nagging. Actually I called because I have a guy who wants to meet you."

"Really? After the guy who spoke Klingon and the one who cried during dinner you think I'm going to let you fix me up again?"

"No, it's not a date. It's a fan. This guy loves your goat cheese. He eats at the restaurant all the time, and he wants to buy the cheese retail. I told him it wasn't available so now he wants to meet you so he can talk you into selling him the cheese directly. He's very persistent."

"Did you tell him—"

"Everything," Sharon interrupted. "It's not part of your business model, you don't sell retail, you've been asked before, you're plenty busy supplying to restaurants. All of it. Look, he's a great customer so I can't be mean to him, but you can, and nobody knows how to shoot a guy down like you. You have a natural talent for nasty looks and withering remarks. So can I leave him in your capable hands?"

Emily sighed, staring out the window. It was getting dark and her wheelbarrow was still in the driveway. "Give me his number and I'll call him sometime."

Sharon said she'd e-mail it and they said goodbye. Emily took her lasagna out of the fridge and popped it into the oven, which she'd preheated before she went outside. A friend who owned a vineyard nearby had traded two bottles of his wine for one of her cheese logs. She put a bottle on the table next to the bread she'd made earlier that day and went back outside to finish cutting the bittersweet.

***

"Now are you sure you'll be all right?" Isabel asked.

Greta hoped her smile was sincere as she said, "Yes, dear. We'll be fine. You have a good time and we'll see you in the morning."

"Bye, Mama," Henry said.

"Bye, sweetie." Isabel went to him and gave him his fifth goodbye kiss. "Be good for Grandma. You know I won't be here at bedtime, right?"

"Tell Auntie Emmy 'hi,'" he said, pressing middle C. "Hi," he repeated, trying to adjust his voice to the sound he'd just made. He moved his hand up several keys and tried again. "Bye." That time he hit the note and Greta wondered if he meant to do it. She herself could only sing off-key.

Isabel seemed to be unable to leave Henry, fluttering around the room and going over instructions, and Greta tried to remind herself that although Isabel was gone quite a bit during the day she almost never missed Henry's evening time, which was typically filled with educational activities.

Tonight Greta had arrived to find them at the piano. Alan was on a business trip and bless Emily, she'd asked Isabel over for dinner. Greta was thrilled that the two girls were going to spend some time together. As she'd said to George earlier that night, she'd always thought Emily and Isabel would get along if they just gave each other a chance. George called her Pollyanna; she called him Ebenezer in return, kissed him on the nose, and left him "resting his eyes" in his armchair.

Finally Isabel left the room to put on her coat and get her purse. She returned once more to get a huge canvas bag and give Henry kiss number six, then left. The house seemed to sigh as she shut the door behind her. Greta waited until she heard the garage door close, then sat down next to Henry on the piano bench and asked, "Do you want to play the piano some more?"

"No," he said. "I already did my practicing. Mommy likes me to practice a lot."

"You play very well," Greta said, although as he was only five it was hard to tell.

Henry sighed. "I like to sing," he said. "The piano sings."

"Do-re-mi," Greta said, and he turned to look at her.

"What?" he asked.

"Do-re-mi," Greta repeated, playing C-D-E as she said it. "Those are the names of the notes." Henry was looking at her so intently she had to smile.

"What else?"

"Fa-sol-la-ti-do," she said, playing F-G-A-B-C.

"More," he demanded, and then added, "please."

"Well, I'm no Julie Andrews," she said. "It's been a long time since I played the piano and I really can't sing."

"Who's Julie Andoo?"

Greta looked at him for a moment and said, "Henry, let's go to the library. I bet they have a movie you're going to love."

Henry's face fell. "Mommy is very careful about movies for me. Is it okay with Mommy?"

"Absolutely. She'll love it and so will you. Come on!"

***

When Emily returned with her armload of cuttings she could smell the lasagna. She was quite hungry and hoped Isabel would be on time, which for Isabel meant five minutes early. Leaving the branches on the beat-up wooden table in her living room, she went into the bedroom to change out of her goat clothes. The milking was done and she was tired but a strong hot shower would revive her. She emerged feeling much better, quickly toweled off and ran her fingers through her hair, and pulled on some jeans and a sweater. She would never miss pantyhose, she thought happily. Pantyhose, pumps, meetings, memos … she still got up early and worked hard all day but she had a different feeling when she crawled into bed, a sense that her day had been worthwhile, and she never laid awake worrying. If a goat needed her she was in the barn all night, otherwise she was sound asleep in minutes.

Hearing a sharp knock on the door, she went back into the kitchen and waved at Isabel standing on the porch. Her face looked pinched and Emily hoped it was the cold. As she opened the door Jake slipped in and began tangling himself around her legs. "Next time just let yourself in," she said to Isabel. "You look cold. Would you like a sweater?" She knew her house was drafty and always had extra clothes on hand.

"Yes, actually," said Isabel, unbuttoning her voluminous coat. "I'm sorry, I just have a chill." She dropped a large canvas bag at the door and shrugged out of her coat.

Emily grabbed one of the sweaters off the row of pegs in the kitchen and handed it to Isabel, who took it gratefully and swapped it for her coat, which was promptly delivered to the empty peg. Emily knew from experience that some people did not enjoy great clumps of cat hair on their clothes. Jake meowed as only a Siamese can and she picked him up, but he immediately got down again. He was hungry and had no time for nonsense.

"I'm going to have to feed him or he'll drive me crazy," she said. Isabel smiled and nodded, looking like she was at a party where she didn't recognize anyone. "Would you like a glass of wine?" Emily ventured. Isabel beamed and Emily handed her the wine opener, and soon Jake was crunching happily while the two women each enjoyed a glass of wine. Isabel was surprised to hear that a friend of Emily's had bottled it and even more surprised to learn that they had bartered for it.

"That's what we're doing," Emily said. "Bartering your wreath-making skills for my raw materials. Speaking of which, they're in there," she said, gesturing with her chin. "See what you think. I want to check on the lasagna."

Isabel was still in the living room when she closed the oven door, and Emily went in to find her already sorting the branches into different piles. "This is great," Isabel said. "We can really do some nice work with these."

"Want to get started now? We have about ten minutes until dinner."

"Yes, but let me get my bag." Isabel returned from the kitchen with her large canvas bag and the wine bottle, handing it to Emily as she emptied the bag onto the table. Emily refilled their glasses, looking curiously at Isabel's tools. She had clippers, green wire, and dark tape as well as a huge assortment of shiny baubles, bows of every material, and what appeared to be little fruits on sticks.

“Hello, Martha,” Emily said.

***

Four hours later three bountiful wreaths proudly displayed their ornaments to two physically full, mentally satisfied, and completely inebriated women. Emily knew Isabel had enjoyed the lasagna because she’d eaten more than Emily had ever seen her put away, and that was counting Thanksgiving. Emily also knew Isabel was as drunk as she was because they’d opened the second bottle of wine and showed no signs of stopping. And Emily was feeling proud of herself for making a wreath, and this was something unusual for her. She’d always ridiculed Sharon at school for wanting to “girlify” their dorm rooms, insisting she had more important things to do. She’d always preferred modern décor because one vivid red vase was all she needed to say she’d decorated her place. When she’d moved into this little old farmhouse she’d chucked all her fancy furniture and taken what was in there already, which was mostly beaten-up (“well-loved” the real estate agent had called it) tables and chairs and sagging couches. She had to admit it all looked a little forlorn, and the thought that now she had a beautiful wreath to hang on her door made her happier than she thought she should be. Maybe Sharon was right; she needed to get out more. Thinking of Sharon made her frown; she still had to call that idiot cheese man.

"What's wrong?" Isabel said.

"Something I forgot to do. Phone call. It'll wait."

"Business? Greta tells me your cheese is really in demand."

"Yes, that's the problem."

"In business they say demand is good."

Emily laughed. "Depends on who's doing the demanding. There's some guy who wants to buy my cheese directly from me."

"And that's bad because?"

"Well, I've finally got the farm and the business humming along after a few years of struggle, and I don't want to add another element right now. Besides, if you can only get my cheese at high-end restaurants it benefits both me and the restaurants. They don't want to be serving something you can find at the grocery store, and I can charge a decent price. I can't afford to charge less because it's so labor-intensive."

"Makes sense. So who's the guy?"

"I don't know. Sharon didn't describe him." Oh shit, Emily thought, frowning again. She shouldn't have mentioned Sharon. "Sorry."

"Don't worry," Isabel said, "I can handle talking about Sharon. I mean, that was before Alan even met me. Why does everyone act like she's a taboo subject?"

Emily looked at Isabel, surprised. Usually she was a clam about Sharon.

The wine in her answered, "Alan said talking about Sharon would upset you and not to mention her around you. He said it made you crazy and you had a jealous streak."

Isabel looked so momentarily shaken that Emily added gently, "But Alan said that years ago. Maybe it was true then?"

"No," Isabel said. "Never. To be honest—"

Emily watched Isabel's face alternate between anger and confusion. Quietly she poured some wine into Isabel's glass, and with that Isabel leaned back, sighed, and continued. "Alan's the one who doesn't like to talk about Sharon. And he's the one with the jealous streak, because—" Isabel shook her head. "What happened between them, anyway?"

Emily employed great self-control in not asking Isabel to finish her incomplete thought. She shrugged and replied, "I don't know, really. I was happy when they got together, you know, because it would be great to have your best friend be your sister-in-law—I mean, I don't mean … "

Isabel smiled. "I know."

"So they were together for almost a year and then they broke up. Sharon never told me why; she just said they were incompatible. Alan said the same thing. It was like they had a code of silence between them. Which really pissed me off, actually, because

Sharon tells me everything. But then Alan met you, and you and Sharon have never met because Alan won't let me bring her to any family functions even though she's known my family longer than you have. Look, why would Alan say you had problems with Sharon when it was him all the time?"

Isabel shook her head and stared off. They sat in silence for a moment then Emily inhaled and blurted out, "Why does Alan have a jealous streak?"

Isabel didn't say anything at first, but finally she turned to look at Emily, shrugged and said, "Because I'd slept around a lot."

"What?" Had she heard correctly?

"Did you?" Isabel asked.

"What?" Yes, she had.

"Come on, Emily. Did you sleep around much?" She said it like she was talking to a three-year-old.

Emily saw Isabel's smile and realized she'd been sounding like an idiot. "Wha-a-a-at?" she said again, ridiculing herself. Isabel laughed and Emily said, "Yes, since you ask, I did sleep around much. That's not something you should share with my mother, by the way."

Isabel nodded. "Greta and I don't discuss sex, believe me."

"When I was a kid she told me how a girl gets pregnant, and then she said, 'Don't get pregnant until you're married.' I think I was ten at the time and I couldn't imagine anyone voluntarily having sex.

Imagine my surprise when I not only had it but liked it and practiced it quite a bit."

"My mother gave me a pamphlet and the dictionary. She told me good girls do not have sex. She didn't even add the married part. Naturally I rebelled."

"Naturally," Emily laughed, only partly because of Isabel's deadpan tone. She was also shocked that she was speaking this way with Isabel, who had always been perfectly correct and unrelentingly nice. Emily would not have been surprised if Isabel had said she was a virgin when she met Alan. She couldn't wait to tell Sharon—then something occurred to her. "Hey, wait. You say Alan is jealous because you slept around? That's not something you did while you were together, is it?"

"No," Isabel said, looking a little hurt. "But I had a lot of partners before we met."

"And how many did Alan have?" Emily asked, unable to help herself.

"One," Isabel said.

"Sharon was Alan's first?"

"Mm-hmm."

Questions mounted in Emily's head. Did Alan get dumped because of his sexual inexperience? Was he jealous of Isabel because he was worried she'd sleep around? Was Isabel a rebound relationship? Was he embarrassed about Sharon being his first? Emily had never understood her brother's romantic life but now at least a part of his personality was making sense to her. And he was probably wildly uncomfortable around her, she thought, because he must have assumed that Sharon had told her everything.

"I see that look on your face," Isabel said. "I told you all this in confidence, you know. Besides, Alan would pass out if you started talking to him about this."

Emily nodded. "I'm sure it's the last thing he'd want to discuss with me. He hates me enough—" Emily stopped. That was another assumption she'd made that she might have to revise. She sighed. "Pass me the bottle?" she asked.

Chapter 3

GOATS WAIT FOR no woman. They also do not gladly tolerate clumsiness around their udders, and so Emily had staggered through a hot shower and choked down two cups of blazing black coffee before she attempted to milk the girls. Her task finally done, her hands scrubbed, her clothes shucked, she was slumped at the kitchen table in sweats, chewing on dry toast and staring at her cordless phone receiver. She had placed it on the table along with a stack of inquiries, each of which represented a business call she had to make. Too hungover to progress beyond this point, she was staring miserably at the phone when it rang.

"Hello?" she whispered into it, having snatched it up after the first ear-splitting ring.

"Emily?" Sharon whispered back.

"Yes?"

"Why are you whispering? Are you okay?" Emily grunted and Sharon's voice got louder. "Oh my God, do you have someone over? Is he still asleep? Who is it?" Now Sharon's voice was at a decibel level that forced Emily to speak quickly just to shut her up.

"Who the hell would I be sleeping with?" she yelled, then groaned and laid her head on the table, adjusting her own volume and continuing before

Sharon could get another ridiculous thought out of her mouth. “I am very hungover, Sharon, hungover like that night in Syracuse, like the weekend in Portland. I’m not sure how I managed to milk the goats but my one task of the day is done and now I can rest in peace until this evening when I get to do it all again. I cannot talk because the sound of my own voice is making my head throb. So if you called to chat I’d like to hang up now.”

“Did you and Isabel get drunk last night? How did it go? Are you best friends now?”

“Hanging up, Sharon.” Emily reached for the Off button but before she pressed it she heard Sharon shrieking, “Call the cheese guy!” Ignoring the cry, Emily disconnected the call and then shut the ringer off. Let the machine deal with the living. She zombie-walked to the couch and collapsed on it, pulling a heavy knitted afghan up to her chin.

***

Two hours later Emily awoke to a purring Jake kneading her chest, his haunches pressing on her stomach and his blue eyes staring right into hers. She felt as warm and lethargic as a humid day in August, and her hand reached up to pet Jake, hitting all his favorite spots. The cat’s rumbling soothed her and her mind wandered as she caressed him. What was it she’d meant to do today? Besides all those phone calls … the cheese man, that was it. What was up with him, anyway? Thinks he's so special, the only person in the world who's going to get her cheese retail. And won't take no for an answer, either. She already had him pegged: obviously rich, in love with himself, thinks money can buy him anything. She'd met enough of those guys when she was in sales, met them in restaurants and on airplanes, and she'd never liked one enough to take his number. She wondered if something about her attracted egoists. Well, she'd put an end to the cheese man, and then she could stop thinking about him. She gave Jake one last scratch behind the ears and shifted onto her hip, tipping him off the couch. Anticipating her next move, he ran into the kitchen meowing. After her bladder was empty and Jake's bowl was full, she made her way through the twelve phone calls patiently waiting on the kitchen table until she had only one left: the cheese man. Irritated, she dialed his number.

After two rings his machine picked up. "Carl Strand's not here, you know what to do," his message said and then beeped. She wasn't ready for an answering machine but she started, "Hi, Carl, this is Emily Lambert. You inquired about purchasing my goat cheese retail and I'm calling to let you know that while I appreciate your interest, I don't sell retail. As you know my cheese is available in a number of—"

"Emily Lambert, Carl Strand here." He was screening his calls, damn it.

"Hello. Yes, I don't know if you heard my message—"

"Loud and clear," he interrupted again. "Listen, Emily, it's not just the retail. Everyone sells retail, but—"

"Not everyone, Carl," Emily interrupted him back. "It's not a business model for everyone." What an arrogant idiot. Did he think she was a bumpkin farmer with no head for business?

"But for someone in your position, it makes—"

"What position is that, Carl?" Emily heard the edge in her own voice but she couldn't help it.

"New to the market, needing publicity, and word-of-mouth is free. What have you got to lose?" He sounded so confident, it made her want to reach through the phone line and hit him.

Emily took a deep breath and explained as if she were talking to Henry that she was not new to the market, that she had a business plan, that she was on track, and that selling retail wasn't a part of her model just yet.

"A lot of my friends are in the restaurant business," he said, sounding awfully pleased with himself, "and I could help you out. What have you got against help, Emily?"

She let five seconds pass as she collected herself. This man was egotistical and stubborn, and she was ready to bite his head off. But if he could help her, she shouldn't shoot him down, no matter how much she wanted to.

"Emily?"

"Listen, Carl, I've got a goat emergency. I'll call you back when I get a chance. Sorry." She hung up and shook her head. Goat emergency? Let's hope he bought that one. She needed time to think, time to Google Mr. Carl Strand and find out if he was worth any more of her trouble. He may be an ass, but if he could get her into more high-end restaurants, she should probably listen to what he had to say.

***

It was rare for Isabel to sleep in, but when she awoke she found that Greta and Henry had already eaten breakfast and taken a quick walk before the cold made Henry's hands hurt. They were sitting at the kitchen counter, Henry clasping a mug of hot chocolate topped with a squirt of whipped cream. Isabel was too groggy to complain about this early morning dose of sugar, and silently took the cup of coffee Greta offered her with what looked like a slightly raised eyebrow.

"Would you like some eggs, Isabel?" Greta asked.

Isabel's stomach lurched and she shook her head.

"French toast?"

This time Isabel made a face and Henry spotted it. "But Mommy, you like French toast! Does your tummy hurt?"

Isabel looked at Henry, smiled wanly, and said, "Yes, it does, honey. I must have eaten too much last night."

"Do you want a Tums?" Henry asked. "That's what Daddy likes."

"No, thanks."

"Toast?"

"No thank you."

"What if I rub your tummy?"

Isabel inhaled deeply. "Henry, you're being very nice. Please don't worry about my tummy. I'll be fine. I just need my coffee, okay?"

Henry nodded slowly. "Is coffee like Tums?"

"No, it's not. It's… " Isabel trailed off and looked at Greta.

"Henry," Greta said, "Would you like to watch the rest of the movie?"

"Yes!" he shouted, flinging himself off the stool and dashing out of the kitchen.

"I'll be right there," Greta called after him. Turning to Isabel, she said, "Would you like me to stay this morning so you can rest? You look tired."

Isabel smiled. "That would be wonderful." She didn't have to mention the amount of wine she'd consumed, or the fact that she didn't remember much of her drive home. Let Greta think that she was tired, rather than pitifully hung over.

"Well, I'm so glad you two finally had a chance

to enjoy each other's company. You must have had a good time."

Isabel nodded and a sentimental and satisfied look crossed Greta's face as she patted Isabel's hand and started to leave the kitchen. "You enjoy your coffee, dear. I'll stay with Henry as long as you like."

"Thanks, Greta." Isabel stood staring out the window for a moment, and then turned to ask Greta which movie they were watching, but Greta was already gone.

***

By the time Isabel showered, dressed, checked her messages and returned a few calls, Greta and Henry were discussing lunch. She joined them for a cup of tomato soup and a grilled cheese sandwich and then, rejuvenated, she asked Henry what he'd like to do that afternoon before his art lesson.

"Sing."

"What would you like to sing?" she asked, smiling. She wondered if the Christmas carols already infiltrating every public area were influencing him.

"Doe a deer."

"'Rudolph the Red-Nosed Reindeer'?"

"He means 'Do-Re-Mi' from *The Sound of Music*," Greta explained.

"Oh. When did you hear that?" Isabel asked. It

wasn't a Christmas carol, was it?

"From the movie!" Henry said, eyes wide open as if she'd just asked an incredibly obvious question.

Isabel closed her eyes for a moment. She felt very fuzzy-headed.

Greta said, "Henry and I went to the library and rented *The Sound of Music*. He absolutely loves it. I thought it would inspire him with his piano lessons. And he wants to play more now, don't you Henry? He wants to learn how to play the songs from the movie."

"Well," Isabel said. She looked at Henry, who was beaming, and at Greta, who had abruptly started clearing the lunch dishes. Although she would rather Henry didn't spend a lot of time watching movies, if it encouraged him to practice the piano, that was a good thing. "Henry, we'll have to ask your piano teacher to teach you one of the songs, okay?"

Henry nodded and said, "Do you want to hear me sing 'Do-Re-Mi'?"

"I'll join you in the family room in a minute."

As Henry left, Isabel turned to Greta and said, "I'm glad you found something to motivate him to play the piano. It's been a struggle lately." She paused. "I've never seen it but I'm sure *The Sound of Music* is fine, but next time … as long as the movie is G-rated and somewhat educational, it's fine. Thank you, Greta. Are you heading out now?"

Greta said, "Yes, I should get back home. If

you've never seen it, Isabel, you should watch the movie with Henry. I'm sure he'd love to share it with you."

"Mmm." Isabel wondered how long the movie was and when she could spare the time. "Greta, thank you so much for staying over, and for taking care of Henry this morning. I got a lot done."

"Any time you and Emily would like to get together, you just give me a call," Greta said, placing the last few items from lunch into the dishwasher.

***

Several days later Greta was sitting in her son's kitchen enjoying a cup of tea and a crossword puzzle while Isabel worked upstairs. The mid-winter sun slanted feebly through the window, the dishwasher was humming softly in the corner, and Henry was allegedly napping. Greta suspected he didn't really nap at all, but Isabel insisted, and it was probably good for the child to have some quiet time to himself. The kitchen was gleaming even in the faint light, and Greta had a real sense of satisfaction for the clean quiet house and the happy people in it.

Nonetheless she felt herself growing frustrated as she stared at the puzzle in front of her. Damn that George, he'd gotten her a book of fiendishly hard crosswords and even though they drove her crazy, she just couldn't leave them alone. He laughed every time he saw her hunched over one, freshly sharpened pencil expectantly poised over the paper. Of course he couldn't do a puzzle to save his life, which she pointed out when he teased her. The only answers he was good for were the sports clues, especially the old ones, and if she wanted his help she had to catch him early because these days he was asleep by nine o'clock every night. Silly old man, she thought, wondering who the 1940's three-season NL MVP was.

"Greta?" Isabel was standing in the kitchen doorway.

"Hello!" Greta said. She hadn't heard Isabel approaching and had started a little at the sound of her voice. "Cup of tea?"

"No, thanks." Isabel looked out the window. "I wanted to talk to you. Henry is refusing to go to his art class this week."

"Why?" Greta asked, surprised. He usually loved to show off his creations, which Isabel displayed in profusion in the playroom. The National Museum of Henry Art, George called it.

"It's the singing." Isabel looked at Greta now. "He says it's what he likes to do, and that he doesn't like art anymore."

"I see." Greta nodded slowly, turning her tea mug around by the handle. She wasn't sure what to say. Normally Isabel didn't consult Greta on Henry's upbringing.

"He's never said no to an activity before."

Greta shook her head, still unsure what to say.

Isabel hesitantly continued, "So I was wondering if you could talk to Henry about going to art class again. Since you and he bonded over the singing, maybe he would listen to you in this regard."

Isabel had spoken slowly, and Greta knew it must have been hard for her to have this conversation. Isabel was not only admitting to a lack of discipline with Henry, but that she needed Greta's help. Greta was secretly pleased that Henry had finally stood up to his mother. For heaven's sake, they were enriching the childhood right out of him.

"Of course, Isabel. I'll speak to him when he wakes up. But," she added, "maybe it's just time to stop art classes. Perhaps he could start a singing class?"

"Maybe," Isabel said softly. "Maybe math … that's related to music and the two taken together can improve both. Well, back to work. Enjoy the puzzle." She left the kitchen and Greta stared after her, wondering what kind of math a five-year-old could perform.

Chapter 4

ISABEL SAT IN her kitchen, staring vaguely out the window, exhausted. Days of fundraising, countless holiday parties, fancy dinners, decorating and baking on top of her usual schedule had all conspired to sap the last bit of energy from her. It had all culminated in hosting Christmas, which she thankfully greatly enjoyed since it gave her a chance to adorn her home with all manner of ornamentation. Isabel loved to decorate; she had a quarter of their basement dedicated to storing her carefully packed and labeled holiday boxes. This year they had three trees, one for the front window for passersby, a family tree in the great room, and a special one for Henry in the playroom, which he'd decorated with paper ornaments he'd made himself. Not in art class, though; he'd flat-out refused to go and no amount of logic would change his mind. But she could still incorporate art into his every-day life, so they'd spent the month of December happily making decorations for his tree. When she pointed out that it was "art," he said no, it was just playing with Mommy. Well, whether he knew it or not, he was receiving art instruction, and that was the important thing.

Work had slowed down considerably now that the Christmas parties and open houses were over. She was glad; she'd spent a lot of time out of the house that month, mostly in the evenings when Alan could be home with Henry. She'd stopped asking Greta to babysit in the evenings because Greta said she wanted to be home with George, who was not feeling well this winter. He had frequent headaches and wasn't eating like he used to. Isabel thought it was just stress; George took on as much work as he could and he was always busier this time of year what with people overloading their systems on tasteless Christmas displays. Isabel had encouraged George to see a doctor but he believed that a doctor's appointment was a sign of weakness. Greta could not convince him to go either, so she chose to hover around him instead, which left Alan and Isabel without their usual babysitter, and no teenager they met could compare to Greta. They'd asked one of Henry's preschool teachers but she was taking night classes and never seemed to be available. Their advertisement for a CPR-certified, early-childhood-education graduate student babysitter had gone unanswered. This meant Isabel and Alan hardly ever went out together anymore, and with their mutual work events they'd barely seen each other all month.

Alan seemed to be busier than she was, but then end-of-the-year financial planning always took up a lot of his time. Isabel was looking forward to New Year's Eve, when Emily was taking Henry for the night and they were attending a black-tie event in the city. They would stay at a hotel and drive back the next day. She was dropping off Henry at Emily's tomorrow morning to give her time for an up-do and a manicure before the party. She felt like a schoolgirl before the prom, and she knew Alan was as excited as she was; he'd been more cheerful lately, more talkative, and certainly more energetic. Isabel smiled to herself and rose out of her chair, restored. She was very much looking forward to tomorrow.

Greta sat in Emily's kitchen while Emily fixed her a cup of tea. It was early but Greta knew Emily would be ready for company because Henry was expected anytime. Greta had been up since dawn and had slept fitfully, worrying about George through the night. He didn't seem well to her, not at all, but he insisted he felt fine and made her feel silly for worrying. She couldn't convince him to see a doctor but she was hoping Emily could, and had just asked Emily to do so. She was concerned that Emily was taking so long to respond.

"Mom," Emily said, slowly dunking a tea bag into hot water, "I'm not sure I could do any good. I might just make him mad."

"He would never get mad at you, Emily. You know that. You may be in your thirties but you're still his little girl."

Emily snorted and shook her head. "Please. He's a grown man, and I can't wheedle him into seeing a doctor. It's not like I'm asking him for a stuffed animal."

"I really believe he's sick."

"Because he has headaches and an occasional upset stomach? No offense, but isn't that what old age is all about?"

"Yes, but these seem different, somehow. I feel … strange about it."

"So you have vague feelings of anxiety and Dad needs to see a doctor? Have you been to see a doctor?"

"Dad's talked to you, hasn't he?" Greta said angrily. "He told you I'm being silly and to humor me."

Emily shrugged and placed a mug of tea in front of Greta, having already stirred in the amount of milk and honey Greta liked. "Mom, I'm not getting in between you two on this one. I'll suggest he goes to a doctor because it's been ages and it wouldn't kill him. And I'll suggest you go because your anxiety is becoming a problem for you, don't you think? I mean, you're not even sleeping well anymore, right?"

Greta was surprised that Emily knew this. She must have pouches under her eyes. "No, I'm not. I think if George goes to a doctor I'll feel much better. And yes, don't say it, I'll make an appointment myself. Okay?"

"Great." Emily glanced out the window and said, "And guess who's coming up the driveway, right on time!"

"Always right on time," Greta smiled. "Always."

Leaving Henry happily entwined with Emily's cat, Isabel drove to her salon appointment. Henry had been so pleased to see Emily and Greta that he'd barely said goodbye to her. Isabel knew that it meant her son was in safe and comfortable hands but part of her wished for a little leg-clinging or pouting, a trembling lower lip perhaps. Still, it made her departure easier and she would be able to relax while she and Alan were in the city, alone together for the first time in weeks. She smiled a little at the thought of the new negligee she'd bought for the occasion. Alan had surprised her with this night away, but she had a few surprises planned too.

The hotel valet took Isabel's keys from her freshly manicured nails and a porter took her bag. Five minutes later she was in their hotel suite, thrilled at the size of the room, which contained a king-size bed and an entire living area as well as a spacious bathroom with a whirlpool tub. Alan had obviously gone overboard on the room, but she wasn't going to complain. She put away her things and thought about stretching out on the bed until she remembered her new up-do. When Alan arrived an hour later she was so engrossed in a book that the sound of his card key startled her. He looked as relaxed as she felt, and he smiled the moment he saw her.

"You got your hair done. Looks nice," he said,

putting his suitcase off to the side.

"Thanks. Nails too," she said, wiggling her fingers at him.

"Are you still drying them?" he asked, coming closer and stopping an arm's length away. "Or are they ready to be used?"

She smiled. "What service do you need my nails to perform, sir?"

"I could think of a few. Shall I make a list?" he asked, moving toward her and putting his arms around her waist.

"I think I'm familiar with the list, but watch the hair, okay?" She hooked her arms around his neck and reached up to kiss him. "I don't want my up-do to look like doo-doo."

"I like the idea of messing up that hair," Alan murmured against her mouth. "You look much too neat right now." He reached down and squeezed her behind.

"Hey," Isabel said, "You taste like something. What is that?"

"I had a shot of Scotch on the way over," Alan shrugged. "Everyone cut out around noon today. A few of the guys hit the bar next door on their way out, celebrating the deal we closed this week. I wasn't driving so I joined them for a drink."

"Oh," Isabel said. It sounded reasonable but it was unusual for Alan to stop off for a drink. On the other hand, it was New Year's Eve, and a special night out for them both. Why shouldn't he start celebrating a little early?

"You should have one too," Alan said, taking her hand and leading her to the mini bar. "Let's see what they've got."

"Alan, that stuff is so expensive," Isabel said. "Let's go down to the hotel bar."

"Yeah, it's expensive, but how often do we do this? Now, I know you don't like Scotch. We've got wine, vodka, gin, champagne. Let's open a bottle of champagne."

He held it aloft, wiggling his eyebrows, and he looked so boyish then that she had to laugh. "Oh, what the hell," she said. They weren't driving anywhere and they were alone in a hotel room. Why not?

By the time eight o'clock rolled around, Isabel was feeling sleepy. They'd consumed two bottles of champagne and tested the springs on the couch and the bed. She had fixed her hair and was struggling to put on the new black dress she'd purchased for the occasion. It had a low back and a lot of crisscrossing straps, some of which she was sure were twisted, but the full-length mirror was in the bathroom where Alan was shaving. Tired as she was, she couldn't quite see how she was going to make it through the night.

"Alan?" she called, opening the bathroom door. It only opened a crack and then stopped.

“Yeah?” he said.

“I need to get in there and fix my straps. Why is the door stuck?”

“Sorry, dropped a towel there. Hang on.”

She heard him kick the towel out of the way and the door swung open. Turning to look at her back in the mirror, she yawned and said, “I’m really tired. Are you sure you’re up for going out?”

“It’s eight p.m. on New Year’s Eve, kiddo. We’re not going to bed now! The night is young!”

“Where are you getting this energy, Alan? Did you have some coffee I’m not aware of?”

“That’s a great idea,” Alan said. “You need coffee.”

“But I’ll be up all night if I have coffee now.”

“Yup. That fits right into my evil plan to try out the tub when we get back. Go make yourself a pot.”

Isabel pulled and untwisted two straps and wandered back into the room to make herself some coffee. Alan spiked it with Kahlua and she had two cups. The caffeine picked her up enough that she was inspired to dance for much of the evening. Songs from her younger days played, the food was tasty and plentiful, and Alan was solicitous and playful. They even capped off their evening with a late-night bubble bath. Really, she hadn’t had that much fun in ages.

***

Emily and Henry celebrated New Year's Eve at seven p.m., when, as she assured Henry, England was celebrating theirs. They wore cardboard tiaras with the year spelled out in gold garland, drank ginger ale out of champagne glasses, and sang "Auld Lang Syne," and Henry kept Emily company while she milked the goats. As she tended to the girls, she thought about how sweet Henry was, how easy he was to spend time with. It was odd to her that they got along so well, when she and Alan fought all the time. She often wondered what Alan and Henry talked about. Whenever she saw them together it was usually a family gathering; she was never invited over to a dinner with just the three of them. She was very much enjoying Henry's company, and not for the first time she wondered if she'd ever have children of her own. Right now this farm took up all of her time, she had no intention of having a child on her own, and she certainly wasn't involved with anyone, so she knew motherhood wasn't in her immediate future. But she truly appreciated the time she spent with Henry, and now that he was getting older, she realized she could form a more meaningful relationship with him. She decided to bring up the idea with Isabel of taking Henry one weekend a month, maybe even a week next summer if he wanted to. It would be a win-win-win, as Alan would say.

As they slowly made their way to the house, Isabel looked at Alan, who was concentrating on avoiding the leafless branches that drooped sporadically into the driveway. She hoped he wouldn't get a scratch on his car's paint, knowing he would be offering to Emily to cut them back almost before they took off their coats. And even though it would be a thoughtful gesture, the two of them seemingly could fight over anything, and once again, they would end in an argument. She sighed quietly and stared out the window, remaining silent until Alan parked the car. As they got out, Alan said, "That driveway is an obstacle course."

"You did a great job avoiding those branches," she said, and quickly changed the subject. "Doesn't the air smell wonderful?"

Alan shrugged but took a deep breath, then held her hand in his. "I had a great time in the city."

"Me too." Isabel thought about the connection she'd felt to Alan while they were away, and how their time alone reminded her of why she'd married him.

"Too bad we can't do it again soon." He squeezed her hand. "We can't ask Emily to babysit all the time with her farm responsibilities, and my mom is still preoccupied with my dad."

"I'm sure he's fine," Isabel said reassuringly.

Alan turned his head away from her and said quietly, "I hope so."

She pulled his hand toward her and kissed it gently. Alan didn't speak about his parents much, so it was obvious concern over his father's health was disturbing him more than he cared to admit. He looked at her and smiled briefly, then said, "Let's not talk about it in front of Henry," as they approached the front porch.

"There's really nothing to talk about yet," she said. Their hands dropped to their sides as the door was flung open by an ecstatic Henry, who threw himself so hard against Isabel's legs that she stumbled.

***

Greta smiled as Henry vaulted himself onto the piano bench, almost sliding over the other side in his enthusiasm. Taking the top page of sheet music from her bag, she placed it in front of Henry on the music stand atop the piano. It was a very simple arrangement of "A Spoonful of Sugar" from *Mary Poppins*, and she thought the lyrics would appeal to a child. Henry stared at the sheet for a moment and then started to hum the notes as he read across the top line. Greta was still amazed how readily Henry had been able to learn to read music, and how easily he could follow a melody. She settled in next to him and put her hands on the keys.

"Can you read any of the words?" she asked.

"Mmm … I see the word 'fun.'"

"Very good," Greta said. She had started coming over to Alan and Isabel's twice a week for what Isabel called singing lessons. The sheet music she brought was encouraging him to learn to read both the words and the notes, which seemed to convince Isabel it was a worthwhile use of his time. "Let's get started. I'll sing it once and then we'll sing it together."

As Greta sang, the idea of medicine made the unwelcome thought of George's possible illness intrude on her otherwise happy afternoon. Usually she was able to put aside her worry when she was with Henry, but not today. She would have to make sure any songs in the future didn't involve doctors or medicine. Not that she could get George to get involved with either one; he was still stubbornly refusing to see the doctor. She had a strong feeling that something was wrong, but George wasn't going to see someone because his wife had a hunch. The headaches he had begun to have with greater frequency he attributed to stress from the job. And occasionally he lost his appetite, but she tended to feed him too much anyway, and he said he was just full of her good cooking. He had an answer for everything, but it didn't satisfy Greta. Unfortunately she couldn't physically drag the man into a doctor's office, so she decided to occupy her mind with Henry's singing progress instead. Except for today, thanks to Mary Poppins.

Greta softly said “Now,” to remind Henry to turn the pages of sheet music for her. He did, and as she finished the song, she resolved to call her own doctor and explain the symptoms George had, to see if it was worth the worry. She did have a tendency to fret, as George often told her. But George also had a tendency to ignore things until they got desperate, like the time his tooth pain wound up putting him in the dentist chair for an emergency root canal. A few simple questions to the doctor would make her feel better, and if the doctor thought there was reason to worry, well, that would convince George to do something.

After an hour at the piano singing a number of songs from *Mary Poppins*, Henry and Greta sat in the kitchen enjoying an afternoon snack. “Grandma,” Henry said, “Why do you drink tea?”

“I like the taste, dear. Isn’t that why you drink cocoa?”

“Yes.” He dunked a cookie into his cocoa and bit off the soft part. “Do you ever drink something you don’t like the taste of?”

“No,” said Greta, curious about what Henry was really thinking. Sometimes with children it was difficult to determine exactly what they were trying to ask. She wondered if he’d tried something recently that he didn’t like. “Do you ever drink things that taste bad?”

"Cough syrup," he said.

"Of course," Greta replied. "I don't like cough syrup either."

"Do grown-ups drink cough syrup?"

"Yes, grown-ups have to take medicines just like children."

Henry nodded solemnly and dunked and bit another piece of cookie. "And grown-ups are bigger than kids. They take bigger medicine."

"Stronger medicine, dear," Greta corrected him.

He looked at her for a moment, and then asked, "Can we sing 'A Spoonful of Sugar' again?"

***

A few weeks into January, Isabel found herself alone in the house, preparing a four-course dinner for two. Greta had taken Henry to see a regional theater production of The Sound of Music. Isabel was familiar with the theater as she'd been instrumental in the fundraising that had kept it from closing several years ago. Back then the theater had been well-regarded but struggled with donations. Now they were solvent, and she hoped the show would be a good one. They were going to the matinee but afterwards Greta had invited Henry to her house for dinner and a sleepover. "It'll do you and Alan good to spend a night together, Isabel," Greta had said. "You two were so relaxed after your last night away, and Emily and I realized that Henry's old enough now to spend some nights away from home. It would do you and Alan some good."

Isabel didn't think to ask what Greta had meant by that until much later. Now she had a nagging suspicion that perhaps Greta had been trying to say something in her usual roundabout way. She wished that just once Greta would be direct instead of hinting at things. Did Greta think she and Alan were too tense, that they needed some time alone? What parents didn't? But she wondered if she was missing signs in Alan's behavior that his mother had noticed. She thought this evening, a glorious evening alone together, might be the time to find out. The meal she was making was from *Gourmet Magazine*, and each recipe had wine suggestions along with it. She'd reviewed it with Alan beforehand, and he'd approved all the wines and was able to locate all but one in their own cellar. The last he was purchasing on his way home at a high-end wine shop two towns over.

Everything on the menu was designed to be made ahead, so that the cook didn't have to spend a lot of time in the kitchen. There was an antipasto plate coming to room temperature on the glass coffee table in the living room, the vegetables bright against the white ceramic platter. She took the flourless chocolate tart out of the oven and set it on the counter to cool, its aroma filling the kitchen. When Alan arrived, she would put a lasagna and a loaf of bread into the oven; their delicious smells would find their way into the living room, where she and Alan would enjoy a glass of wine and the antipasto. She was just putting on a jazz CD when the sound of Alan's car in the driveway surprised her. He was an hour earlier than she'd expected, and she hoped nothing was wrong. But as she heard his steps on the stairs from the garage, she could tell he was in a good mood. When he was upset, he tended to stomp his feet when he walked, much like Henry, she thought with a smile.

Alan opened the door from the basement and grinned, a bottle of wine in his hand. "Here's our first course!" he said, putting the wine on the kitchen counter.

"You're early," she said, pleased. She watched as he retrieved the wine opener from the kitchen drawer and began to uncork the wine. Taking two glasses from the cabinet, she joined him at the counter. "I'm so glad your mother suggested a date night."

"Date night? She called it that?"

"No, but she said it would be good for us." She watched as Alan poured a small amount of the wine he'd just uncorked into a glass. "Why do you think she said that? Do we seem unhappy?"

Alan shook his head. "The wine is excellent." He filled both glasses, took a generous swallow and said, "She's got nothing going on so she focuses all her attention on us, and then she starts imagining things. I'm not unhappy, are you?"

"No," she said, "not unhappy at all." She took a sip of wine and glanced at the clock, wondering if she should put in the lasagna earlier than planned. "But it is nice to have an evening together, just the two of us. Of course saying that makes me feel guilty."

"Guilty?" Alan asked, settling onto a kitchen stool.

"It sounds like I'm saying I don't want to be with Henry." She sat across from him, the cool granite supporting their wine glasses between them.

"Of course we want to be with Henry, but sometimes I like to just be with my wife. There's nothing wrong with that. Think about the old days. My parents never spent any 'quality time' with their parents. They were on their own from an early age. And they turned out okay."

"Well … " Isabel teased.

Alan laughed. "Hey, they're functional adults, and that's all we can hope for, right? That our child will be a good citizen and a productive member of society?"

"That sounds so boring! How about 'happy and healthy'?" Isabel suggested.

"Same thing in the end. Do we have any of that cheese left?" Alan asked. "I had a light lunch."

"Oh, of course, I made an antipasto plate," Isabel said, surprised she'd forgotten about it. A few sips of wine and her head went right out the window. “It’s in the living room. Let’s head in there and get a little more comfortable. Just let me put the lasagna in the oven first.” She rose and walked around the island to the refrigerator.

“A little more comfortable? Does that mean you’ll be slipping into a negligee?” Alan asked, reaching out as she passed him and pulling her to his side.

“If you’re lucky,” she said, smiling and putting her arms around his neck.

He pulled her down to him for a kiss and then let her go, saying, “Unfortunately my appetite is stronger than my other urges right now. Can I help you?”

“No, it’ll only take me a second. Go ahead into the living room; I’ll be right there.”

Alan left and Isabel took the lasagna out of the fridge, uncovered it, and put it into the oven along with the loaf of bread she’d prepared. She was happy and relaxed, and she could tell Alan was too. Isabel was grateful to Greta for suggesting their night alone. She thought perhaps she and Alan should take advantage of some overnight babysitting more often.

***

Emily hadn’t realized how much she enjoyed solitude and quiet until she started tending goats, but now she became irritated when the phone rang or some hardy, or more likely lost, soul came to her door. Unlike some fellow farmers, she didn't play music or listen to talk radio when she was working in the barn. A barn had its own undercurrent of noise, a low hum of animals breathing, chewing, rustling in the hay. Crows cawed, the old wood in the barn creaked, the wind blew. Even in the house, snuggled with Jake on the sofa, she liked the silence, although sometimes, though she would never admit it, she had entertaining if brief conversations with Jake, who never failed to meow back. So it did not take her long one afternoon, lying on her couch covered by Jake and an afghan, to become irritated by an awful whining hum, much like the sound of a giant and bloodthirsty mosquito.

What was that? She paused from her reading and waited a minute to see if she could identify it, and when she couldn't, she shut the book, trying to ascertain if the noise was inside her house, which would be very bad, or outside, which would be better but still annoying. It was getting louder and now she could tell it was coming from outside. Shifting her hips slightly, she sighed and gently lifted the mounded afghan that was Jake off her lap, sliding out from under him and sitting on the edge of the couch, hands on her knees, listening. There was a large machine of some sort outside, that was certain. It didn't sound like a truck or a tractor; it sounded more like an airplane. She often saw small prop planes flying overhead but rarely did they come so low that she could hear them this loudly. Concerned, she decided to investigate. Grabbing her fleece coat from a hook by the door, she stepped out onto the porch and peered up into the sky.

A small silver airplane was flying low over her farm, sweeping in an arc from the east. Emily watched a little apprehensively as it began to circle her land. Why on earth was it doing that? Was the pilot in trouble? Was there something strange on her property? Idly she wondered if she should call the police, but that seemed ridiculous. What could she say: There's an airplane in the sky over here? After a few minutes she decided that the plane wasn't doing anything extraordinary, aside from flying over her house, so she went inside to make a cup of tea. She was dunking a tea bag of Earl Grey into one of her many goat-themed mugs, all given to her as gifts, when the sound of the airplane changed from a high whine to a slower lower roar. Hurrying back outside, she watched as the plane began to descend slowly to the right of a row of trees separating her property from an old access road that used to bisect her farm long ago. It hadn't been used in years and wasn't paved, but it was flat and at least two miles long. She zipped up her fleece and started jogging slowly toward the access road.

Moving over the hardened terrain was difficult. Hillocks of sod interspersed with clumps of frozen grass dotted the land; sometimes her feet would sink, sometimes not. It was awkward going and she quickly slowed to a safer walk. No fireball had appeared above the trees, and from the sound of the engine, the plane had landed. Another minute and the engine whine stopped completely. Emily rounded the line of trees in time to see a man climbing out of the airplane and dropping to the ground. She stopped for a moment and thought to herself. She was far from her house, obscured from view by trees, alone with a strange man. Did serial killers often drop out of the sky? Probably not. She started walking again, slowly, toward the pilot, who was checking some instruments in a panel on the side of the plane.

As she neared the man, he turned and watched her approach. He was solidly built, had closely cropped dark hair, and was wearing an old brown leather jacket and a pair of jeans too crisp and blue for a farm. His expression was neutral and she tried to remain impassive as she came within speaking distance.

"Are you okay?" Emily asked, stopping a little more than arm's length away.

He grinned and said, "You bet. Great landing. Is this your farm?"

"Yes," she said. He was staring directly at her with disarmingly friendly brown eyes and she felt slightly uncomfortable, which made her angry. She crossed her arms and continued, "Is something wrong with your plane?"

He glanced at the open instrument panel and said, "No."

"Then what are you doing here?" she asked. She knew her tone was not very friendly, but who was this guy and if his plane was fine, why was he on her property, disturbing her otherwise extremely relaxing afternoon?

"Oh, sorry. You're Emily Lambert, right?"

"How do you know that?" she asked, taking a step back and lowering her arms, tensing her hands into fists.

"Hey, take it easy," he said, his smile crinkling his eyes. "I'm Carl Strand." He said this in a tone that implied she should not only know who he was but be honored by his presence.

"Who?" she said, completely irritated.

"Carl Strand. I called you about buying your cheese, remember?"

"I remember I said 'no,'" Emily answered, wishing she'd Googled this guy already.

"I didn't like that answer. I'm here to change your mind."

"And you don't own a car?" Emily asked, folding her arms across her chest, wondering if this man was slightly insane.

He shrugged. "I like to fly. I take my plane out a lot, and I haven't been up this way in a while, so I figured I'd stop by."

Emily stood staring at him for a moment. She had no idea what to say; Carl sounded so reasonable and yet he had just landed a plane on her property on what was basically an errand. Shaking her head, she said, “You must really like goat cheese.”

“I do. I’m also curious about your business. Think you could give me a tour of the farm? You’re not having any goat emergencies, are you?” He cocked his head as he said that last bit, grinning at her.

Emily flushed, reminded of her embarrassing phone message to Carl. “No, not today.” She looked at him, standing there so full of himself, with an arrogance bordering on the socially unacceptable. She sensed that he wouldn’t leave until he got something. She thought for a moment and then said, “I’m busy this afternoon. I can give you a quick tour, but then you’ll have to go.” He nodded. Emily turned and marched back up the access road, Carl unfortunately easily keeping pace.

Chapter 5

GRETA URGED HENRY to stand as the cast came out for their final bow, the boys in knickers, the girls in dirndl skirts, the echoes of "Climb Every Mountain" hovering in the air. "I can't see anything," Henry called over the applause, standing on tiptoe and dancing from side to side, peering around the man in front of him. Nonetheless his little hands slapped together as fast as he could make them, and Greta saw that the wide smile that had jumped onto his face during every musical number had returned. He'd been singing along quietly during the entire play, his eyes riveted on the actors. Greta had never seen Henry so transfixed, and thought that perhaps this experience would remind him of her when he was older; she briefly imagined him sharing the story with his own children some day. As the actors left the stage and people began to rise from their seats, she placed her hand gently on his head and said, "I guess you liked it, huh?"

He looked up at her and said, "Yes! Oh yes! But where did they go?"

Greta picked up their coats and her purse and ushered him along the row of seats. "The show is over, darling. They've gone backstage to collect their things."

"What's backstage?"

"Behind the stage," Greta explained patiently as they slowly made their way into the aisle.

"I want to say goodbye," Henry said, turning and darting down the aisle toward the stage. Greta called, "Henry!" but he was out of earshot, and within seconds she'd lost sight of him completely. She hurried toward the stage, fighting the tide of people heading out. Arriving at the stage she didn't see any actors but some of the musicians in the orchestra pit were still there. "Excuse me," she asked loudly, "did anyone see a little boy up here?"

No one answered, although she had everyone's attention. She realized she must have sounded panicked because the pianist offered to check the bathrooms and a violinist said he'd check backstage. Five agonizing minutes later, the violinist returned along with Henry, who was hand in hand with a gangly older man with long grey hair and wire-rimmed glasses.

"Did you lose this?" the older man asked with a smile. He drew Henry over to Greta and left his hand extended, saying, "My name's Stan. Director. Did you enjoy the play?"

"Oh," said Greta, torn between giving Henry a fierce hug and returning the man's offer of a handshake. Good manners won and she shook his hand, reaching down with her other hand and putting it on Henry's head. "Greta. Henry's grandmother. I'm terribly sorry; he disappeared so quickly I couldn't keep up."

"No need to apologize. Enthusiastic kid. Outgoing. I found him shaking hands with the actors back there, then he tells me his favorite song is 'Do-Re-Mi,' then he proceeds to sing a bit of it. He's got quite a voice on him. Says he's five; is that true?"

Greta was overwhelmed with the polite desire to answer all of this Arthur's questions, but decided Henry's behavior needed to be attended to first. "Henry is very sorry he went backstage where people are not allowed, aren't you, Henry?" Henry contritely agreed and Stan winked at him. Greta frowned at Stan, who cleared his throat and added, "Backstage can be dangerous, kid. Next time ask me for a tour, okay?"

Henry nodded and sat down abruptly in a front row seat, crossing his hands in his lap and looking at Stan expectantly.

"Now, in answer to your question, Henry is only five and doesn't understand theater protocol, which is why you found him backstage. I'm glad you like his voice; I think it's quite nice."

"Does he do commercial work?"

"What's that?" Henry asked, jumping to his feet.

"I don't understand what you're asking," Greta said. "He's five years old."

"He's got a presence. Unassuming, outgoing, and I think he'd be easy to direct. Also a fine singing voice for a kid. He being taught?"

Greta couldn't help but feel flattered, although she knew fine singing voices were born, not made. "Yes, I've been teaching him to sing, but I hardly think you can tell at his age—"

Stan interrupted her again. "I can tell. Used to work Broadway a thousand years ago. Lots of musicals. But my point is you should get him into acting. Commercials." He reached into his back pocket and pulled out a worn brown leather wallet, extracted a card and handed it to Greta. "Call me if you want to pursue it. Pleasure to meet you, Henry," he added, and left. In seconds Greta and Henry were alone, the theater transformed into an empty, dusty, quiet place. Greta clutched Stan's card in her hand, staring dumbly after him as he disappeared behind the curtain. She looked down at it. "Stan Campbell, Campbell & Associates, 45 South Washington St.," she read aloud.

"Can I see Stan again, Grandma?" Henry asked. "Can I see the play again?"

"Let's talk about it at dinner, okay, honey? Grandma's got a lot to think about." Greta took Henry's hand in hers and they slowly made their way up the aisle and out into the cold.

***

George waited until Greta was finished blowing kisses and waving to Henry and Isabel, the blue

Volvo out of the driveway and into the snow-packed street, before he closed their front door to the cold. He knew Greta felt like he did: sorry to see the kid go. Still, while George thoroughly enjoyed spending days with Henry, he was always tired afterwards. And this headache he'd had all week wasn't helping his mood. He looked at Greta, her smile faded, her arms crossed, staring at the small pile of brightly colored Legos Henry had left on the brown carpet near George's easy chair in the living room. Henry had been playing at his feet while Greta cleaned up the breakfast dishes and George flipped through the paper. "Let's take a load off," he said, putting his hand on her shoulder.

"I should clean up," she said, but she starting walking towards the couch with him.

"We'll get them later," he said. "I wouldn't mind a break."

Greta gave him a funny look. "Aren't you rested from reading the paper?"

He guessed he should be, but he wasn't, and he realized if he admitted that, Greta would worry and insist he call the doctor. Again. He was just getting older, that was all. "Sure I'm rested. I mean a break from playing with a five-year-old. I'd like to sit down and talk to my beautiful wife." He took her hand as they sat on the couch together. They'd had that couch a long time but it still felt comfortable, supportive, not like Alan's enormous sinkholes of furniture. He could barely get out of those.

Greta squeezed his hand and smiled. “Still sweet after all these years.”

“Still my wife after all these years,” he said.

“Would you like to take a walk this afternoon? We’ve been cooped up all day.”

“Later. Got a bit of a headache.”

“A headache? Since when? Would you like an aspirin?” Greta looked worried.

George sidestepped her concern once again. “I didn’t have the reading light on earlier, and my eyes are tired, that’s all.” Not true, but much easier than listening to her go on about his health.

“Would you like to take a nap?”

“Jesus, Greta, I have a headache, I’m not a hundred years old,” he snapped, and immediately regretted the look on her face. “Sorry.” He raised her hand to his lips and kissed it. “I’ll close my eyes to rest them, and we can sit and talk for a minute.” He hoped a few minutes’ rest would revive him, otherwise he’d have to soldier on and pretend everything was fine.

“All right. I wanted to tell you about something anyway. Last night Henry made a mad dash for the stage after the show ended—”

“What? Henry doesn’t usually misbehave like that. Did you talk to him about running off?” George didn’t think he could keep up with Henry if the boy suddenly decided to run off in a crowd, or even in an apple orchard.

"Yes, we talked, and he wasn't misbehaving, exactly, he was just so excited about the show and he really wanted to meet the littlest girl."

"Five years old and his first crush," teased George.

"In the end he met the director, a nice man by the name of Stan Campbell, who gave us his card and told us that Henry could be an actor. I think I might give him a call."

Alarm bells went off in George's head and he opened his eyes. "What do you mean, an actor? The kid's five. What does this guy want? Did he seem legit? Did he look like a pedophile?" He'd gone from alarmed to angry in about three seconds, and he knew Greta wouldn't like that, but it was his job to protect his family, not to be open and friendly to every nut job that crossed their path. He tried to smooth the anger out of his face.

Greta had turned her head to look at him with an expression of amusement. "For heaven's sake, George, of course he was legitimate. His name was in the program. He has a company that I would imagine represents actors. And he said that Henry would probably be a good actor for commercials."

"You sure he wasn't interested in Henry for some other reason?" George was beginning to feel a little silly but his protective instincts were still running high.

"First of all, I don't think pedophiles go around handing out business cards. And second, George, you've heard Henry sing. You can't deny he's good."

"I think he is, but I'm tone deaf and he's my grandson. Maybe he's not as good as you think, maybe this Stan guy's a weirdo. Maybe he was interested in you. How old was this Stan guy?"

"I don't know … sixties?"

"Same age as me, same sex drive," George said, half serious that this guy was after Greta. She silently pursed her lips, which meant she didn't find him amusing. If she added a quick roll of the eyes it meant she thought he was being ridiculous. Ah yes, there they went.

Greta said firmly, "Monday I'm going to call 'this Stan guy' and find out exactly what he thinks Henry could or should be doing with his voice. If Henry truly is talented, we wouldn't want to stand in his way, would we?"

George knew defeat when he heard it. Greta would have her way. But he would tag along, keep an eye on things, and make sure both his grandson and his wife were taken care of. It occurred to him that Greta hadn't mentioned anything about this to Isabel when she came to pick up Henry.

"Why didn't you tell Isabel?"

Greta sighed and leaned into his shoulder. "I thought I'd get more information before presenting it to them."

"You're making a presentation now?" he teased, putting his arm around her, leaning his head back, and closing his eyes again. George figured Alan would probably say whatever made Isabel happy, and Isabel would probably be thrilled that someone had finally noticed her incredible genius of a son. Not that Henry wasn't a bright kid, but there were lots of bright kids, and he wanted Henry to enjoy being a kid, with less focus on the bright.

"I want them to have all the facts, and I'm sure they'll do whatever's best for their own son," Greta said.

Once again Greta was seeing the best in people, and all he was doing was giving himself stress. He grunted, and said, "Okay, but if you meet Mr. Director for coffee I'm coming along. Just in case he has any ideas about you."

Greta snuggled deeper into his side and George fell asleep wondering if his grandson really was talented, if some stranger wanted his wife, and if his damn headache would ever go away.

***

Isabel tried to concentrate on Henry's excited chatter as she navigated home, avoiding frost heaves and icy patches, the car's tires crunching in the snow. Her head was still pounding slightly and her mouth was dry, although that felt like a small price to pay for last night. She'd enjoyed herself tremendously, forgotten all the stresses of her life, and remembered how funny Alan could be when he was relaxed. They'd eaten, laughed, danced, and gone through quite a bit of wine, slept in this morning, had a leisurely breakfast … she was thinking how nice another cup of coffee would be when she became aware of Henry saying, "Mommy?"

"Yes?" she responded, hoping he wasn't mid-story.

"Did you and Daddy watch it?" Henry asked.

Damn, he'd been mid-story. "Watch it?" she stalled.

"The Sound of Music. Did you watch it last night?"

"Oh, no honey, we didn't. We were busy."

"What did you do?"

"We had dinner, and listened to music, and … " She didn't quite know how to describe her slightly decadent evening to a five-year-old. "Danced."

"Oh."

He sounded so disappointed. Isabel recalled Greta suggesting that she watch the movie with him ages ago. It was a cold winter afternoon and she had a bit of a hangover. What the hell, she thought. Her email could wait until later. "Henry, would you like to watch it with me after lunch?"

"Yes yes yes!" Henry cried, bouncing in his seat. "With hot chocolate?"

"Sure, that sounds great," Isabel smiled. He was a good negotiator like his Dad.

***

When Isabel and Henry entered the warm kitchen from the cold garage, Alan was at the table where she'd left him, reading the paper and sipping a cup of coffee, steam still rising from the surface. He'd brewed a fresh pot of coffee and even cleaned up the breakfast dishes. She and Henry both paused and stared at Alan, and she wasn't sure why until Henry asked, "Daddy, are you sick?"

"No, kiddo, why?" Alan smiled at Henry and waved him over, pulling him to his side with one strong arm.

"Because you're sitting down and you're in your pj's and you're not on your computer."

"I'm just relaxing. Now tell me, how was your time with Grandma?"

"I saw The Sound of Music on the stage, it was great, and everyone was clapping, and then I met Gretel." His eyes were shining and he put the arm that wasn't pressed against his father across Alan's chest.

Alan looked at Isabel and she answered his look with raised eyebrows. She had no idea what Henry was talking about; this must have been what she missed in the car. She didn't want to admit it, though, so she said, "Henry and I are going to watch The Sound of Music together. Would you like to join us?" thinking that would send Alan running for a shower and some work, but she was shocked and delighted when Alan agreed. The three of them spent the afternoon nibbling on popcorn, drinking hot chocolate, and watching the movie. Occasionally she peeked at her husband, still in his plaid pajamas and sweatshirt, his arm around their son, his features relaxed, and felt happier than she had in weeks, while outside it grew dark and flurries swirled around their porch light.

***

The heavy barn door creaked shut behind Emily. The barn itself was hushed and quiet; there were a few goats inside resting but most of them were outside, oblivious to the cold, happily eating the dense prickly brush on the far side of the winter-barren pasture. She inhaled deeply the mingled scents of goat, hay, and manure, and something else, maybe the scent of contented mammals, and glanced at Carl, who stood to her right, taking off his gloves. He had a strong nose, strong chin, military short black hair, and, she couldn't help noticing, no wedding ring … what was she thinking? This guy was obnoxious, arrogant, used to getting what he wanted. And right now it seemed like he wanted her cheese, which meant he wanted her to change the way she ran her business. Well, she'd worked in the business world, she knew how to negotiate, and she knew how to say no. If he thought he was getting what he wanted today, he was going to be one disappointed businessman, she thought as he met her gaze. A businessman with the most gorgeous eyes, so dark they were almost black, and those lashes … .

"So this is the barn?" Carl asked with one corner of his mouth raised, not breaking eye contact.

Emily flushed and nodded, looking away toward the end of the barn with the processing equipment. "Come this way," she said, hoping she sounded brusque, and embarrassed by her desire for this man. She'd run away from the business world years ago, and she didn't need to be dragged back in. Besides, he was here because of her cheese, not because he was looking for a date. A guy with his own plane probably didn't lack for dates anyway. She purposely refrained from pointing out the goat manure that dotted the floor and hoped that Carl would step in some.

When they reached the processing area she explained how the goat cheese was made and he asked intelligent questions; he not only knew about cheese-making but seemed impressed with her operation. Emily tamped down her usual enthusiasm when she gave her tour; she didn't want him to think she was at all interested in any propositions he was going to make. Well, there was one proposition she'd accept, she thought, but it was doubtful he'd make it. Too bad, he had quite a nice—

"You have a bathroom out here?" Carl asked, turning to face her; he'd been looking at the cheeses aging on the shelves, his hands shoved in the pockets of his jacket, the brown leather so old he must have owned it since high school.

"What?" Emily asked, hoping he hadn't caught her staring at his butt.

"I need to use the bathroom. Do you have one in the barn?"

There wasn't one, and it wouldn't be good business practice to tell him to pee outside, would it? She supposed inviting him into her home was a bit risky, but he seemed pretty safe. In fact she felt completely at ease with him, as if they were old friends. Of course sociopaths often seemed perfectly nice, but she wasn't going to start thinking that way. "You'll have to come inside. Follow me."

***

As they entered Emily's kitchen, Carl shrugged out of his jacket, dropped it on the back of a chair, and asked her where the bathroom was before she even shut the door.

"It's around the corner," she said, pointing toward her living room. "It's not a very big house, as

I'm sure you saw." She knew sometimes people expected a rambling homestead when they heard "farmhouse," but hers was small, just two bedrooms, a kitchen, and her cozy living room. She loved the smallness of it. Luckily Carl was only average height; taller people always seemed to stoop a bit when they came to visit. She enjoyed an unrestrained look at his behind as he disappeared around the corner, wondering what he looked like in clothing a little less bulky.

This was not good. She should send Carl on his way, make a cup of tea, and curl up with Jake and a good book, because what she really wanted to do was pour a glass of wine and make out with him on the couch. But his was a business-related visit, not a lunch date. He was only there for her cheese, or maybe her business. Going retail wasn't part of her business plan at the moment, but it might be someday, and he would make a useful contact, not to mention a potential business partner or investor, albeit an incredibly arrogant one. She glanced at the breakfast dishes still stacked in the sink and put them in the dishwasher, finishing just before she heard Carl's voice saying, "Well, hello." She turned but didn't see him, then heard, "Aren't you friendly?" and realized he'd probably just met Jake. Sure enough, Carl came around the corner with Jake draped over one shoulder, only the cat's creamy back and dark brown legs and tail visible, his traitorous front half lounging on Carl's back. Carl's big hand slowly stroked Jake's back.

Jake, you're so easy, thought Emily. There was something sexy about a man petting a cat. "Sorry about that," she said, taking a step toward Carl to relieve him of the cat. She should really get Carl out the door.

"No need to apologize. Love cats, Siamese especially. Great personalities. So," he asked, "any chance of a cup of coffee?" He pulled out the chair with his jacket dangling off the back and sat down. "Just to warm up? The barn was pretty cold." He smiled, still petting Jake, looking directly into her eyes.

He probably wanted to sit her down and make her a business proposal, and she just wanted to jump in his lap. This was ridiculous. "No, I don't have coffee. I don't drink it."

"You don't offer it to guests?"

"It's a breakfast beverage," she said, crossing her arms.

"You don't offer it to guests after sleepovers?"

Was that flirting? "I have some tea," she said, trying to sound unenthused.

At the offer of tea most men would leave. Carl was not most men. "Sure. Strong black tea would be great, thanks." He didn't stop petting Jake and he didn't stop staring at her.

She flushed and turned her back on Carl,

nattering on about the origins of different kinds of tea as she filled the kettle, got out her basic black tea bags and two mugs, and reached for the sugar tin after ascertaining that he would indeed like some. She felt like a high school girl on her first date and that irritated her. She reminded herself that it just had been too long since she'd had a good—

"With your knowledge of tea I'm surprised you don't have any loose leaf," Carl interrupted her long stream of chatter.

"Tea bags are faster," she said without thinking.

"Are you in a hurry?"

She turned to look at him and he was in that same damn position, her stupid cat purring madly on his shoulder, except now Carl had a very knowing grin on his face, damn it. She would not let him know how much he was confusing her. "No hurry," she said.

"I thought you said you were busy this afternoon."

Damn it. Emily knew she could think fast on her feet, but right now her brain had stopped working. She sighed. Truth must be told or she'd embarrass herself more.

"Look, Carl," she started, carrying over two mugs of tea and sitting down across from him at the table. She slid a mug across to him. "I'll be honest with you—"

"You mean you've been lying to me? I'm hurt,"

he said with a small smile, reaching for the mug with his free hand.

She waited a moment to let him know she was not amused, then continued. “I have goats to milk. At seven. But I don’t want to waste your time because I don’t want to change the way I do my business. I have a five-year plan and it’s been working well for me. I’m sure you can understand, since I assume you’re a businessman yourself?” She hoped he was; she’d never had a chance to Google him, and what if he turned out to be some crazy person?

“I’m an entrepreneur. When I see something worth investing in, I go for it. After having seen it, I think your operation is worth investing in.”

“I thought you wanted me to sell retail.”

“I did at first. But it’s more than that, which I tried to tell you over the phone, but if you remember, you had a goat emergency.”

Emily remembered. “What exactly have you invested in?” she asked.

“A ski shop in Colorado. A surf shop in Hawaii. An organic cocoa bean producer in Costa Rica. Things like that.”

“Were you born rich?” came out of Emily’s mouth before she could think, further evidence that her brain was on the fritz.

Carl looked at her, and his hand stopped on Jake’s back. “No.” He looked down at the cat and started petting him again. “Surprisingly direct, but a fair question. You have a right to know if I'm legitimate. I take it you didn't try to Google me?"

"I planned to but I haven't done it yet. Now I can ask you directly."

Carl nodded. "I had some success with an IPO when I was in my twenties. It gave me the freedom to invest. So far my investments have been small but in people whose work I admire."

"You admire a surf shop?" Emily asked.

"They do work with at-risk kids."

Emily felt like a jerk. Some guys would have cashed out in an IPO and spent everything on cars or girls, but this guy put some thought into the good he could do with his money. "Sorry. That's admirable. So what exactly do you expect from your investments? You can't be sitting on the boards of these operations."

"Not at all. I'm more of an angel investor. But you'd have to be willing to at least listen to my thoughts about your business. You might actually find them interesting."

An angel investor? Someone to give her money, no strings attached, just because he liked her business? Trying to play it cool, Emily sipped her tea and looked at Carl. "All right. Tell me one of your thoughts and I'll listen. If I think it's interesting we'll talk about how an investment might go."

Carl smiled at her. "You want me to give you money and free advice? That's going to cost you a dinner. Meet me at La Famiglia this Friday night, 8:30. You free?"

Emily wondered. Obviously he'd chosen La Famiglia because that's the restaurant Sharon owned, and Sharon had gotten them in touch. But did he know that Sharon was her best friend, and that he couldn't have picked a more comforting place for her? And Sharon's place could be romantic; was he possibly asking her out? If this was a date wouldn't he have offered to pick her up? So was this a business dinner? She decided there was only one way to find out. She made a laughable show of checking her completely empty calendar, then said, "You're in luck. I'll be there."

"Excellent." He gently displaced Jake from his shoulder and gave him one last long stroke before standing up and shrugging into his jacket. "Thanks for the tea. I'll see myself out."

He was gone before she could respond. Jack meowed once and hopped into her lap, stretching his nose up to touch her chin. "You were awfully nice to that pain in the ass," she said to the cat, but he merely purred and curled into her lap. She thought about Carl's surprise visit. If his plan was to go into business with her, he'd managed to get her to at least to think about it. It made her question once again what exactly Mr. Carl Strand wanted, her or her business? And did it matter to her what the answer was?

***

"Would you like a glass of wine?" Alan asked Greta as he took two out of the cupboard, one for himself and one she presumed for Isabel, who was putting Henry to bed. Greta didn't normally drink wine except on special occasions, but she agreed to a glass. She needed some fortification to talk to her son and his wife about turning their son into a commercial actor. She'd been worrying the idea in her mind like a dog at a bone, and she'd finally concluded that the right thing to do was to have Henry try his hand at acting. One should not pass up opportunities like the one Stan had offered to them. She was fairly certain that Isabel would agree, because Isabel believed her son was gifted in every endeavor unless proven otherwise. Alan tended to agree with Isabel where Henry was concerned. Greta sometimes uncharitably felt this was because Alan was not very involved in Henry's life, but she understood the demands of high-level jobs these days. An electrician could make his own hours, but a finance man like her son had no choice in the matter.

As she accepted a glass of wine from him, she noticed that Alan looked tired. He had dark circles under his eyes and he appeared to be thinner in the face. "How are you feeling?" she asked, wondering if he was coming down with something.

"I'm fine, Mom, great. Work is good, busy. I just picked up another client with a portfolio in the tens of millions." He placed a glass of wine in front of the chair next to him and sat across from her, silently taking a sip from his own glass. She heard the soft closing of a door overhead and knew Isabel had just left Henry safely tucked into his expensive cotton sheets. The dishwasher hummed quietly with the detritus from the dinner she'd cooked and then eaten with them. Alan sat back in his chair, hands resting on the table. "Thanks again for dinner, Mom. Chicken piccata's one of my favorites."

"I know, and you're welcome. Your father is playing poker tonight anyway, pretending he's not smoking cigars and drinking whiskey. He's taken to bringing mints with him, but I can still tell."

Alan laughed. "When Henry's a teenager, Dad'll be giving him tips on how to get away with smoking cigars." He played with his glass, hesitated, then said, "How is Dad?"

"He's fine." Greta saw a brief look of concern in Alan's eyes and added in what she hoped was a reassuring voice, "Just fine."

Alan nodded. "That's good to hear. Emily said he seemed kind of tired on Thanksgiving. But she overreacts to everything, right?" He smiled and drank some wine.

Greta cursed Emily for sharing her concerns about George. She'd told Emily because she needed to confide in someone, but Alan and Isabel always seemed stressed to her and she didn't want to add to their worries. She'd have to ask Emily to keep things to herself, at least regarding George. That girl did have a tendency to share her thoughts with everyone.

Greta was saved from having to change the subject by Isabel's arrival in the kitchen. She was still wearing her soft blue tailored suit but she'd removed her heels. Isabel looked tired too, but her eyes lit up when she saw the wine awaiting her. She slipped into the chair next to Alan and said, "Just what I needed," taking a sip and sighing.

"Fundraising never takes a day off, does it?" Greta observed.

Isabel hooked a lock of blond hair behind her ear and shook her head. "I was so busy today. Thanks again for coming by this afternoon. Dinner was delicious, by the way." She took another long drink of wine and said, "We really do appreciate you so much, Greta."

Greta was acutely aware of Alan and Isabel watching her, smiling, and she realized at that moment that they'd never before expressed much emotion when thanking her for babysitting. They were always in a hurry, flinging words of gratitude over their shoulders as they departed, but tonight they were not going anywhere, they were simply sharing her company and expressing heartfelt thanks. Greta was glad she'd decided to stay and have a glass of wine with them.

"It's such a pleasure for me. Not only because I enjoy Henry's company, but because I see how hard you both work, and it makes me happy if I can help you out even a little."

"A lot, Greta. Cheers to you," Isabel said.

Glasses were raised and everyone took a sip. Greta thought this was an excellent opportunity to bring up Henry's foray into acting, so she explained who Stan Campbell was, how they'd met, and what he'd suggested for Henry. Alan and Isabel listened intently but asked far fewer questions than she'd anticipated. Isabel knew the theater troupe's reputation and was impressed, and in the end they decided it would be a good idea for Greta to meet with Stan and report back, if she didn't mind, because they were both quite busy. Greta readily agreed, because being out of the house meant not worrying when George took a nap or complained of a headache. She turned down their offer of another glass of wine—she'd barely had half of her first one—and set off for home, resolved to call Stan in the morning.

***

George was still sleeping off poker night the next morning when Greta called Stan, but he wasn't in and she had to leave a message. She wiped down the red linoleum countertop and moved her breakfast dishes from the white porcelain sink to her creaky old dishwasher, a little the worse for wear but still running fine. She was sipping hot coffee out of a mug Henry had painted for her, and working a crossword puzzle on the little wooden table where Alan and Emily had once done their homework, when Stan called her back half an hour later.

"Greta Lambert? Stan Campbell here. Great to hear from you! Listen, can you bring Henry in tomorrow afternoon?"

"Tomorrow?" Greta asked. She would have to check with Isabel. "I'm not sure."

"Not sure? We can do it after school. What time does he get out?"

"He usually gets home around 3:45, but—"

"How's 4:15, then?" Stan interrupted.

"It's probably fine, but—"

"We have snacks and drinks here for the kids, no need to worry about that."

"That's very thoughtful of you, Stan, but—"

"Okay, I'll put you down for 4:15, I want him to look just like he would going to the grocery store, no fancy clothes, stuff in his hair, makeup, got it?"

"Makeup? Why on earth—"

"You'd be amazed, my dear, just amazed. Okay then, enjoy the day, see you tomorrow!"

He hung up and Greta stared at the handset for a minute, listening to the buzz of the dial tone, before pressing the Off button and putting the phone down. That man was absolutely exasperating. She felt like she was always two steps behind in their conversations, and by the time she caught up, he was gone. She would have to check with Isabel right away and call Stan back if Henry was unavailable. Luckily, when she called, Isabel answered, and said that if Greta could get Henry from school and bring him to Stan's, Isabel would be able to conduct a second meeting in the city and thus maximize her time there. Greta was just hanging up from that phone call when George entered the kitchen and silently poured himself a cup of coffee. She waited until he had seated himself across from her before asking, "Would you like a cheese omelet and some greasy bacon?" She said it with a teasing smile, knowing that after a night of poker his stomach would be unsettled.

"Very funny," he said, wincing at the thought. "Some dry toast would be nice." He rubbed his face with one hand and yawned. "Late night but a good time. I made twenty bucks."

"Now we can retire," Greta smiled, standing to get some bread from the refrigerator. "I just spoke with Isabel. I'm going to bring Henry to meet Stan tomorrow."

"She thought it was a good idea?" George asked, taking a gulp of coffee.

"She knew of the theater troupe and said they

had a good reputation, so she was comfortable with it, yes. They asked me to bring Henry over since they're both so busy."

George snorted.

"George," Greta warned. She knew what was coming; they'd had this argument so many times.

"People shouldn't be too busy for their own kids."

"I know how you feel, George, but keep it to yourself, especially after the barbecue last summer."

"I was just giving them some advice. I think Henry'd be a lot better off at home, running around outside, with his mom around if he needed her." George shrugged. "It's the whole generation, Greta. How'd they end up like this?"

"Like what? Focused, hard-working, smart?"

"Greedy. They want a bigger house, newer car, more of everything. We did just fine with our small house and our old cars. Did you ever feel deprived?"

"Of course not, George," Greta said, standing up as the toaster beeped. "But it's unfair to call Alan and Isabel greedy. Things are different now. You know very well our house was only five thousand dollars, and what do houses cost nowadays? Not to mention cars. But look at all the opportunities available to Henry that weren't even dreamt of when Alan and Emily were kids." She gave him a piece of toast, spread lightly with strawberry jam, and sat down with him again.

"Do they need such a big house? New cars every few years? Does Henry need all those classes he takes?" George took a large bite of his toast.

"I think life is stressful for young couples these days. If they want to reward themselves with a nice car or a fancy vacation, why not? They're working hard for it."

"It wouldn't be so stressful if they didn't live beyond their means."

Greta sighed. "Should they be living in refrigerator boxes on the street? A house costs what a house costs, George."

He grunted an assent and licked some jelly from his top lip. "Okay, I'll stop, Pollyanna. Don't worry, I won't say anything to Alan and Isabel again, but you know I enjoy a good argument with you. Now tell me about Stan."

Greta told George about her phone call with Stan, and they both decided it might be nice to have George along since Stan was like a steamroller with Greta. Then they sat companionably at the table, Greta working her crossword and occasionally asking George for help with a sports clue, and George idly flipping through the newspaper, until he was roused by an emergency electrical call which he decided to take, he said, because he could work just as hard as this younger generation, even hungover.

***

George took one look at Stan and thought, hustler. But the man had a firm handshake and a steady gaze, and hustling wasn't necessarily bad if you were selling, so he decided to keep an open mind and listen to what Stan had to say. George sat in one of the many chairs scattered around Stan's messy office while Greta helped Henry out of his coat and hung it up on a crowded coatrack along with her own. George glanced around at the folders haphazardly stacked on shelves, the theater posters hung just a bit crookedly, the various coffee mugs left to congeal around the office. He didn't much care about neatness but he knew Greta was probably already itching to straighten the place up.

"Thanks for bringing Henry in, Greta, George," Stan said, nodding to each of them. He was wearing black jeans and a black turtleneck, and had a long ponytail compensating for the lack of hair on top of his head. "Henry, do you know why you're here?"

Henry asked, "For commercials?"

"Sure. What's your favorite, Henry?"

"My favorite?"

"Favorite commercial. Cereal? A toy? A movie?"

"I don't know," Henry said, frowning.

"He doesn't watch much mainstream TV," Greta said. "His mother thinks it's a corrupting influence."

George could see Stan was letting that sink in a

minute, and he couldn't wait to hear what the man was going to say. How could he hire a kid who didn't know anything about commercials for a commercial?

But Stan surprised him, coming out with, "Excellent. No preconceived notions about how he should be acting. Fresh. Love it. Listen, Henry's going to need head shots."

George figured Stan meant photos of Henry's face and said, "They did pictures at preschool this year. Got one in my wallet." He started to reach for his back pocket but Stan said, "No, no, not necessary," waving his hand at George. "I mean professional photos of Henry, done in a studio. You'll have to get some. Here, I can recommend this place," he said, handing George a business card.

"They do them for free, do they?" George asked sarcastically.

"Do you work for free?" Stan retorted.

George liked the response, although he could tell from Greta's intake of breath that she thought one or both of them was being a little rude. She didn't understand men when it came to business; they didn't come to terms over tea, that's for sure. "How much?" he asked.

"Four hundred." Stan held up his hand like a police officer stopping traffic. "I know it's expensive, but it's an investment."

"Poor kids don't act? Or is there a charity out there for them?"

Stan sat back and folded his arms across his chest. “Are you in need of charity?” he asked George.

George shook his head. “That explains why there are no real kids in commercials.”

“You know, George,” Stan said, “that’s exactly right. Exactly right. That’s why I think Henry would be a great asset for a director. He’s a down-to-earth kid, no B.S. I think that’ll come through on the camera.” He pressed a button on his phone and asked someone named Carla to come in and get some video. A young woman arrived, Stan introduced her as his granddaughter, and she took Henry into another room to shoot some video of him talking, making faces, eating and drinking—he’d promised Henry a snack after all—while Stan went over the particulars of how his business worked, what percentage he took off the top, and what he would do for Henry. George asked what kind of jobs Stan had gotten his clients and was impressed with the commercials Stan mentioned, some of them national spots. When George had asked all of his questions, Stan told them to sit and think about it for a few minutes while he left to check on Carla’s progress.

They were silent for a moment, and then Greta said, “The head shots seem expensive.”

“Sure do, but I know Alan can afford it. The question is, is it worth it? My guess is they’ll say yes.”

“I think they will too. They probably spent that

much on their New Year's Eve night out."

"Yup. I'd like to hear from Henry whether he'd like to sit around all day waiting for an audition."

"I know," Greta agreed, "Stan made it sound very boring. I thought they'd have a quicker system for children; I didn't realize that's what filming a commercial is like as well. If you can't suffer through an audition, you can't make it through the shoot. I think Henry can handle long waits, though. He has a good imagination."

George nodded. "But can you handle it? You'll be with him, you know; all the auditions are during the day."

"Yes, I don't mind. It'll keep me busy," she said, smiling. "You can take your naps without me worrying."

"Greta," George started, but Stan interrupted him, walking in with Henry, who was holding an enormous half-eaten candy bar and a juice box. Henry looked happy, almost excited, and George guessed it wasn't because of the forbidden candy.

"Here he is, folks. Did great. Now no rush, you can think about things all you want, but talk to Henry too, because I only take kids who want to get into the business, no stage mothers, or grandmothers as the case may be."

"Are the head shots a deal breaker?" George asked.

"Pretty much," Stan said. "They're part of the

job description."

"We'll need to talk to his parents. How much time do we have?"

"All the time in the world. I'm here to represent Henry should he want representation, which is up to you folks. But if you think you'll go forward with it, let me know and I'll keep him in mind as I get requests."

"We think his parents will probably want to go ahead with it. If Henry wants to do it, too, we'll let you know." George stood up and winced at a sudden pain in his chest. Luckily Greta couldn't see his face but Henry and Stan did, and Stan asked, "Everything okay?"

"Why do you ask?" Greta said sharply. "George?"

"I'm fine. Just my knee. They wear out after a while, you know," George said, wishing Stan had kept his mouth shut.

"Had one replaced last year, George. I feel your pain," Stan said, extending his hand. "Pleasure to meet you, sir."

They shook and Stan was just turning to Greta when Henry piped up with what sounded like "na-doo-ee." George looked at his grandson, whose mouth was full of chocolate, and said, "What?"

"Henry," Greta scolded, "no talking with your mouth full. I believe he said he wants to do it," she added.

Henry smiled around his mouthful and nodded vigorously.

"Excellent," Stan said, and gave Greta a firm handshake and Henry a hair tousle because he was still clutching his now more-than-half-eaten candy bar and the juice box. "Get me those head shots and we'll get the process rolling. It's been a pleasure, folks." He held the door for them as they filed out, George greatly relieved that the pain in his chest had only happened once. Probably just a sore muscle; he'd been crawling around attics yesterday. He might try some stretching when he got home.

***

Isabel reviewed her list of donors, finishing the task of personally calling and thanking them for their always generous end-of-year donations. Tax deductions is what the donations really were, although she believed most of her donors would give even if it weren't tax-deductible. Regardless, it was important to maintain a cordial personal relationship with people when you were asking for their money, and that was where Isabel excelled. She made sure her donors felt like kings and queens as they were writing checks, and it paid off; she was always able to pull in a significant amount of money for a cause. This gave her both discretion as to what she would fundraise for, and an unassailable reputation. Of course, although she had built up her own fundraising consulting business over the past several years, what clients she had were needy and there was never enough money raised to generate more than modest commissions for herself. Still, she very much enjoyed the work.

She sighed and sat back in her chair, rolling her shoulders and moving her head from side to side to release some tension. Feeling slightly chilled, she rose to get some tea, slipping her feet back into her chocolate brown suede pumps and smoothing down her close-fitting camel wool skirt. Greta and George had told Alan and Isabel about their meeting with Stan; Alan had said it would be a great adventure for Henry, and Isabel was reassured that both Henry and Greta wanted to proceed. The cost of the head shots was inconsequential, although neither she nor Alan ever spoke of their income that openly with his parents; they merely said they would be able to handle it.

Greta was with Henry at the photographers right now, after having spent the entire morning accompanying him on the piano as he sang. Isabel wished she could accompany Henry on his new adventure, instead of staying here in the house alone, working in silence. But she understood that the auditions, callbacks, and shoots would each take hours, hours she didn't have, hours that Greta would happily spend. And she and Alan had a family dinner with Henry most nights, during which they heard about his new experiences. He really was excited about being an actor, she thought as she filled an empty mug from the hot water dispenser and added a tea bag. Her little angel. She smiled to herself and looked out the window at the bare trees and hard ground, and the little chickadees flitting around the bird feeder. A squirrel was scheming near the feeder, but the baffle she'd purchased was thwarting an easy meal. There was a solution to every problem, she thought.

Her problem right now was that she was awfully tense, and she didn't really know why. The holidays were over and Henry was happily involved in something productive. Greta and George were more than generous with their childcare, and Alan's job was going well. What did she have to worry about? Not a thing, but she still found herself clenching her teeth a lot. She looked around the spotless kitchen and saw nothing to straighten, nothing to clean. The donor list beckoned. She sighed, musing that a glass of wine would be lovely right now. But you couldn't have a drink in the middle of the afternoon, could you? Alan always said it was five o'clock somewhere, but still, the thought of having wine by herself during the day seemed wrong. On the other hand, she recalled in college having a roommate who made herself hot toddies when she was sick, just a bit of Scotch and honey in her tea. And Isabel did feel a chill. She went into the living room and rummaged through the liquor cabinet—always locked, of course—for some Scotch. Her hot toddy carried her through the remainder of her phone calls, and she thought she sounded more warm and friendly thanks to the toddy. She was also relaxed enough to lie down on the couch and take a quick power nap before Greta returned with Henry.

She awoke to Henry's little hand on her cheek, and she was disoriented for a moment. The room was darker than she expected, and she wondered what time it was. She pulled Henry to her for a hug. "Hi honey, how did it go? Did you get some pictures taken?"

"Yes," he said, climbing up on the sofa and snuggling into the curve of her body.

"Where's Grandma?"

"She's making dinner. Spaghetti."

Isabel smiled; it was one of Henry's favorites. But had she really slept so long that Greta was making dinner? She felt completely refreshed, if a little groggy. "I should help Grandma, Henry. Would you like to have a little rest before dinner?"

"Grandma says we could read a book together. Can we?"

Isabel thought about it. Normally she'd ask Greta to stay for dinner, not to make it. But what mother could resist reading a book to her child? "Of course. Run upstairs and pick one out. I'll just say hi to

Grandma and then we'll read a story."

Henry quickly disappeared upstairs and Isabel rose and stretched before walking into the kitchen. Greta was putting some breadcrumbs into a bowl and there were already two pots over flame on the cooktop.

"I'm so sorry I overslept," Isabel said. "Looks like you've been busy in here."

Greta turned to look at her with an odd expression on her face that Isabel couldn't quite read. "I tried to wake you. You seemed very tired." She wiped her hands on a dishtowel and asked, "Would you like another cup of tea? I washed out your teacup."

"Oh, no thanks. I'm feeling quite refreshed after that nap." She paused. "You tried to wake me?"

Greta looked uncomfortable and hesitated before saying, "I shook you on the shoulder a few times, called your name. You were sleeping very deeply. Finally I told Henry to come in and help me with dinner. He filled a pot with water and put sauce from the freezer into the microwave, then went in to try to wake you. I guess he has the magic touch." She smiled and said, "Will you be reading a book together?"

"Yes, he's upstairs getting one. Thanks again Greta, your making dinner is a nice treat."

Greta shrugged. "I'm just making some meatballs." She turned back to the bowl, reaching in to mix everything together with her hands. She told Isabel that Henry had had a productive session with the photographer, who said he was photogenic and, unlike most children, easy to pose, so they'd gotten everything done in one session. The pictures would be ready in four weeks, and Greta had already called Stan to let him know. Henry returned with a precarious stack of books in hand, and Isabel surrendered her kitchen to a capable Greta, something she'd never done before, but she was feeling awfully relaxed, really not quite herself if she thought about it.

***

Emily stood outside La Famiglia, surreptitiously checking her reflection in the window. She'd called Sharon earlier to ask her opinion about whether her scheduled meeting with Carl was business, pleasure, or both, and to get some idea of what to wear. Sharon had suggested something demure that could easily convert to date wear, so Emily was wearing black tights and pumps, a grey wool skirt, and a soft pink blouse unbuttoned to showcase a cleavage that was discreetly covered with a scarf, which could be removed if events warranted it. The entire outfit had taken Emily thirty minutes to assemble after three phone calls to Sharon and an excavation of her closet, and now she was late. She hated to be late, especially for Carl; she didn't want him to think her unprofessional.

The front door to La Famiglia opened and Sharon stuck her head outside, saying, "Get in here and stop preening. He only got here five minutes ago so don't let him guilt trip you about the time. I put you in one of the cozy little booths in the back."

"How do I look?" Emily asked.

"Fine," Sharon said, giving Emily a quick once-over. "Actually, I'm surprised you did this well with such little time. Bet your bedroom looks like a disaster area. Okay, go," she added, gently pushing Emily into the restaurant.

By the time she got to the booth, Carl was standing up to greet her. "Goats hold you up?" he asked, extending his hand for a shake.

Emily shook his hand, reminding herself to stay focused on the business at hand, and slid into the booth, saying, "Yes, sometimes it goes smoothly, sometimes it doesn't. I'm sorry I'm late."

"Don't worry about it. So was I. Got a call from Costa Rica and didn't want to miss it. You clean up very nicely, by the way."

Clean up? Was he implying that she'd looked a mess the last time they'd seen each other? "Thanks," she said, frowning slightly. What did she care, though, since this was a business meeting?

Carl cleared his throat. "Okay, I've been told I give back-handed compliments. I think that was one of them." He leaned forward and rested his hands on the table. "What I meant was, you look beautiful."

Emily felt a cursed flush moving up her face as she acknowledged his compliment. "Thank you," she said, and reached for her water glass. Was it still business only? Goats were so much easier to read. She took an overly enthusiastic gulp of water and immediately started coughing, causing Carl to stand up and pound her on the back until she stopped. She dabbed under her eyes with her napkin, probably erasing whatever mascara she'd managed to get on, and smiled weakly at him, nodding yes when he asked if she was okay. His hand was still on her back, one knee on the bench seat and the other hand firmly planted on the table. She could smell his cologne as he said teasingly, "I wouldn't want to lose you before dinner," then returned to his seat.

They were thankfully distracted by the arrival of the waiter, who left to fulfill their request of an inexpensive bottle of red wine. Carl had wanted a more expensive one but Emily had insisted on the cheaper bottle because she planned to split the bill. She perused the menu, occasionally making what she hoped were interesting comments about different dishes. The waiter returned with the wine, which he uncorked and poured, then he went over the specials and left them to make their final choices.

"I love the roast chicken here," Carl said. "I get it every time."

"Creature of habit?" Emily asked.

"I guess I am, but it's also really great roast chicken. Have you tried it?"

"Once."

"You didn't like it?" Carl asked, sounding surprised.

"It was good, but when I eat out I like to try things I wouldn't make for myself. Roasting a chicken is easy."

"Maybe for someone who knows how to cook."

"Even if you don't," said Emily, "it's important to have some variety in your life. For instance, this wild mushroom ravioli has four different kinds of mushroom and the sauce over it reduces for half an hour. That's not something I'm likely to attempt at home."

"Do you work for the restaurant, by any chance?"

"The owner is a friend of mine. She would absolutely recommend the ravioli tonight. If you're feeling adventurous, that is."

Carl nodded. "So you're telling me I'm boring and predictable, and that I'll regret it unless I order the ravioli."

Emily laughed. "Basically, yes."

She and Carl both decided to order the wild mushroom ravioli with a salad of winter greens.

That task accomplished, Emily reached for her wine and said, "Cheers."

"To a successful partnership," Carl said.

"I haven't agreed to anything yet," Emily said, but she clinked his glass.

"To the beginning of a beautiful friendship?" Carl ventured.

"Like in Casablanca," she said.

"Maybe a slightly different kind of friendship," he smiled.

"In what way?" she asked, hoping she'd just pinned him down.

"I believe theirs was of a slightly criminal nature, although it was in service of the resistance. And of course they were two men."

"Men and women can't have the same kind of friendship that two men can?" Emily asked, raising an eyebrow.

"Of course they can. But you and I are not both men, to my relief."

"It's a relief that I'm a woman? Why is that?"

Carl shook his head. "You should have been a lawyer. I feel like I'm on the witness stand. If there's this much discussion about a toast, we'll be here until midnight talking about your business."

Carl leaned back in his seat and stretched his legs out under the table. One foot brushed against her shin and she shifted slightly, moving herself out of the way. Now they were back to business, where she felt comfortable and not overwhelmed by the proximity of a man's body to hers. She launched into a discussion of what an angel investment in her business would entail; she'd given it plenty of thought and was ready with a number of questions and a few suggestions of her own. Carl had the answers she wanted and had even brought a list of references and a contract.

They were halfway through their ravioli when Emily put down her fork and said, "Give me a week to check out your references and review your contract. I'll let you know next Friday. So far I have no reason to say no, as long as we're agreed that you'll be invisible in the day-to-day operation, and that your ROI won't kick in for eighteen months." Carl had some intriguing ideas and didn't want control of her company, and after talking to him tonight she felt there was no downside to accepting his money. He agreed to wait a week, and she leaned back and breathed deeply, relieved that their conversation had been mutually satisfying.

"You're quite a businesswoman," Carl said, "although I already knew that."

"Thanks," Emily said, wondering if he'd researched her old days in the corporate world. "You're not bad yourself."

"And next on the agenda of the Mutual Admiration Society," he said, "a discussion of the meal. This ravioli is really tasty."

"There's a secret ingredient but I can't divulge what it is."

Carl looked surprised. "Is it your goat cheese? It doesn't taste like it."

"No, no. I don't know what it is, I just know there is one." Carl was looking at her quizzically so she added, "Sharon told me once there's a secret ingredient, but she would say no more."

"Hmm," Carl said. "Were you friends before or after you started selling your cheese here?"

"Does it matter?" Emily thought it an odd question.

"Just curious if you got your foot in the door as a favor or because you're pushy."

"Or maybe because my product is excellent?" she demanded.

"That goes without saying. Look, I think I'm upsetting you again. Let's just enjoy the rest of our meal, okay? Friends?"

He leaned forward and reached out his hand and she clasped it, expecting a handshake, but he held onto hers in a firm grasp and covered it with his other hand. "Listen, Emily," he said, clearing his throat, "I'm enjoying myself. I'm glad we got our business out of the way, because I'd like to get to know you better."

She sat immobile, sitting there staring into his dark brown eyes with those thick lashes, feeling the strength in his hands, startled by his directness. She opened her mouth to speak, made an embarrassing little choking noise, and then managed to get out,

"Oh. Um. Okay."

He let her hand go and smiled. "Okay?"

She was growing very warm and reached up to remove her scarf, which suddenly felt like it was strangling her, forgetting its original purpose. He glanced down at her newly exposed cleavage for half a second and then returned his gaze to her eyes, smiled briefly, and said, "Okay."

Well, at least the cleavage plan worked. She looked down at her plate and studiously cut a ravioli in half with the side of her fork, wondering what Carl meant by getting to know her better, hoping it meant what she thought it did.

***

Greta watched as a young woman powdered Henry's face to keep the shine down. The lights were bright and very hot. Had she known she would have dressed differently; she was stewing in her winter clothes. Henry didn't seem bothered by the heat at all. He wasn't doing much, really, just sitting at a table in the set kitchen, playing a game with a few other kids while a fake mother put snack food on the table for them. The snacks were called "D'Oh Nuts," a name that made no sense to Greta, and consisted of little balls of dough with different sweet fillings. Henry bit into it like it was ambrosia, and Greta wondered whether he was acting or truly enjoying one of his first encounters with processed food. She watched the adults gathered around the pretend kitchen, adjusting lights, moving microphones, focusing cameras, and was struck by the oddity of the scene. With the constant stopping and starting, the reapplication of makeup, the sound checks, and the camera angles, it was hard to believe the end result would appear to be some children having an afternoon snack in a neighbor's kitchen. She hoped she'd get to see it someday, whether it made it to television or not. Stan had warned her that not all commercials that get shot get used, and that although Henry would get paid for the day, they may never see the ad. She didn't think it mattered that much to Henry; on the way over all he'd done was ask her about how commercials were made, and when she didn't have many answers, he'd speculated on his own.

Greta had a small crossword puzzle book tucked into her purse, which she pulled out when she realized there would be no one to talk to. Most of the other parents had immediately opened laptops or cell phones and were busily tapping away. She found it hard to concentrate, however, and often just sat watching Henry or the general activity in the room. After a few more hours of retouching melted makeup, making minor adjustments to light reflectors, and settling down one particularly overactive child, they finally finished. There was a time limit on work for children of Henry's age, and they'd managed to complete everything, announcing they wouldn't need the kids again tomorrow. They told the kids to visit the snack table, where most of them reached for the little dough balls lined up on trays like soldiers. Only Henry shied away from them, reaching for a juice box instead. As Greta watched, the man who'd introduced himself as the director walked over to her and said, "We got out of here in an afternoon thanks to your grandson. Usually this takes longer because filming kids is like herding cats."

"Thank you," Greta said, assuming there was a compliment in there somewhere.

"No prob. I'll ask for him again if I need his type. Made my job easier, thanks." He gave her a thumbs-up and walked away, and Greta turned to see Henry running towards her.

"Grandma! Did I do a good job? I got a juice box but I'm hungry and I don't like those snacks. They taste weird."

"Yes, dear, you did a very good job. The director said he liked working with you and he'll ask for you again some day. You must be tired after all that acting."

"I was acting, Grandma. Did you see me? I didn't make a yucky face even when I had to eat those things."

Greta laughed. "Were they really that awful, Henry?"

“It tasted like paper and glue with sugar on top. I got paper and glue in my mouth once in art class, and that’s what it tasted like, except sweet.” He looked down at his still unopened juice box and then up at her.

Greta smiled and took Henry’s hand. “Let’s sit down and I’ll help you with the straw.” She led him back to a cafeteria table off to the side where someone had put a large array of D’Oh Nuts along with some prepackaged snacks. They unearthed a package of trail mix and sat next to each other in the row of chairs that had been provided for the adults during the shoot. Most people had left, the crew was tidying up, and the bright lights had been turned off. Greta wiggled the straw into Henry’s juice box and opened his snack, which was advertised as Healthy Trail Mix and which she belatedly realized contained chocolate candies. She made a mental note to bring her own snacks should they do another commercial shoot.

“Henry,” she said once he’d settled in, “I know you didn’t like what you had to eat today, but did you have fun making the commercial?” She was worried that what turned out to be the tedium of shooting a commercial would be difficult for a small child to endure.

“I loved it, Grandma! Did you see all the cameras? And the microphones? And did you see them putting the powder on my face?”

Greta smiled at Henry's enthusiasm as he continued to talk about every small aspect of his experience. Clearly he'd been paying a great deal of attention to all that had gone on that afternoon, even more than she had. If he enjoyed it that much, she was sure it was the right thing to do, bringing him to auditions and pursuing this course of action. She would tell Isabel when she brought Henry home, guessing that Isabel needed the reassurance as much as she did.

Chapter 6

GEORGE DIDN'T KNOW at what point the pain had become something he could no longer ignore. It had been creeping up on him all morning. At first he thought it was indigestion from the sausage he'd picked up from the butcher whose exterior lights he'd fixed last night, and which he'd fried up with some eggs after Greta left to pick up Henry. After cracking the window and studiously washing, drying, and putting away all evidence of his unhealthy eating choices, which was far easier than listening to Greta scold him when she returned, he'd headed out to a job at one of the big houses out near where Alan lived. It had taken him ten minutes to figure out that the lady of the house didn't know where the electric panel was and consequently hadn't been able to flip the circuit herself, which had tripped because she'd attached a CD player, a video player, a large radio, and a many horse-powered mixer to one outlet. She'd used an outlet extender of a type he hadn't seen in twenty years and which had sparked and caught fire moments after she turned on the mixer. She looked so sheepish that he felt bad charging her, but not bad enough to tell her it was on the house. That he reserved for elderly folks and women in small homes with lots of children hanging off them. Besides, parting her and her money would serve to remind her of the mistake she'd made, one which could have been disastrous had she turned on the mixer and left the room. He pocketed the check and headed home, not having another job scheduled until after lunch.

Turning into his driveway George felt a burning in his chest and cursed the sausage he'd eaten for breakfast. Popping a couple of antacid from his glove compartment after he shut off the car, he opened the door to get out when a weakness in his leg made him hesitate for a moment. Same thing that had happened in the apple orchard, but that had gone away pretty quickly. He boosted himself up and out, hung on to the door for a moment, and assessed himself. Burning sensation, gone. Weakness, gone. Greta's constant worry was turning him into a hypochondriac. He slammed the door shut and headed for the house. It wasn't until he was sitting in his armchair with a coffee and the paper that the burning sensation came back, but this time there was a pressure on his chest too. Damned heartburn. He decided he'd look for a stronger antacid next time he went to the drugstore. But an hour later he was the proverbial frog in the pot of hot water, sitting in his chair and suddenly and acutely aware that he was not well. Trouble was, he wasn't sure what to do about it.

What were his symptoms, really? Just a bit of heartburn, some weakness in his leg, a little chest pressure. Each of these alone was something he could handle, and had in the past, but all of them together added up to a sense of unease he couldn't quite shake. He knew heart attacks came with arm pain, which he didn't have, but he clearly had something that over-the-counter medicines and rest could not fix. He decided to call his doctor. Five minutes later he was very much regretting his phone call, because the nurse who answered the phone had decided he should report to the nearest Emergency Room immediately and that he should not attempt to drive there himself. But Greta was with Henry at the commercial shoot, Alan was in the city, and all the neighbors he was acquainted with worked during the day. So he had two choices, neither of which appealed to him: call Isabel or call an ambulance. He decided to try Isabel first, and was oddly relieved that she didn't answer either of her numbers. He didn't leave a message.

He pondered his next move. He figured that medical people were always conservative, and that the nurse probably told him not to drive because she wanted to cover her own ass. Getting to the Emergency Room was mind over matter, really; he needed to get a hold of himself and drive the damn car. He slid on his jacket, picked up his keys, and headed out the door.

***

Isabel's home phone rang twice before the

machine picked up. No message, she noted, relieved. Would there ever be an end to telemarketing, she wondered. At least there were answering machines to fend off the undesirable. She recrossed her legs and returned her attention to the novel she'd received from a satisfied client months ago. She never sat and read a book in the middle of the day, considering it a little too self-indulgent. After all, she had a child and a job, and neglecting either one was wrong. But every time she spied that book sitting on her desk, she had a little mental argument about whether she was virtuous or ungrateful for not reading the book. Also, she worried that someday her client would ask her if she had liked the book and she would be embarrassed to admit that she hadn't yet read it. That fact, combined with the lingering cold she still had, resulted in her deciding to do something she rarely did, relax and read in broad daylight. The fact that she had made this decision after two hot toddies was something she preferred not to think about. But she had deferred three tasks on her to-do list until tomorrow, turned down her cell phone to the softest possible ring, and finally picked up that novel. Her legs were stretched under a blanket on the oversized couch in their living room, her back rested against two large pillows, and a bright light behind her illuminated the pages she was finding so interesting that she didn't notice that her cell phone had slipped in between two cushions until much later, after fifty more pages, one more hot toddy, and a lengthy nap.

Emily could not believe how right it felt to be sitting on the couch with Carl's arm around her, his left hand draped casually on her shoulder. Carl had been traveling, and they'd only managed to see each other a few times over the last couple of months. This was the first time she'd cooked dinner for him. After they ate, she'd lit a fire in the fireplace and they'd sat down side by side, chatting and looking at the flames. Jake had jumped up on Carl's lap, Carl had put his arm around Emily, and there they sat, like they'd been that way forever. They were sipping a port Carl had brought over. She'd never tried port before but she was enjoying it. She was enjoying everything, really, but she felt almost immobilized by the questions running through her mind. She had no more questions about whether Carl was attracted to her, of course; that was obvious. There had been plenty of kissing and hand-holding, but this was the first time they'd been alone together. Was tonight the night? Should she discuss it, or maybe just climb into his lap? She was thinking like a teenage girl. She sighed and took another sip of the port.

"Everything okay?" Carl asked.

"Yes. Very okay."

"Like the port?"

"Delicious. Thanks for bringing it over." She glanced at him and found he was looking at her.

Startled, she stared back at the fire.

"Emily." Carl tapped on her left shoulder with his finger.

She turned her head to the right again and there he was, his face inches from hers. She tried to sound composed. "Yes?"

He just sat there looking at her, a little smile dimpling one corner of his mouth. Then he lifted his hand from her shoulder to the back of her head and with the softest touch gently urged her toward him.

That was all she needed. Before she could stop to think about it, she pressed her lips against his. With a sharp intake of breath he pressed back, and before she knew it they had their arms wrapped around each other and Jake had been unceremoniously dumped on the ground. They'd been kissing long enough for another fire to start inside her when Jake jumped on the back of the couch behind their heads and sat there, periodically twitching his tail into their faces. After the third slap of Jake's tail, Emily giggled and pulled back slightly, looking at Carl. His hair was pushed up on one side and he looked quite pleased with himself. She wondered what to do next. What she wanted to do was drag him into the bedroom, but instead she said, "Should I put another log on the fire?"

"Only if I'm invited to stay and enjoy it," he said, running his hand through her hair.

"Oh, yes," she said, and rose to tend to the fire.

"Do you think Jake is jealous?"

"I usually spend the evening petting him, so yes, he probably is." That made her social life sound pretty exciting. She put a log on the fire.

"You must not have the chance to do many evening activities with the milking schedule," Carl said.

"What kind of activities are you talking about?" she teased, moving the embers around with a poker.

"No, not … I mean … you know, things like book clubs."

Emily put the poker away and turned to look at him. He had an embarrassed expression on his face. "I know. I was kidding. Every twelve hours is a tough schedule. I've been looking for a backup person so I could take a night off, but so far I haven't found anyone. There aren't many part-time goat milkers out there." She returned to the couch and sat next to him. "I knew up front this business would be time-consuming, but I'd love a vacation."

He grinned and pulled her to him, saying, "As your angel investor, I strongly recommend it."

Carl's shirt was unbuttoned and Emily's was completely off when her phone rang. She felt Carl hesitate for a moment mid-kiss, and she knew he was wondering if she needed to answer it, but who ever called her at this hour? She pulled him to her again, but they both stopped a few moments later when they heard a voice speaking from her answering machine.

It was Isabel.

***

For a silent room there was a lot of noise. That was what struck Greta as she sat in one of two metal and foam chairs pushed up against the wall next to George's hospital bed. A white cabinet and countertop faced her on the opposite side of the bed. The overhead lights hummed, machines beeped, footsteps came and went in the hallway. She heard a murmur of voices from the room next door. They'd given George some kind of sedative, and he was snoring gently, his head turned slightly to the side. She wanted to wake him but knew that, like with a sick child, it was best to let him rest. She wanted to shake him, really, and ask him what he'd been thinking, driving himself to the hospital, and why he hadn't called her, and why he hadn't gone to see the doctor months ago, and why he was scaring the hell out of her. She looked at him, and saw the young man she'd married, the energetic father of her children, her robust husband of so many years, and now he was diminished, lying in that excuse of a bed, a thin blanket covering his frame, medical paraphernalia attached in various places.

She didn't even know what was wrong with him. She'd dropped off Henry and stayed to chat with Isabel, who was once again napping on the couch when they arrived. She had a nagging suspicion that something was wrong with Isabel but it flew out of her head when Isabel had gone to retrieve her cell phone from the couch and announced that George had called her. Both women knew the unspoken truth that something had to be wrong for George to call Isabel, and Greta immediately called both home and his cell phone and got no answer. Although George could have been out on a job, Greta had an uneasy feeling and went home right away, where she found a note on the kitchen table that read, “Gone to hospital. Back soon.” There was only one hospital in town and that was where she went, and after a minor outburst at the hospital’s registration desk, she was ushered in to George’s room, where she was told he’d been given something to help him sleep and was resting comfortably. She had used her cell phone directly under the “No Cell Phones Please” sign to call Isabel and tell her what was going on. She’d told Isabel to stay home with Henry, and Isabel promised to call Alan and Emily for her. A nurse had poked her head in to say the doctor would be with them momentarily, but that felt like ages ago. Her mind raced but she couldn’t stay on any thought longer than a few seconds, because all her thoughts were laced with fear.

The metal click of the door opening startled her as Alan walked into the room. He was still in his dress pants and shirt but was holding his suit jacket as if he were already warm. She was greatly relieved to see him, although disappointed he wasn't the doctor. Alan looked almost angry, his eyes wide, his eyebrows down, and he said loudly, "Mom, what's going on? I got a call from Isabel. What's wrong with—"

"Shh! Let your father sleep," Greta whispered quickly. She stood up and went to Alan, giving him a hug.

He squeezed her briefly and said quietly, "Sorry. I'm just upset. Let's step out in the hallway." He opened the door again and they slipped outside. "What happened?"

The lights were brighter in the hallway. Several doors down there was a nurses' station staffed by one harried-looking nurse. Occasionally nurses would bustle in or out of a room, and a janitor was quietly mopping at the far end of the hallway. A red-faced older man lay on a gurney with an IV drip near the elevator doors, and a nurse was wheeling a young woman in a wheelchair down the hall. Greta wondered where George's doctor was. "I don't know anything yet. He called Isabel this afternoon—"

"Why did he call Isabel?"

"We don't know. But he couldn't reach her—"

"Why not? Wasn't she working?"

Greta paused. "She didn't answer right away and he didn't leave a message. She noticed a missed call when I brought Henry back from his commercial—"

"How'd it go? Did he like it?" Alan ran his hand through his hair and rubbed the back of his head.

Greta put her hand on Alan's arm. "I understand you're upset, dear, but please let me finish. We'll talk about Henry later. I tried to reach Dad but I couldn't, and when I got home I found a note saying that he was going to the hospital. I came right away and they brought me here, and said the doctor would be with me soon."

Alan took a deep breath and asked, "And how long ago was that?"

"Half an hour? I don't know."

"That's ridiculous. I'm going to find the doctor now. You go back in and sit with Dad."

"Alan, the nurse said the doctor would be in—"

"I'll be right back." He turned and stalked off toward the nurses' station.

Greta didn't like the idea that Alan was going to bother the obviously busy staff, but she didn't want to argue with him either, and she didn't think it would have made a difference. He seemed very tense, which was understandable, but it made him almost belligerent. Hoping he wouldn't antagonize anyone, she went back into George's room. He still lay there, sleeping. At least his face was a good color, and his breathing was deep. He looked so healthy, she couldn't imagine what was wrong with him.

She heard the door open again but it was neither Alan nor the doctor. Emily quietly entered the room, followed by a solid-looking man with an almost military bearing, shut the door gently, and quickly came over to Greta, who stood and hugged her. "Hi dear," she whispered, holding her for a moment and then pulling back and suggesting they step outside. Greta expected to see Alan in the vicinity but he'd disappeared. She wondered if he'd followed some poor doctor into another patient's room.

"Mom, this is Carl Strand," Emily said. "Carl, this is my mother, Greta."

He shook her hand firmly. "I'm sorry we couldn't meet under better circumstances, Mrs. Lambert."

Greta nodded. "It's very nice to meet you, Mr. Strand. Please call me Greta."

"And I'm Carl." He hesitated, and added, "I hope you don't mind me coming along. I realize it's a family matter, but I was with Emily, and I wanted to offer my support."

Greta was impressed with Carl's poise and manners, and she noticed he was rather handsome, even in these terrible fluorescent lights; he reminded her of George as a young man. She wanted to ask Emily all about him, but it would have to wait. She thanked Carl for being there, assured him he was welcome, and told both of them everything she knew about George being in the hospital, which wasn't much. "And your brother," she finished, "went off to find out what's going on, although I don't know where he's disappeared to."

"Alan's here?" Emily asked.

"He was very intent on getting answers immediately. I told him not to bother anyone," Greta shrugged. "I don't really see any doctors around."

Carl said, "When my father was stabilized in the hospital after his heart attack, we didn't get a visit from the doctor for three hours. I'm sure they'll be in as soon as they can. Your husband looks like he's resting comfortably."

"He does look good, doesn't he? I suppose if something were terribly wrong we would have heard already."

Carl assured her she was right and offered to get them something to eat or drink. Greta admitted she was thirsty and a little peckish; she hadn't had any dinner. He told them to keep George company and headed out toward the elevators. As they turned to go back into George's room, Greta said to Emily, "Carl seems very nice."

Emily put her arm around Greta's shoulders and squeezed. "I've been dating him for a little while. He's an entrepreneur, which means he's rich enough not to work. He made a lot of money on a start-up. He's from around here, he has no siblings, and his parents live in Florida. I think our relationship has potential. Does that answer the questions you were about to ask?"

Emily smiled and Greta knew she was trying to

cheer her up. She smiled back. "For the most part. Let's go in and sit with your father."

***

Emily sat and watched her father's chest rise and fall. She thought he looked fine, just sleeping; but she wanted to know exactly what was wrong with him. She could understand Alan's desire to hunt down a doctor and find out right away. Her mother was trying as best she could to quietly eat a packet of peanut butter crackers; little dots of cracker had fallen onto her thick wool skirt. Carl was standing behind Emily with his hand on her shoulder. His presence there was a real comfort to her, and she could tell he'd been able to reassure her mother as well. She took a sip of the water Carl had brought her and sighed. Alan had been gone now for close to twenty minutes, and she wondered where he was. Whether or not he'd been able to find a doctor, wouldn't he have returned by now? She was considering getting up to find him when he came in. Alan was a little pale and looked almost distracted. Emily stood up and hugged Alan quickly, then stepped back and introduced him to Carl.

They shook hands and Carl said, "Sorry about your father."

"Thanks. I couldn't find out anything, except that if you raise your voice the battle-axe nurse will remind you the hospital has security." Alan wiped under his nose, looked around the room, and extracted a thin tissue from a nondescript cardboard box, blowing his nose quietly and tossing the tissue into a trashcan.

"Did she call security?" Emily asked, surprised.

He shook his head. "No, but she read me the riot act." He draped his suit jacket on the back of Emily's chair and walked to the bed, staring at George for a moment then turning back to them. "Anyone want some water?"

"You can share mine," Emily offered. "Carl brought us some."

"That's okay. I could use a walk," Alan said. "I'll stay away from the staff." He glanced at his father and slipped out into the hallway again.

Alan wasn't usually this antsy, Emily thought. This must be the way he responded to stress. She glanced at her mother, who looked surprised and disappointed at Alan's behavior. "I think he's just really worried, Mom," she said.

Carl cleared his throat. "I think I'm a little hungry after all. I'm going to get myself something. Anyone else? Emily?"

They thankfully declined and Carl left. Emily tried to smooth over Alan's strange behavior, attributing it to nerves. Then Greta told her about George calling Isabel, and how that's when she knew something was wrong. They both smiled; they knew

George hated to ask for help, and certainly Isabel would not have been his first choice. It's not that he disliked her; she just brought out the worst of his pride.

"But why didn't Isabel answer her phone? She brings that thing to the dinner table, for God's sake."

Greta hesitated. "She'd fallen asleep."

"Our Energizer Bunny fell asleep? Is she not well?" Emily was very surprised. Isabel was one of those people who was constantly available, always working, always in touch.

"Maybe. She said she's just getting over a cold. She was napping when I returned with Henry." Greta started to say something else and then stopped.

"What?" Emily asked.

"It's just … twice in the last few weeks she's been napping in the afternoons. Of course there's nothing wrong with that, but it's so unlike her. It makes me worry."

"Mom, everything makes you worry," Emily said. "You know what it makes me think?"

Her mother looked at her hopefully.

"Maybe she's pregnant. Sleeping in the afternoons, low energy, it fits. And that could explain Alan's weird behavior, too."

"Oh, Emily, wouldn't that be wonderful?" Greta reached over and put her hand on Emily's forearm. "That would explain everything, wouldn't it? And I was worried that … " she trailed off.

"That what?"

Greta sighed. "Nothing. I hope you're right. We'll find out in time, I suppose. I remember with Henry they didn't tell anyone until she was four months along."

"And even then you could barely tell, she dressed so carefully."

Greta nodded. "She always does. Now, tell me about Carl. How did you meet?"

Emily answered all her mother's questions about Carl, realizing it would help distract her until the doctor arrived. She found she didn't mind so much talking about him, anyway. It had been a long time since she'd had anyone in her life, especially someone who felt like he was here to stay. She was mid-sentence about their first date at La Famiglia when the door opened, revealing a young blond doctor in light blue scrubs.

***

Greta's breath caught in her throat as the doctor entered the room. She thought about those moments in one's life when everything changes because of the words that come out of one person's mouth. It might be "I'm pregnant" or "your aunt died" or "I'm in love with someone else," but good or bad, it will change your life. She fervently hoped this would not be one of those moments.

The doctor stopped and looked at his chart. “Mrs. Lambert?” he asked.

“Yes?” Greta said, standing up. Emily rose and Greta added, “This is my daughter, Emily.”

“I’m Dr. Weatherbee. Your husband has a tumor on his spine, which is causing an autonomic neuropathy of the leg. It’s manifesting itself as an irregular heartbeat and digestive upset. Mr. Lambert also admitted to occasional numbness or possibly paralysis in his right lower extremity. We’ve stabilized his heartbeat. We’d like to keep him here and run some tests. A surgeon can see him the day after tomorrow to determine the feasibility of removing the tumor. The prognosis is good in cases like this, and he seems relatively healthy.”

The speech flowed over Greta and all she was left with was “tumor, irregular heartbeat, paralysis, surgeon.” Through the fog she heard Emily’s voice.

“So the tumor is doing what? Pressing on a nerve?”

“Basically,” the doctor said. “The nerves being pressed determine the symptoms the patient experiences. In your father’s case, it’s mainly interfering with his gastrointestinal tract and his heart, although at some point his leg was being affected.”

“And the tumor isn’t cancerous?” Emily asked.

“We’ll do a biopsy. That will determine the surgeon’s course of action, that and a closer look at the tumor." He paused, looking at them both, then continued. "The nurses' station can give you all the information you need on the tests that are scheduled for tomorrow. Your husband has been given a sedative and won't be waking up again tonight. I would suggest you go home and get some rest."

Greta thanked him and he left the room. The two of them stood in silence for a moment, then Emily said, "It sounds like he's going to be okay."

Greta looked at her. She didn't know what to think. Awful words were still floating around in her brain, and she hadn't heard "he's going to be okay." But Emily seemed reassured. The thought of surgery scared Greta, but if that's what it took to make George well, that's what they would do. She didn't want to leave George's side, but she was tired, and she couldn't possibly sleep in these chairs. "Do you really think he'll sleep all night?" she asked.

"Yes," Emily said. "Mom, you should go home and get some sleep so you're refreshed tomorrow when Dad wakes up. I'll find Alan" —she paused for effect, because where the hell was he? —"and tell him what's going on. You just go get some rest. You want to be in great shape tomorrow, okay?"

Greta thought that Emily was probably right. George really hadn't stirred once since she'd arrived, and the doctor did say he'd been stabilized. She wanted to be at her best tomorrow, when George would be awake and decisions would have to be made. “All right,” she agreed. “Thank you, honey. I will go home and get some rest, but I’m going to be back here very early in the morning. I’m just going to stay a few minutes longer.”

She gave Emily a hug and watched her leave, waited until the door clicked shut, and walked over to the bed. Leaning in close to George’s ear, she said quietly, “George Lambert, you better get well quick. I’ll be back tomorrow. You get a good night’s sleep,” and kissed him on the cheek. She smoothed the blanket over him, rested her hand on his shoulder briefly, and quietly left the room.

Chapter 7

ISABEL STUDIED HER face in the mirror. She was adept at covering the nascent crow's feet and making her pale skin look radiant, but the bags under her eyes were going to take some extra effort. She'd been so busy since George had taken ill, although to their great relief his tumor had been benign and he was on the mend. Since George's hospital stay, Alan had become another person entirely, one she wasn't enjoying living with. Sighing, she unscrewed the cap on the concealer and went to work. Alan was already gone, and Henry was happily watching a video while eating a bowl of cereal. She had a busy day today; after her morning phone calls she had a business lunch to which she would have to bring Henry, and then they went straight to an audition. Henry loved his budding career in commercials, but it had been so much easier when Greta was accompanying him. Sometimes she had to choose between Henry's schedule and her own; she'd had to cancel more than one meeting. Evenings she usually made dinner and got Henry to bed on her own, because Alan rarely showed up for dinner anymore. He usually claimed a heavy workload, arrived home after Henry was in bed, and disappeared to his office. Even when she left him a plate of food, he rarely ate it. She wasn't sure if George's illness was triggering some sort of personality change in Alan, but whatever it was, it wasn't good.

She had tried to talk to Alan about the situation once or twice, but he was so busy these days, and if she did manage to corner him, he was edgy and unreceptive. The only reason he craved her presence lately was for sex, and although that alone left her feeling connected to him, it was often when she was already half asleep, further contributing to her exhaustion. She'd taken to having a few glasses of wine with dinner. It put her in a better mood and enabled her to forget about everything for the time it took to clean up and get Henry into bed.

Isabel surveyed her face. The concealer would have to do; she didn't have any extra time this morning. Henry was moving around downstairs, which meant his cereal was finished and he was probably putting his things in the dishwasher. He tried hard to help out, although lately he'd been a little fussy with all the changes in his life. She began to apply mascara, greatly missing the days when Greta had provided so much of their childcare, and she could leisurely apply makeup and get dressed because her workday didn't start so early. Now that Greta was caring for George, she was simply unavailable to watch Henry. Greta had suggested that Isabel drop Henry at their house occasionally, but Isabel realized that Greta was very busy assisting George with his physical therapy and doing most everything else George used to do. Isabel did like to bring them dinner sometimes, to give Greta a break from cooking and also because seeing Henry cheered them both up. But taking Henry to an audition or a photo shoot, cooking, laundry, all the things that Greta had happily done for them in the past, was now up to Isabel. She'd asked Alan to pitch in and he'd suggested they should look into hiring someone, which had become another task on her to-do list. It had occurred to her as she fell asleep last night that Emily had just interviewed a number of people for a part-time goat-milking job; perhaps one of them would be interested in a part-time housekeeping job. She would call Emily later; right now she had to fly.

***

"I'm glad you're going to be with me for this," Emily said to Carl, looking at him as he drove to Alan and Isabel's. She loved to look at him, his strong arms under the old leather jacket, his competent hands on the steering wheel.

"You make it sound like a trial," he said, glancing at her and smiling a little. "It's just dinner. And I'm looking forward to meeting Isabel and Henry."

"And hopefully Alan will be in a better mood."

Carl shrugged. "People respond differently to stress. I'm sure he's back to normal now that your

Dad is recuperating. The surgery was successful; he's off the meds. A few more months of rehab and he'll be as good as new. Nothing for Alan to worry about now."

Emily stared out the window, hoping Carl was right. She got the sense after talking to Isabel a few days ago that something was amiss with Alan, but she wasn't quite sure what. Isabel was never very forthcoming, although tonight she hoped to get a few glasses of wine into her and have a little heart-to-heart while the guys watched the basketball game. Plus she planned to take Henry aside and make sure everything was all right with the little guy. Henry was busy with his acting, if you could call it that, and she didn't think he had much time to be a kid any more. She'd been completely distracted by her father's illness and had never acted on her decision to invite Henry to the farm more often, but that was going to change. Now that she had part-time help, she'd have more time to spend with her extended family. Having confronted, however briefly, the idea of losing one of them, she realized she needed to make an effort to bring them into her life.

She couldn't credit herself with this realization, though; a lot of it was Carl. He'd been surprised at how little she saw her family; being an only child with far-away parents, he thought she was very lucky to have them around. He'd jumped at the chance to accompany her tonight; apparently a family dinner and a televised sporting event were his idea of heaven. She looked at him again.

"You're quiet," he said.

"You're great," she replied.

He grinned and reached his right hand out to caress the back of her head. "So are you."

***

Before they headed up the walk, Carl grabbed Emily and kissed her hard, and she reciprocated just as fervently. When they came up for air she said, "We should go in before Henry peeks out the window and sees us."

Carl let her go and squeezed her behind as she turned to head up the walk. She swatted his hand away, then grabbed it and held it in hers. "Behave," she said, sure she was grinning like an idiot.

Henry was the one who opened the door, stepping onto the porch before they reached the top step. "Hi, Aunt Emmy!" he yelled. "Hi, Mister Stand!"

"Hi, Henry," Emily said, scooping him up into a hug. "Hey, kiddo, my friend's name is Mr. Strand," she added, emphasizing the 'r.'

"You can call me Carl, okay?" Carl said, as Emily released Henry and they all stepped into the house. He bent forward to offer his hand but Henry went right to him and gave him a hug, and Emily was suddenly and overwhelmingly moved by the look on Carl's face. He looked very happy, and Emily was blinking back tears. She must be getting her period, she thought, turning to surreptitiously wipe them away.

She'd just dabbed at the corner of her eyes when Isabel came into the foyer. "Hello!" she called, approaching and surprising Emily with a big hug. She then proceeded to give Carl a handshake, thanked him warmly for their offered bottles of wine and port, and tousled Henry's hair before she took his little hand in hers and led them all into the kitchen.

Emily wondered who this Isabel was, as she and Carl were ushered onto stools at the counter. Grocery-store cheese and crackers were spread on a paper plate and there were two wine glasses awaiting them, although Isabel offered Carl a cold beer if he preferred. He did and she retrieved a frosted glass from the freezer, filling it with an imported beer and spilling it a little as she put it down in front of him. Carl took a paper cocktail napkin from a pile next to the platter and placed it on the spill, then put his glass on top of the napkin. He looked at Emily, whose mouth she belatedly realized was hanging open, and raised his eyebrow quizzically. Closing her mouth, she shook her head slightly and looked at Isabel, who was opening a bottle of red wine.

"Please, open the bottle we brought," Carl said.

"I'll save that one for later," she said. "Alan

wanted me to open this one first."

"I insist," Carl said. "My guy says it's what we want to start with. The port's for the end of the evening."

Isabel frowned a little but politely agreed and opened Carl's bottle.

He was very sure of himself, Emily thought. She admired how Carl was able to convince people.

As Isabel poured a glass of red wine, Henry pulled a bowl of grapes from the refrigerator. "I washed these all by myself," he said, proudly lifting them onto the island.

"Great job, Henry. I love grapes," Carl said, standing and pulling out the stool next to Emily. "How about a lift?" He deposited Henry on the seat and Henry thanked him sincerely before taking a bunch of grapes and popping a few into his mouth.

Isabel took a seat opposite them and began talking to Carl. She was warm and friendly, and Carl was his usual outgoing self, so in a short amount of time Isabel knew everything about Carl and about his and Emily's relationship. Carl and Isabel even had some acquaintances in common, people they both knew from social events. Emily wondered if Isabel was chatting up Carl as a prospective donor to some cause, but she didn't think so. Isabel seemed more relaxed, almost like she'd been the time she came over and they'd gotten drunk together. Maybe it was her and Alan's father getting sick, maybe it was

Henry's excitement over his new career, but Isabel was definitely loosening up. Also, Emily noticed, she'd yet to pour herself a glass of wine. Perhaps she was pregnant after all.

"If you'll excuse us," Isabel said, "Henry and I are going to go upstairs so he can get washed up."

"Awwww," Henry whined, kicking under the counter.

Emily was surprised; Henry rarely acted up.

"Before dinner?" Carl asked, probably trying to angle for Henry to stay a little longer.

"He's already had his dinner," Isabel said. "The grapes were his dessert. Now it's off to bed." She frowned at Henry, who was still kicking under the counter.

Henry tried a different approach, stopped kicking, and said in as grown-up a voice as he could muster, "I think I'm old enough to stay up a little later now," but Emily could tell from his tone of voice that he knew he wasn't going to win this fight.

Isabel scooped him off the stool, Henry said his goodnights and they left the room. The moment they were out of earshot Carl turned to Emily and said quietly, "Is everything all right? You had such a strange look on your face before."

Emily nodded. "Isabel was behaving so strangely, I didn't know what to think."

"She seemed fine to me. Very nice."

"I know, but she's usually more uptight. I was

shocked to see only one kind of cheese from a regular grocery, on a paper plate, with paper napkins. She's generally very upscale, everything's presented in a fancy way," Emily shrugged. "She's just different."

"Sounds like a change for the better, though, right?" Carl asked.

Emily agreed as she stood and walked around the island to put Henry's napkin in the trash. She was pushing the trash bin back under the counter when she heard the basement door open and Alan walked in.

"Hey, Em!" he said, putting his briefcase down on the counter and shrugging off his coat. "Carl, nice to see you again." He draped his coat over one arm and went over to shake Carl's hand.

He looks much better, Emily thought. His face was still thin but it had some color to it.

Alan told them briefly about the traffic he'd run into as he dumped his coat and briefcase onto a kitchen chair. Taking in the island, with the crackers, cheese, and grapes, he said, "Is that our appetizer?"

Emily nodded and said, "Henry washed the grapes himself."

"Henry. Let me run up and say goodnight to him. Be right back." Alan darted out and up the stairs.

"He looks better, doesn't he?" Emily asked Carl.

Carl nodded slowly. "Yeah, he looks better."

"That wasn't a resounding yes. You don't think so?"

Carl looked at her as if he were debating whether to say something. At that point Isabel returned and said, “Alan’s reading a story to Henry before bed. Isn’t that sweet?”

“Doesn’t he usually?” Emily asked. “I thought that was a ritual around here.”

“He’s been awfully busy lately,” Isabel said. “So have I. But Darlene will be a big help. Thanks for sending me her contact info, by the way. She said she’s much happier doing housekeeping than milking goats. Do you like your new assistant?”

“Anyone who gives Emily a night off is a hero,” Carl said. “Eventually I hope to work my way up to a whole weekend.”

“Whoa, a whole weekend,” Emily said, smiling. “That’s a big step for me. And my goats. Let’s see how Miranda works out first. But yes,” she answered Isabel’s question, “I do like her. She grew up in 4H and already knows how to milk, she’s in graduate school for agriculture, and this fits into her schedule really well. I couldn’t have dreamed up a better fit.”

They were discussing weekend getaways when Alan returned to the kitchen. He picked up the bottle, looked at it, and said, “What’s this?”

“Supposed to be a great wine on its own, so I thought it’d be a good bet for appetizers,” Carl said.

Alan glanced at Isabel and she said, “He insisted.”

“Thanks,” Alan said. Emily knew him well

enough to tell that he was slightly annoyed. Alan was too used to being the boss man, she thought. It wouldn't kill him to acquiesce occasionally.

They sat and chatted for a while. Eventually Alan said, "Isabel, help me pick another bottle from the cellar."

"There's one right there," Emily said, pointing to the bottle Isabel had planned to open earlier. She was surprised they'd gone through a bottle; Alan must have had at least two thirds of the first one.

"That one doesn't follow well after the one we just had. I know just which one I want."

Emily knew Alan was rebuking Carl for changing the wine. Two alpha males, she thought. Alan and Isabel went downstairs, and Isabel returned quickly with a bottle of wine. "Alan's gone to get some antipasto. He had a craving. He was thinking about these stuffed peppers all day and he just had to have some."

"Maybe he's pregnant," Emily joked, and immediately regretted it, but Isabel had no reaction to the comment. Okay, maybe she wasn't pregnant after all.

"They must be pretty tasty," Carl said.

"Cheese-and-herb-stuffed Peppadews," Isabel said. "Yummy. I suggested them yesterday but didn't have time to pick them up. He'll be back in a jiff. Another beer?"

"Thanks," Carl said. Both he and Emily received

a drink refill, although Isabel was still not drinking.

Curious, Emily decided to push the issue. "Isabel, you haven't poured yourself one yet. Are you feeling okay?"

Isabel shrugged. "I'm getting over a cold. I might have one with dinner."

They chatted until Alan returned with the stuffed peppers, which they all sampled and agreed were worth the extra trip. Carl and Alan seemed to get along well, and Emily didn't feel obligated to watch the game with them, so when they left with their bowls of chili and beers, she stayed behind in the kitchen with Isabel. Turning down a third glass of wine, she happily tucked into the vegetarian chili. It was delicious and she thanked Isabel for making it without meat.

"You know, it's fewer calories than regular chili anyway, and I've put on a couple of pounds."

"You sure don't look it," Emily said. "And Alan looks like he's losing weight."

"It's all the work he's been doing, and the stress he's under."

"You're under a lot of stress too, aren't you? With my mom being busy with my dad, you must be swamped. I know she helped you out a lot." She quickly added, "Happily," seeing the concerned look on Isabel's face. "Now that you hired Darlene, things should ease up. But Isabel, I've been thinking for a while that I'd like to take Henry more often, bring him to the farm, maybe even do some sleepovers. He's such a good kid, and I enjoy having him. That might give you and Alan more time together too. What do you think?"

Emily's offer was so gratefully received that she wished she'd done it a lot sooner. Isabel admitted to feeling overwhelmed with her schedule. Then Isabel asked if Emily could possibly fill in for one photo shoot in two weeks that she just couldn't do, and when Emily said she'd be able to, she could see Isabel's shoulders drop as if she'd been holding them up for weeks. They compared schedules and picked out a night when Emily could take Henry, and continued talking until the men returned at halftime for another beer. Alan was animated, talking about the first half of the game and drawing them all into conversation. Isabel had poured herself a glass of wine and was giggling at everything. They all watched the second half of the game, and Emily and Carl stayed for an hour or so afterwards. It was the most fun Emily had had with her brother since they were little.

***

"Damn," George said to the empty room. His back hurt. His legs were sore. His arms ached. He'd never been an exerciser. He thought working had kept him in shape, but the month of physical therapy was killing him. If he opened his eyes he'd see that same water stain on the ceiling. The bulb in the lamp was buzzing; he should have swapped it out ages ago. He had to go to the bathroom but that would require asking Greta for help. His stomach grumbled for lunch, but again, he would need to ask Greta. Christ. Greta was a saint, as usual, and he was so damned tired of asking her for help he wanted to go into a voluntary coma. He'd never had to ask anyone for physical help, least of all his wife. He knew she was trying to keep his spirits up, but they were down for the count. He wouldn't be in a good mood again until his back was healed, and according to the doctors that was going to be maybe two more months, unless he really worked at his physical therapy.

As if he wasn't already? He busted his ass when the PTs came to visit, he struggled, he agonized. When he was recovering from the surgery in the hospital, he thought that was going to be the worst part. He was in a hell of a lot of pain then, he wasn't getting any sleep, and he had no privacy. But that hell was a paradise compared to this. Now he was in pain, he wasn't getting any sleep, he had no privacy, and he was pissing off his entire family. And he knew it. And he couldn't do a damn thing about it. How could he? He'd been on his own since he was a teenager. He apprenticed at seventeen, started his own business at twenty, married young, had kids, sent them off into the world, worked hard, paid his taxes, and for all that, the world said screw you, George. Thanks for all your effort; here's a tumor. Now you can't work, your kids think you're a helpless pain in the ass, and even your wife is ready to smother you with a pillow.

He heard Greta walk softly into the living room where they'd set up the hospital bed he was currently pretending to be sleeping in. He figured that she knew he was pretending to be asleep, and further that she would let him pretend, because he'd yelled at her this morning for nothing at all.

"George?" Greta said quietly.

He didn't move.

"I know you're awake. I heard you curse. It's time for lunch and you probably have to go to the bathroom." She spoke a little louder now.

He sighed deeply. "I hate this. I've never been laid up before. Not one sick day in 30 years."

"I know. You tell me every day. And every day I tell you you're getting a bit better. The nurse said she noticed a marked improvement from just a few weeks ago."

"I still hate it."

"My goodness, Henry. Try to look at the bright side."

"The bright side? What exactly is—did you just call me Henry?"

"Did I? Perhaps you're reminding me of a five-year-old." Greta's voice had a distinct edge to it.

She hadn't been anything but kindly in the weeks

since he'd landed in the hospital. George opened his eyes and looked at her. She was standing over him, arms crossed, one eyebrow raised. It was the same look she used to give the kids when they were misbehaving. He looked at the ceiling.

"George Lambert, are you rolling your eyes at me?"

He looked at her again. He'd been hoping to complain a blue streak but now he wasn't so sure she was going to put up with it.

"You listen to me, old man. I've had enough out of you. The nurse says you're to start moving around more on your own. She says I'm being too careful. You are going to get out of this bed and go to the bathroom. Use your walker; call me if you need help. Then meet me in the kitchen for lunch. And run a comb through your hair; it's sticking up on the left side." She yanked the blanket clean off the bed, threw it on the couch, and left the room.

After she left George allowed himself the first smile he'd had since he got sick. He did as he was told, and although he never would have admitted it to anyone, he was terrified he would fall. He made it, though, and it felt damn good to be doing something on his own. Joining Greta at the kitchen table for tomato soup and grilled cheese, he kept his mouth shut and listened as she told him that she was inviting everyone over that weekend for lunch, and that he'd better be on his best behavior. George hadn't seen anyone for a long time; the few times they'd had company he'd pretended to be asleep or claimed to be in too much pain, and he could see now that it had been affecting Greta. It was so important to her to keep the family together, and if he'd been avoiding the family, it must have been hurting her more than he realized.

"How's Henry doing?" he asked. He missed that kid, he realized.

"Alan took him to the bank and they opened a savings account for Henry. He was so proud of his passbook, he showed it to everyone at the bank."

"Five years old and making enough money for a bank account," George said. "Things have changed since we were kids." He couldn't believe how much money a kid could get paid for looking cute.

"Emily's found herself a boyfriend," Greta said.

"Who? Do I know him? Did you meet him yet?" George was instantly suspicious.

Greta smiled at him. "Yes, I met him. His name is Carl Strand. He'll be coming along to lunch this weekend."

Good thing, thought George. "What's he do for a living?"

"Emily says he's an angel investor. From what I can gather it means he has a lot of money and gives it to deserving companies. In fact that's how they met; he invested in Emily's farm."

"Really? He thought that was worth investing

in?"

"George! Don't you think Emily's business is worthwhile?"

George shrugged. "Seems like a lot of hard work. She was making more money and working less at her old job."

"Well, she's happy, and Carl thinks her business could really grow. In fact he's already convinced her to hire some help."

"No kidding?" George was impressed. Any man who could convince Emily to do something must be worth his salt. "Who'd she hire?"

"A nice girl called Miranda. She's studying agriculture and loves the work."

"Didn't think there were people out there these days who'd want a job working on a farm."

"There were quite a few who called, actually. One of them ended up working for Alan."

"From farming to finance? How does that work?"

"Working for Alan at home. Her name is Darlene and she keeps house for Alan and Isabel. She's wonderful. She cleans, cooks, does the laundry and even the grocery shopping if they need her to."

"You mean the things Isabel should be doing?"

"George, stop it," Greta said. "Why is it okay for Emily to be working, but not for Isabel?"

"If a woman's got to work, by all means, go ahead. But Alan makes plenty of money and they've got a kid at home. So that's where Isabel should be. Home." He looked at Greta's face; she was about to explode. "But the one time I offered my opinion I caught holy hell for it. So I'll never say it again, except to you."

Greta's face softened. She stared at him a moment then reached across the table and said, "Somehow we're going to have to drag you into the 21st century, George."

He put his hand on hers and squeezed. For the first time in a month, he felt all was right with the world, except for his goddamn back. But he'd have to keep the complaining to himself from now on, because the light was back in Greta's eyes and he wanted to keep it that way.

***

"Henry, you wait here for me. I'll be down in a minute." Isabel left Henry with his latest picture book and went upstairs to grab a different pair of earrings; the ones she was wearing were catching on her scarf every time she turned her head. They were on their way to lunch at George and Greta's, the first time the whole family had been together since George had been in the hospital. Alan was meeting them there; he had a client meeting beforehand. It wasn't unusual for him to have oddly-timed meetings; his clients were wealthy, elderly and demanding, and didn't like to drive during the week or at night. And Sunday parking was free. Still, she hoped the meeting would go quickly; she didn't want to be at the lunch alone. If only Greta would serve mimosas. She remembered how fun it had been when Emily and Carl had joined them for dinner and the basketball game; a few drinks before they arrived and she was relaxed and happy. She knew Emily had noticed a difference in her; she had felt it herself. As she attached the back of a pierced earring, she remembered the bottle of port Carl had given them. Would it hurt to have a glass before they left?

After popping in to check on Henry and giving him another of his favorite books, she told him she'd be ten more minutes and went into the kitchen. She poured a little port into a juice glass and sipped it. It was quite delicious. She sighed happily and leaned against the counter. Her kitchen gleamed. The housekeeper kept the house so spotless that dust seemed to have given up and left. She even cleaned the inside of the dishwasher. She had a look of unabashed pride every time she left with a "See you next time, Mrs. Lambert."

The fact that she was also able to do the grocery shopping and laundry and leave frozen meals for them made Isabel's life more like it was before George got sick. And because she was an employee, Isabel didn't feel like she had to make small talk with her, or pay any attention to her at all. Not that Greta had ever said anything, but Isabel knew that Greta often felt snubbed by her, just because she was busy working. And she also knew that George didn't approve of her working at all. She finished the port, rinsed out the glass and put it into the dishwasher, and went to get Henry into the car.

***

Carl held the door open for Emily as she smoothed her skirt underneath her and sat in the passenger seat of his old Porsche. She liked the way he did that, even though it was old-fashioned and flew in the face of her feminist sensibilities. He climbed in next to her and started the car.

"I really appreciate your coming today," Emily said.

"I'm looking forward to getting to know your dad."

"Don't be surprised if he's a little gruff," she said. "He can be that way but he's harmless." She sighed. "I hope we can get through this."

"You're more worried about it than I am," he said. "I'll be fine."

Emily sighed. "I know. I'm worried about Alan. We always end up fighting when we're together. It drives my mom nuts."

"How about some good news to relax you?"

"Good news?"

"Yes. I've floated ideas for a few new products and the response has been great."

Emily was confused. Was he talking about one of his other companies? "What products?"

"Fruit-flavored goat cheese and goat cheese fudge." He said it with such a flourish she could tell he was very pleased with himself.

"What are you talking about? Who came up with those gems?"

"What's wrong with them? They're good ideas. People are interested."

"Before we even discuss if those are good ideas," she said angrily, "why don't we talk about how this is a partnership and you're supposed to discuss things with me first?"

"Who cares who comes up with the idea? You should be pleased."

"You don't understand. It's not up to you to present ideas to my clients."

"But they're getting a great response. We should put them intro production as soon as possible. Especially the fruit cheese; that'll go great with salads in the summer. And I've already got a chef friend of mine thinking about how to use it in winter dishes. Too bad he lives in California, otherwise he'd be a big customer."

"Carl!" Emily yelled, "are you listening to me? What happened to partnership? Remember the contract we signed? You can't just do this!"

He slowed the car slightly as he turned his head to look at her, his eyes wide and genuinely surprised. "Do what? Come up with a great enhancement to our business? Do the market research? Pump up the potential sales?" He returned his gaze to the road, but not before she saw him rolling his eyes.

God, he sounded so smug. She pounded her fist on the armrest and growled, not trusting herself to speak.

"Seriously, Em. I can't run to you every time I have a great idea. Part of being successful in business is not hesitating when the time is right. And you," he added, "have a tendency to hesitate."

"Stop the car," Emily said. "Now."

"Are you going to be sick?" Carl asked, alarmed.

"No, I just can't be in the car with you another minute."

"Don't be ridiculous," he said, not slowing the car at all.

She opened her door and Carl slammed on the brakes, yelling, "Hey! Shut the door!"

"Stop the damn car," she said. He did and she got out, stalking angrily off down the road. She could hear Carl pulling over behind her, then he got out and caught up with her, grabbing her forearm and stopping her progress.

"What the hell are you doing?" he demanded. "It's a long walk to your damn parents house."

"My 'damn parents'?" she asked. "Nice

attitude."

"Sorry. Didn't mean it. But you're really pissing me off."

"I'm pissing you off?" she laughed, incredulous. "You're unbelievable."

"Okay, tell me exactly what's upset you," he said, letting go of her arm. "Please. Because as far as I can tell all I did was tell you you'll soon be making more money. How is that a bad thing?"

"Because I'm the boss, Carl. Me. It's my business, and you're an investor. And if you want to change my business, you run it by me first. You don't tell me anything. You ask."

Carl stood looking at her, silent, frowning. Finally he nodded. "Got it. Let's go."

"That's it? 'Got it.' What do you get?" Emily could not go from furious to calm in two seconds. She couldn't understand how Carl had been angry two seconds ago and was perfectly fine now.

"You're right," he said. "You are the boss. I crossed a line. It's the first time I've ever slept with a founder. Clouded my judgment. It won't happen again."

She looked at him for a few moments. Finally she said, "How about a 'sorry'?"

"I apologize." He took her hands in his. "I'd rather pull out my investment than give you up," he said.

She allowed him a small smile. "First time

you've slept with a founder, huh?"

"I don't recommend it as a business practice," he said, pulling her to him.

She felt the length of him against her and saw the simple honesty in his eyes and relented. Furious to calm was easier with a kiss in between.

***

Greta opened the door to greet Isabel and Henry, surprised not to see Alan with them.

"He's got a meeting with one of his bigger clients, an elderly couple who doesn't like to drive. They invite him over for tea and scones once a year so he can tell them how rich they are," Isabel explained.

Isabel was uncharacteristically flippant about Alan's job. Perhaps she really was pregnant and the hormones had mellowed her out. "Would you two like something to drink?" she asked.

"No, thank you," Henry said, darting into the living room to see George.

"I'll take a mimosa," Isabel said, smiling. Greta hesitated, and Isabel added, "Just kidding. I'd love a coffee."

While Greta made herself a cup of tea, Isabel pulled out a chair at the kitchen table, sipping coffee and chatting to Greta about Henry's latest adventures in the advertising world. Greta listened gratefully; it was not often Isabel volunteered to sit and talk. Greta could hear the murmur of George and Henry talking in the next room and smiled to herself, thinking Henry was the best medicine for George right now.

They hadn't been in the kitchen long when there was a knock on the door and Alan let himself in. He entered the kitchen, gave Greta a hug, and then went to Isabel.

"Babe," he said, kissing the top of her head and pulling out the chair next to hers.

Isabel put her hand on his shoulder. "Glad the meeting wasn't too long."

"When they brought out the scones I told them I didn't want to spoil my appetite for my mother's brunch, and they hurried me out of there." He winked at Greta and she smiled. Alan could be such a charmer, although she hadn't seen that side of him in a while. She was also glad to see that he and Isabel were getting along; they'd seemed a little disconnected lately.

She offered Alan a cup of coffee but all he wanted was orange juice, and he gulped down two glasses in quick succession. The three of them had just filed into the living room when the doorbell rang and Emily let herself in, followed by Carl. Greta rose to greet them and was surprised to see that Emily was wearing a pretty flowered skirt, form-fitting sweater, and heels, something that actually showed off her figure; Carl had on dress pants, a dress shirt, and a tie. Before she could offer them coffee, Carl made a beeline for George. He introduced himself confidently, firmly shook George's hand, and told him how happy he was to see him out of the hospital. George gruffly accepted the gracious manners, but Greta knew he was impressed.

Greta watched Alan's face as he hugged Emily and shook Carl's hand. He looked surprised and oddly a little nervous, although she couldn't imagine why. Emily had told her about having dinner at Alan and Isabel's and how well that had gone. Greta had been thrilled at the news. She often worried that she was the only reason her children got together, and she hoped that after she was gone they'd still see each other. She mentioned her fears once to Emily, but Emily just laughed and told her to stop being morbid. She was Henry's aunt, she said, and she'd always be in Alan's life because of that alone.

Greta excused herself to check on the breakfast casserole and Emily got up to help her.

"You look lovely," Greta said, taking an oven mitt out of a drawer.

Emily shrugged. "Carl insisted I wear something nice."

"He insisted? Is that all I needed to do? You always told me what you wore was your business."

"Carl can be very persuasive. That's one thing I like about him," Emily said.

Greta poked a fork into the casserole, pulled it

out, and touched the fork with her finger. "Have you given any thought to asking Henry for an overnight visit?"

"Funny you should ask. I told Isabel I'd like to have him over and she jumped at the chance. I was just asking Carl about it on the way over."

"Asking him what?"

Emily had the grace to blush a little. "Well, he's been staying at my place most weekends. And I wanted to make sure he wouldn't mind Henry being there."

"You asked him permission to have your own nephew in your own home?" Greta was bothered by this; she didn't want her daughter feeling controlled by this man.

"It's not like that, Mom," Emily said.

"It certainly sounds exactly like that," Greta said, putting the hot casserole onto a trivet. "You have control over your own life. He has no business making you ask his permission."

"He didn't. Look, he's not going to turn out to be an abusive boyfriend. But he knows he wants, he's certain about his opinions, and he appreciates that I check in with him. Let's just say we both have strong personalities, okay? Anyway, he's already looking for baseball mitts so they can play catch together. I also have to make sure Alan and Isabel won't mind having Carl there while Henry's over, although I think they'll be fine with it now that they've met him.

But if the overnight goes well, I might even have Henry over for a whole weekend. With all the activities he does during the week, he could use some communing with nature. And now that Miranda's helping me out with the goats, I have some free time."

Emily looked her in the eye, smiling and confident. Greta saw the old Emily then, the one she didn't worry about, except when it came to finding a man. Now she had one and Greta was worried about that. Silly. Emily was probably besotted, and that's why she was simpering around him. Well, that would change in a few months when the bloom wore off the rose.

Greta nodded. "Alan and Isabel could use some time alone. That's very generous of you to offer, Emily. A weekend is a long time with a five-year-old."

"I know, but I think Carl will be a big help. And Henry's such an easy kid. Most of the time."

"Most of the time?" Greta was surprised. She'd always found it a pleasure to be with Henry.

"He was a little out of sorts the last time I saw him; he didn't want to go to bed when Isabel told him to and he was kicking under the counter in the kitchen."

"Is that all? Henry's very well-behaved, believe me. Good thing he doesn't take after his aunt." Greta smiled fondly. "My goodness, don't you remember hiding when it was time for bed, making us look all over creation for you?"

Emily grinned. "Nope. I was the model child."

Greta laughed. "Well, Miss Model Child, tell everyone brunch is ready in the kitchen. It's buffet style and we can all sit in the living room. And tell your father he can rest; I'll bring him in a plate."

***

George watched everyone file out of the room to the kitchen. He had to admit he liked Carl. He was the first one of Emily's boyfriends who knew his ass from his elbow. Turned out Carl flew his own plane, which meant he knew all about engines. He'd also managed to get Emily to free herself up from the farm and enjoy herself a little. She looked happier today than he'd seen her in a while. She didn't look like she'd just stepped off a farm, either. Greta appeared with a plate and some coffee for him, put it on the end table to his left, and said, "Here you are, dear."

He reached out and touched her lightly on the hand. "Thanks."

She smiled at him and he watched her go, picking up a cinnamon raisin bagel with cream cheese and taking a bite. He was a lucky man.

Emily came in and sat next to George on the small couch to his left, placing her coffee next to his.

She held her plate on her lap and smiled as Carl came into the room. He joined her on the couch, setting his coffee down on an end table and balancing his plate on his lap. They both turned to look at George at the same time.

"You two look nice today," George said. "Off somewhere else this afternoon?"

"No," Carl answered. "Meeting Emily's parents was occasion enough."

George nodded, pleased with Carl's manners. When he met Greta's parents he'd worn a full suit, vest and all. Of course things were more relaxed these days, but it never hurt to put some effort into your appearance.

"So, Dad," Emily said, "Mom said physical therapy's really paying off."

George picked up his coffee cup, saying, "Between the nurse and your mother I'll be running a marathon soon," and took a sip of the strong coffee, one cream, two sugars, just the way he liked it.

Carl said, with the tone of someone who knew, "Physical therapy's torture, though, isn't it?"

"Yes, it's tough. Have you done it?" He was surprised someone as young as Carl would have needed physical therapy.

"Yes, I blew out my knee skiing a few years ago. Surgery followed by physical therapy. The PT was more painful than the original injury. It was worth it, though; my knee is better than ever. Although no more skiing for me."

"What happened?" Emily asked.

"Some kid came out of nowhere and spilled right in front of me. I managed to avoid smacking into him, but I tore up my knee doing it."

Emily put her hand on his shoulder. "So no cross-country skiing for us next year?"

George saw the care on Emily's face and the concern in her voice and realized that she really liked this guy. And judging from the way Carl kept looking at her, he figured the feeling was mutual.

Greta came in with Henry; each was carrying a plate and a drink. They sat on the larger couch to George's right, and Alan and Isabel followed soon after, sitting in two chairs Greta had placed opposite George. They formed a family circle, everyone eating, drinking, and talking. George understood deep down that this was Greta. It was her doing, of course, she'd organized it, but it was more than that. This circle of people, their connection to each other, it was what defined Greta, made her who she was, and she in turn was the one who made them a family in the genuine sense of the word. He looked at her, at the contentment on her face, and was once again gratified that he'd made the wise decision to ask her to marry him all those years ago.

***

Emily couldn't believe her luck. One of the goats was due to give birth any day now, and it was quite possible that Henry would get to see, if not a live birth, at least a brand new baby goat. He'd been hoping for that all winter but so far the timing hadn't worked out. But now Emily had him for Friday night and Saturday morning, and it looked like Francie would probably have her baby while Henry was there. Carl thought it would be best if he didn't sleep over, so she and Henry would be on their own, although Carl was joining them for dinner and would be back bright and early to play catch. Emily couldn't wait to watch that; Alan tended to do more cerebral things with Henry, like educational computer games, number puzzles, or word searches. She smiled to herself as she shut the barn door and stepped out into the late afternoon sunshine.

Fearless crocuses braved the chilly spring air all around the barn, and the buds of hyacinth dotted the area near her front door. The fields of grass were resurrecting themselves, stretching toward the sun like a sleeping giant finally roused. She could smell the earth, the millions of organisms in the soil called by the light, beginning to work their yearly magic. Her garden had lost its winter coat of hay and was dressed in a nutritious layer of compost, polka-dotted with cold-hardy plants. She'd even planted a few warm weather vegetables in complete defiance of Mother Nature. She knew planting anything before

Memorial Day was asking for trouble, but she could always throw a blanket over them if a late spring frost arrived. Not many weeds were growing yet, but she and Henry had spent some pleasant afternoons quietly talking and pulling up unwanted sprigs in the garden. He usually liked to weed while eating his fill of cherry tomatoes and cucumbers, but he wouldn't be seeing those again until July.

Emily wondered if Henry's schedule would ease up as the weather got warmer. It did seem like everything slowed down in the summer; the days lengthened, people played hooky from work, gentle breezes took their time coming over the hill. Her goats, on the other hand, were filled with energy, constantly trying to get out of the pasture, vying for her attention, and romping with each other well past bedtime. She hoped to give Henry a taste of that freedom and exuberance, a respite from his orderly and busy life. Of course he loved his little career, but should any child have a career? Shouldn't children have childhoods, and what would they become if they didn't? For Emily, childhood had been a time to experiment, to learn about failure and success, to discover who you were. If you were shepherded from one adult-defined experience to the next, when did you learn to amuse yourself?

She puttered in the yard, picking up snapped branches left over from winter, wandering over to admire the purples and yellows of the crocuses, dropping debris in a pile near the fire pit. Henry would love to make some s'mores there tonight, and it was finally warm enough to suggest it. She heard a low mechanical rumble and turned to see Isabel's blue Volvo approaching up the driveway, Henry's little face peering out of the back seat. She waved and walked over as Isabel pulled up. Henry leaped out of the car and ran to hug her; she bent and hugged him back, smiling up at Isabel. After depositing his overnight bag next to him, Isabel bent down and hugged Henry, kissing both his cheeks several times, told him to be good, thanked Emily, and left after another hug and round of kissing.

Emily was pleasantly surprised to see all the blatant signs of affection. Normally Isabel was not a demonstrative person, and Emily had often wondered if she was cuddly with Henry. Apparently she was; maybe she was finally feeling comfortable enough around Emily to show it. She reached down and put her hand on Henry's small shoulder. "Let's put your suitcase in the house, and then I'm guessing you'd like to see the goats?"

Henry nodded. "Can I see Belle's baby? And Belle? And did Francie have her baby?" When he saw Emily shake her head, he said, "Will she have it tonight? Can I see?"

"I think there's a good chance she'll have it while you're here," Emily said as they walked into the house. Jake came running over to Henry and immediately began weaving in and out of his legs so that Henry had to stop and pick him up. Jake was quite an armful for a little boy, but Henry was quite good at holding him, and gentle too. He didn't put Jake down until Emily dropped his suitcase next to the couch and said, "Do you need to use the bathroom? Are you hungry?"

Henry shook his head, put down Jake on the couch with a little scratch behind the ears, and said, "I want to see Belle. And her baby. And Francie."

"In that order?" Emily smiled.

"Yes, please."

They went to the barn and Henry greeted Belle like the old friend she was, admired her baby, and carefully approached Francie, who was greatly rounded in the abdomen and clearly tired. Henry did not give her a carrot as he had the other two; Emily told him goats weren't very hungry when they were about to have a baby.

"When will she have the baby?" Henry asked.

"The vet says she's due any time now," Emily replied.

"Six o'clock?"

"No, sweetie, not any o'clock. Just whenever the baby's ready to come."

"Mommy's friend had a baby at ten o'clock," Henry said.

"Today?"

Henry shook his head. "In the winter. She said

her friend was having a baby at ten o'clock, and I wanted to go see the baby, just like I see the baby goats here, but she said no because she didn't want the new baby to get sick. That baby came at ten o'clock. So what time will Francie's baby come? And will Belle's baby get sick from me?"

Emily took a breath. "Okay, first of all, when people have babies in hospitals sometimes they," she hesitated, wondering how to explain scheduled C-sections to a five-year-old, "they have a special way of knowing when the baby will come. But goats aren't born in hospitals and they don't have that special way. And you won't get Belle's baby sick, or Francie's baby, so don't worry about that."

Henry frowned and said, "Will the baby come when I'm awake? Or after I go to bed?"

"You really want to be there, don't you, kiddo?"

Henry nodded.

"Okay, if she starts having the baby when you're sleeping I'll try to wake you up, and if you're not super sleepy you can get out of bed. But if I have trouble waking you up, you can see the baby in the morning, okay? Deal?" Emily stuck out her hand for a shake.

"Deal," he said, putting his little hand in hers.

She pumped his hand way up and way down, twice, smiling. "Now let's see what we can rustle up for dinner. Carl is going to join us."

"Yeah, he's nice. He has baseball mitts."

Emily nodded, thinking that life was very uncomplicated when a friendship could be based on the possession of baseball mitts. She led Henry out of the barn and into the house, where they decided on Henry's favorite, breakfast for dinner. By the time Carl arrived they had a fruit salad made and the pancake mix was ready for the griddle. Afterwards Carl and Henry went outside to play catch while Emily cleaned up the kitchen. She finished and then joined them. As she stepped onto the porch she heard spring peepers, for her the first real sign of spring.

"Gentlemen," she said, walking over to stand next to Carl, "how about we all take a walk to the pond and see if we can spot any peepers?"

"The spring frogs?" Henry asked.

"Yes," Emily said, surprised that he knew what a peeper was. She didn't think Henry was very familiar with the natural world.

"I told him what was making that noise," Carl said to Emily. "It's pretty loud; he noticed it right away."

Emily nodded, pleased that Carl could identify a spring peeper. "After the pond you can come back and play some more while I milk the goats. And then we can all make some s'mores, okay?"

"Yes!" Henry said, running over to Emily. Carl took the mitts and left them on the porch and they all walked to the pond, over a small ridge about a half-mile from Emily's house. In the summer she loved to sit out there and read, at least midday when the mosquitos weren't too bad. When they got close to the pond they moved very quietly and slowly, "creeping on the peepers" as Emily put it. You could never get close enough to catch one, Emily explained, but you could get close enough to see them jump into the water. They walked around the perimeter of the pond, Henry repeatedly tiptoeing to the water's edge and running away with laughter whenever the frogs jumped, Emily and Carl quietly following behind him, holding hands. At one point he tiptoed up onto a small rock, and Emily saw it wobble.

"Careful, Henry," she said, but too late, as Henry fell sideways and landed in the muddy earth just shy of the water. He popped up quickly but his pants were a mess.

Henry looked at them, stricken, trying to wipe off the mud and only making it worse.

"That's okay, buddy," Carl said. "If you're getting dirty you're having fun!"

Henry looked at Carl, his hand in mid-wipe, then he smiled and proceeded along the edge of the pond.

"You don't know Isabel," Emily said. "She gets upset if he drips water on the counter. She's going to flip over those pants."

"Soak them in laundry detergent tonight and rinse them out in the morning. There won't be a stain." Emily raised her eyebrows in surprise and he added, “My mother was a laundry queen.”

Good with kids, knows how to clean his own clothes, flies a plane, Emily thought. Everything a girl could want. She said, “Do you cook, too?” without thinking.

He looked at her quizzically for a moment and then said, “Nope, hopeless in that department. Although I think I could handle the s’mores tonight.”

When they had scared every amphibian in the area they made their way back to the house. Emily milked the goats while Carl built a fire in the fire pit and dragged some ancient beach chairs outside along with the fixings for s’mores. Emily knew Henry was tired because he sat down to toast his marshmallow, rather than walking around the fire like he usually did. But it was a good tired, one born of fresh air and exercise, one she thought every child should have, every day. After two s’mores his eyes started to close, and she said, “Henry, I think it’s time for bed.”

“No, Aunt Emmy, I’m not tired. I’m wide-awake. See?” He leaned forward and opened his eyes as far as he could, staring at her.

Carl laughed. “Wow, he is wide awake, Em. Let him stay up a little longer, okay?”

Henry beamed at Carl, their friendship now cemented.

Emily smiled, shaking her head, and said, “All right, Henry, fifteen more minutes.”

Henry sank back into his chair and within thirty

seconds his eyes were closed.

Carl said quietly to Emily, “Down for the count.”

“I know,” Emily said. “He’s been great today. I’m glad I asked him over.”

“I bet his parents are too. Are they doing anything special tonight?”

“Nope, just cooking dinner together, renting a movie.”

Carl reached over and took Emily’s hand. “That sounds like a nice night to me.”

“Me too.”

They sat together holding hands, talking quietly by the fire, Henry sleeping beside them, for a long time.

Chapter 8

ISABEL DIDN'T REALIZE how drunk she was until she stood up. Alan had paused the movie, a fun combination of action and romance, so she could use the bathroom, and as she rose she wavered a little, putting her hand on his thigh to steady herself. He patted her behind as he gave her a push to her feet, saying, "Hurry back." She wondered whether he was as drunk as she was. She'd lost track of how much wine they'd consumed; Alan had been very generously refilling their glasses all evening. She was definitely unsteady on her feet, and was glad for the light and quiet of the bathroom where she could take a few deep breaths. After she went to the bathroom she would get herself a big glass of water, and bring one to Alan as well. She didn't want to pass out when the movie ended; she and Alan hadn't really talked much during the evening and she was still feeling a little disconnected. He'd been working so much that they'd had fewer opportunities to sit down and talk lately. As she washed her hands she noticed her makeup was smudged on one eye, but she couldn't remember having done it. She dabbed some water on the back of her neck and dried her hands.

Feeling marginally more sober, she went into the kitchen, filling two large tumblers with water. She was still a little unsteady on her feet as she returned to the living room, handing Alan a tumbler.

He raised his eyebrows, asking, “Water?”

Isabel nodded. “I’m feeling pretty out of it.”

“I was just going to suggest another bottle of wine,” he said, nonetheless taking a large gulp.

“Are you kidding? Last time we had this much to drink you were standing on a chair singing.”

“You want me to start singing?” He smiled and took another long drink.

Isabel sat down next to him and said, “Maybe I drank more than you. I think I should stick to water for a while.”

“Too bad,” he said. “I was hoping to take advantage of you.”

She smiled at him. “Right here, right now?”

“Okay,” he said, plucking her water out of her hand and putting it on the table. He pulled her on top of him and before she knew it they were at it like teenagers, right there on the couch.

***

“Wow,” she said later, as they lay in each other’s arms on the floor.

“Yeah,” Alan replied, hugging her to him with one arm. “Still feeling drunk?”

“No.”

“Better than a glass of water?”

“Yes,” she said, laughing. She stood up and

started looking for her clothes.

"Going somewhere?"

"No, just a little chilly."

"Covering up that body?" Alan said. "That's a cruel thing to do to your husband."

Isabel smiled at Alan, flattered. He'd been more attentive this evening than he'd been in weeks. Maybe it was the fact that they were alone, maybe it was the wine. She knew they were more connected after sex, but was that the only way they were connecting lately? That must be typical of parents of young children; it wasn't like they had romantic weekends away anymore. She pulled on her underwear and her shirt, leaving her bra on the floor where it had landed. Alan stood up and slid on his boxers, saying, "I'll be right back. Still want to watch the end of the movie?"

"Sure." She leaned back and waited for him, finishing the rest of her water. She heard him go into the bathroom, and then down to the basement, which meant he was getting another bottle of wine. Now she felt much better, and she decided she could probably have another glass. But did that mean Alan would have the rest? Should she say something? He'd certainly been very capable on the couch, not impaired in the least. She smiled to herself, thinking that would be an interesting alternative to a Breathalyzer test.

"What's so funny?" Alan asked, walking into the

room with a freshly opened wine bottle in his hand.

"I was thinking your recent performance on the couch would be a great substitute for walking a straight line or touching your nose with your finger."

"If it's you pulling me over, officer, I'll go for that alternative every time," he said, refilling their glasses.

As they watched the rest of the movie, Isabel nursed her glass of wine and refused Alan's offers to refill it, so at the end of the night she knew that he'd had three more glasses. But he was alert, his speech wasn't slurred, and he followed the plot of the movie. Same with her, but she'd switched to water a while back. She was impressed. Maybe she should start having wine every night like Alan, just so she could keep up. After all, having a few drinks together was keeping them connected, and maybe more relaxed as well. That would be good for them, and for Henry as well.

***

Emily awoke suddenly just before dawn and didn't even bother changing, only tucking her pajama pants into some boots before quietly slipping into the barn to check on Francie. Standing apart from the rest of the does, Francie had pawed a nest in the straw bedding, and was standing next to it, head down, breathing heavily. As Emily approached Francie lay down heavily, and Emily could see she was close to giving birth. This was not Francie's first pregnancy; she had had twins twice before, and Emily expected the birth to be easy and relatively fast. A minute later the restless Francie staggered up again and Emily knew it was time to get Henry.

She went back into the house, stepping aside as Jake bolted through the front door, happy to be out so early. There was a stillness to the house, still dark in the pre-dawn light. She could hear Henry's shallow breathing from the futon on the floor, could see his slight form under a thin flannel blanket and an old afghan. She stared at him a moment, wondering what it would be like to have her own child here in the house. She would certainly need more than a futon. As she padded across the room Henry stirred and he said groggily, "Aunt Emmy?"

"Henry, do you want to get up? Francie is having her baby."

The boy was up in an instant, momentarily tangled in his blankets and then standing, his hair sticking out on one side.

"You don't have to get dressed, just put on your sneakers."

Henry shoved his feet into his shoes, not bothering to tie them. "Did the baby come yet? I don't want to miss it. Is Francie okay? When is the baby coming?"

"Don't worry, I woke you up in time. Let's go!"

She took his hand and led him out to the barn.

They reentered the barn, Henry still in his pajamas but all the sleep out of his rounded eyes as he stared at Francie. The doe was down again, and this time Emily could see the water bag between Francie's hind legs. She pointed it out to Henry and told him to be very quiet, and as they looked the water bag broke. Clear fluid spilled out and Francie began licking the bedding where the bag had broken.

"Is she thirsty?" Henry asked quietly.

"No, she's just getting the bed ready for the baby," Emily whispered. "We should be seeing it soon."

The goat labored quietly on her side, panting slightly. The barn had gotten quiet, as if the other goats knew what was about to happen. Within minutes the kid's nose and front feet appeared. Henry breathed out, "Oh" but didn't say anything else. Emily was relieved to see that the kid wasn't in a breech position. Goats had breech babies but sometimes she had to participate a little more than she wanted to with Henry there. Then the head emerged, its shape obvious but its features indistinct, and Henry gasped, "What's wrong with it?"

"Nothing," Emily said. "It has a special film over its face. It'll come off when it's born." The thin membrane that covered the kid's head tore and they could see its face. Because this was not Francie's first time giving birth, the rest of the kid emerged quickly.

It spilled out onto the hay-covered floor and Francie stood up, severing the umbilical cord in the process.

"Stay here," Emily whispered to Henry. She slipped into the stall and wiped the baby's tiny head and nose off with a towel, then waited for a moment to make sure Francie began licking the baby clean. When she did, Emily left the stall, satisfied that Francie was bonding with her baby. She and Henry watched in spellbound silence as the goat's rough tongue licked the baby's new wet hide. Finally Francie lay down again, the new kid half clean and already struggling to stand.

"Is she resting?" Henry asked.

"No, she's having another baby," Emily said.

"Now?" Henry asked. "Like twins?"

"Yup. Seems like she always has twins. Lots of goats do. Not like people." They watched in silence as another kid was born, again without complications. This time Francie stood to break the umbilical cord but lay down again almost immediately.

"She's tired now," Emily said. "I'll be right back." She went in to check on the newest kid. It was breathing normally, and she lifted it gently.

"Where are you taking it?" Henry asked, alarm in his voice.

"I'm moving it closer to Francie so she can clean it without getting up again," Emily explained.

"Look!" Henry cried, pointing to the first-born, already wobbling on its feet in search of a meal.

"Did you start walking that fast?" she said, checking that Francie's teats were open.

"No way!"

Emily smiled and looked at Henry thoughtfully. "Do you want to come in and help me do something?"

"Really?"

Emily nodded. "Come on in here slowly, okay?"

Henry took short deliberate steps into the enclosure, almost like he was sneaking up on Francie. Emily said, "We're going to wipe off the belly buttons. Let's do one together." They approached the older kid, already steadier on its feet. Emily gave Henry a clean cloth dipped in iodine, covered his hand with hers, and gently wiped the belly button. Then she said, "Now you can do the other one yourself."

Henry nodded, looking as serious as a cardiac surgeon before his first heart operation. He carefully did as he was told and then returned the cloth to her, pride wrestling with excitement on his face.

"Nice work," Emily said. "Now let's leave the new mom alone." As they left she softly swung a gate into place, creating a kidding pen for the three goats. They would spend the next few days there, where Emily could make sure they were bonding and that the kids were nursing and healthy.

"Let's go," she said to Henry. "Francie needs to rest."

She took his hand and they stepped out of the barn into the new morning. Birds were carrying on as the first streaks of daylight crossed the sky. The air was cool after the warmth of the barn, and Henry's pajama pants were soaked with morning dew by the time they reached the porch. Henry shivered a little and Emily led him to the couch, tucking his feet under an afghan and leaving to make him some hot chocolate. She returned with a mug for him, some coffee for herself, and a toasted cinnamon raisin bagel for them to share.

Henry took a giant bite of bagel and said around the food, "What are the names going to be?"

"I don't know. Do you have any ideas?" Emily sipped the hot coffee, curious what Henry might come up with.

Henry frowned, chewing and staring at Jake, who had just appeared.

"Jack?"

Emily smiled. "They're girls. Do you like the name Jack for a girl?"

"No." Henry patted the couch next to him and Jake leaped up and curled against his leg, purring. "What about Fee-fee and Foo-foo?"

Emily burst out laughing. "Fifi and Foofoo? That's what you want to call them?" Henry nodded and she said, "Okay, then, Fifi and Foofoo it is."

Henry grinned and picked up his hot chocolate, taking a sip and remaining silent for a moment before asking, "Aunt Emmy? Where did the baby come out of?"

Oh, crap, thought Emily. She'd hoped Henry wouldn't ask that question but she was prepared. "There's a special place in the mommy goat where the baby comes out of."

"But babies grow in the tummy," Henry persisted.

"Babies grow in a special place, too. It looks like they're in the tummy, but they're not."

Henry looked at her, frowning, then said, "How do they get in the special place?"

"I think you should ask your mom and dad about that," she said.

"Do people babies grow in a special place too?"

"Your mom and dad will be able to tell you," Emily reiterated.

Henry sat for a few long moments, petting Jake slowly. Finally he asked, "Will they tell you too?"

Emily laughed. "I expect they will," she said.

Greta sat at her kitchen table, surveying her daughter. Emily was looking down at her cell phone, having apologized to Greta for her rudeness and explaining that she had to respond to an email right away. She had offered to leave the room but Greta had told her to stay, pretending to work on her crossword until Emily was fully occupied. Now she could examine her daughter at leisure. Emily's brow was clear, not characteristically frowning as it had been in years past. It looked like she was wearing the tiniest bit of mascara, and her hair was full and shiny. Greta noticed that Emily was paying a little more attention to her appearance now that Carl was in her life. Certainly her clothes were more form-fitting than usual, something men always liked. She had even opted for a tailored cardigan instead of the shapeless sweaters she usually wore. Greta looked back up at Emily's face to find her staring back.

"Yes, Mother?" Emily said, smiling a wry smile.

"Yes, what?"

"Do I pass inspection? Hair? Clothes? Makeup?"

"So you are wearing makeup?" Greta asked before she could stop herself.

"Not really. Now tell me, how's Dad? And more importantly, where's Dad?"

"You know that new hardware store that opened up two towns over? That's where he is."

"Ah, heaven on earth. He could be there for hours."

"I'm counting on it," Greta said, and then lowered her eyes, immediately guilty.

Emily reached across the table and put her hand on top of Greta's. "Mom, it's okay to want Dad to get out of the house. It's for his own good. And even happy couples need an occasional break, right? You can't be expected to spend every minute together for months on end."

"I know," Greta said, squeezing Emily's hand, amused that her daughter was giving her relationship advice. "I am glad he's able to go out now, but I'm so terribly worried that something will happen to him."

"The doctor encouraged him to get out and walk around, didn't he?"

"Yes, and he cleared him for driving too. Just no work yet. But your poor father is worried sick about not being able to work for this long."

"Is he worried he's going to lose clients? Because I can't imagine his customers forgetting about him. He's had some of them for decades."

"I know, but I can't convince him that his whole business isn't going under while he recuperates."

"Could he do some easy jobs? Like installing new switches or changing bulbs? I bet the doctor would approve that."

Greta nodded. "You know, Emily, that's not a bad idea. I'll call his doctor tomorrow." She knew George wasn't yet ready to climb into attics or squirrel into crawl spaces, but certainly he could work while standing on his own two feet. Her concerns about George momentarily eased, she asked Emily about her weekend with Henry.

Emily enthusiastically recounted the weekend, which Greta thought sounded wonderful until Emily said, "He finally got to see a birth. It was an easy one, twins. He was thrilled."

"He saw the whole thing?" Greta asked,

surprised. "Wasn't it a little … unseemly?"

"'Unseemly'?" Emily laughed. "Yes, it was. It was also the miracle of birth, and if everyone witnessed it at least once, maybe we'd all have a little more reverence for each other."

Greta held up her hand, sensing Emily was about to go off on one of her rants. "I'm sorry, dear, I didn't mean it that way. I just thought maybe Henry was a little young to grasp the importance of what he was seeing. And maybe he'd have a little trouble understanding the mechanics of it all. I don't think he knows anything about the birds and the bees."

Emily exhaled deeply and recounted her conversation with Henry, concluding with, "So I told him to ask his parents."

"An excellent answer," Greta nodded. "Let Isabel handle that one."

"Or Alan," Emily added.

Greta smiled. "I think it's better coming from a woman. Your father could never talk about that sort of thing."

"But a man should tell his son, don't you think?"

Greta shrugged, not wanting to get into this discussion either. "I don't know. I don't even remember how we told you two." She saw Emily open her mouth and added, "And I don't want to be reminded of it now. But I'm very happy that Henry got to see the birth with you. It's an experience the two of you will never forget. Tell me about everything else you and Henry did."

Greta knew Emily loved to talk about Henry, and indeed, Emily told her in detail about Henry's visit. It sounded to Greta like Henry must have had an excellent time, and she was looking forward to seeing him and asking him all about it. Greta noticed that Emily lingered over the image of her and Carl, sitting by the fire, while Henry slept next to them. Greta could picture her daughter with a family of her own, living and working on her farm, and she realized for the first time that Emily could picture it too.

***

In the bathroom, hairbrush in hand, Isabel was feeling a bit woozy. She wondered about the days when office workers had three-martini lunches. How had they functioned afterwards? Did any work get done before they left at five? And once they returned home, for a pre-dinner cocktail and then some wine with dinner, and maybe a nightcap, how did they manage to get their children to bed, much less feed themselves? Maybe they all had a higher tolerance for alcohol back then. But she did not have the stamina for afternoon cocktails, and that was exactly what she and Alan had had: they'd slept until almost noon, gone out for a late lunch, and consumed two martinis apiece. Now they were home, waiting for Emily to drop off Henry. She was glad Alan handled alcohol better than she did, because she wouldn't have been comfortable driving home. But he seemed fine, and when he offered to go outside and wait for Emily and Henry, she went upstairs to freshen herself up. After washing her face, reapplying her makeup, and brushing her hair, she felt much better, although still tipsy. That was all right; it was Saturday night, after all.

The sound of Henry's voice came floating up the stairs and she hurried down, eager to see her little boy. He was talking excitedly to Alan about something when she entered the kitchen, "… and the straw got wet, and then—Mommy!" He rushed over and she crouched down to give him a hug, but she must have been a little off-balance because when he came into her arms they both toppled off to the side, and she twisted and pulled him down on top of her to break his fall.

"Are you okay?" she asked, lying on the floor, surprised but not at all hurt.

Henry, his face inches from hers, laughed and hugged her, saying, "That was fun!"

Alan came over and looked down at them, shaking his head. "I think Mommy's a little too relaxed, don't you, Henry? Do you think she should get up off the floor?"

Henry rolled off Isabel and lay next to her, looking up at his father. "You look very tall now, Daddy. Come down on the floor too."

Alan grinned and lay down next to Henry, then said, “You know what I’d like now, Isabel?”

“What’s that?”

“A Henry sandwich!”

He used his shoulder to push Henry into Isabel and she reached over and started to tickle Henry, who laughed and then wriggled away and jumped up, yelling, “Two pieces of bread, that’s what you are!”

“Where’s my Henry sandwich?” Alan growled, sitting up and looking from side to side before letting his gaze fall on Henry.

Henry screamed and ran upstairs, laughing all the way.

Alan got up and said to Isabel, “You better hurry or he’ll get away!” and followed Henry up the stairs.

Sitting up, Isabel laughed out loud in her empty kitchen. She and Alan hadn’t played with Henry like this in months, and she’d forgotten how fun it was. Wondering why that was, she got to her feet, scooped up Henry’s little backpack and ran up the stairs. She could unpack his clothes later. Right now she had a Henry sandwich to make.

***

Alan and Isabel didn’t stop playing with Henry until it was well past his normal dinnertime, but he hadn’t said a word about being hungry. Isabel finally noticed the time and went to the kitchen to make grilled cheese and tomato soup for Henry while Alan unpacked Henry's backpack. She burnt the first one, but when they came into the kitchen a decently made second sandwich was on a plate with some grapes. Alan slipped downstairs to open a bottle of wine; they'd agreed to eat something light after Henry went to bed but these days not a night passed without a glass of wine. Alan had showed Isabel an article about the health benefits of red wine. She'd pointed out that chocolate had antioxidants, but Alan said he felt much more relaxed after a glass of wine.

Henry started to say something around a large bite of food, but Isabel interrupted him. "Don't speak with your mouth full."

Henry chewed frantically as Alan returned with the wine, then gulped his food down and said, "Francie had her babies. I saw them being born."

"You what?" Alan said, handing a glass of wine to Isabel and giving her a look of concern.

"I saw them being born. She had two of them. And I got to name them. Fifi and FooFoo." He took another large bite of his grilled cheese, a proud look on his face.

"Those are interesting names," Isabel said. "Whatever made you come up with those?"

Henry shrugged, swallowed, and said, "I don't know. They were in my head so I said them. Aunt Emmy said she liked them."

"I bet she did," Alan said.

"They stood up really fast. People babies don't stand up fast like that."

"You didn't start walking until you were almost one year old," Isabel said, smiling at him fondly. "And human babies practice for months before they get it right. Like playing the piano."

"Why don't the goats have to practice?" Henry frowned. Isabel suspected he was jealous that goats didn't have to play the piano.

Isabel explained in a basic way that prey animals need to be able to run right away, which led into a discussion of which animals hunt and which are hunted. As they talked, Henry's eyes began to close, and although he struggled to hide it, he was falling asleep at the table. She promised Henry they could go to the library the next day and look for a book about animals on the savannah, and then led him upstairs. He fell asleep as she was helping him into his pajamas, and she decided to tuck him into bed without even brushing his teeth.

***

Isabel and Alan were watching a movie later, having eaten some cheese and crackers and polished off almost two bottles of wine. She thought she heard a noise and said something to Alan, who paused the movie and listened for a moment. Nothing. They resumed watching but a few moments later Alan thought he heard something too. They were both listening intently when Henry appeared in the doorway, squinty-eyed and yawning.

"Henry? What's up, kiddo?" Alan asked.

"I had to go to the bathroom," he said.

Isabel nodded. "You didn't have your trip to the bathroom before bed." She was having trouble shifting to Mommy mode, trying to sound sober.

"Back to bed then, right?" Alan said. At least he sounded more together.

"I have a question," Henry said. "Aunt Emmy said I should ask you."

"Ask us what?" Alan said, standing up, obviously preparing to lead Henry off to bed.

"Where does the baby come out of?"

Alan sat down again. "Come out of?" he repeated.

"The baby is in the tummy but it doesn't come out of the tummy. Aunt Emmy doesn't know where it comes out of. She said to ask you."

Alan sank back onto the couch and looked at Isabel. His expression was so helpless that she laughed out loud. "Aunt Emmy doesn't know where it comes from?" she said.

"No. She said to ask you. Maybe you can tell her too."

"Sweet Jesus," Alan said to Isabel. "Santa Claus and the Easter Bunny are bad enough."

"Santa Claus?" Henry asked, clearly confused.

"Does the goat have a chimney?"

"Yeah," Alan laughed. "A chimney."

Isabel started giggling. It was all so ridiculous. "He flies the baby in on his sleigh, drops it off with the Easter Bunny, who puts it in his basket and hops it on over to the chimney."

Alan burst out laughing and then they both lost it, laughing and making ever more outlandish explanations involving whatever mythical childhood characters they could think of. By the time they were finished, chuckling and wiping their eyes, Henry looked very tired again, and completely confused as well.

"So Santa and the Easter Bunny, they bring the babies?" he asked.

"Yeah, sure," Alan said, still laughing.

Isabel thought fleetingly about telling Henry they were joking, but she wasn't prepared for the birds-and-the-bees conversation, especially inebriated and at such a late hour. She figured if Henry really wanted to know, he'd ask again. Sometimes kids forgot all about things. They put him to bed and returned to the movie, forgetting about Henry's question within minutes.

***

George watched Henry dig into his second slice of turkey meatloaf. The kid had already put away a pile of broccoli and a plain baked potato, served with a thick yogurt and no butter. George had to admit that Greta's health food tasted pretty good, and her efforts to make George eat healthier were paying off; he'd lost ten pounds and that was helping him with everything. Tonight in honor of Henry they were having dessert, but even that was light ice cream. George was happy to see Henry; he missed the kid, and finally felt well enough to handle Henry's level of activity again. He wasn't quite ready to get down on the floor yet but he could play with trucks and cars on the living room table, although Greta made them put a blanket down first so they didn't scratch it. Bunching up the blanket made good hills.

"Did you enjoy your visit with Aunt Emily?" Greta asked Henry.

He nodded, chewing and saying, "I'm not supposed to talk with my mouth full."

Greta smiled at George. "You have very good manners, Henry. And you can always hold up a finger, or cover your mouth if necessary." She demonstrated as she spoke.

"Okay," Henry said, swallowing. "I played baseball with Carl. And we saw peepers. And I saw the baby goats being born."

"Baseball?" George asked. "That's great. How'd you do?" He should get the kid a mitt. He'd love to toss a ball around with Henry.

"Good. I learned to throw and to catch. It's hard,

but Carl says I'm a natural."

Pride filled George. Of course his grandson was a natural. It skipped a generation, though; Alan was never very athletic. Still, Alan should have introduced his own son to baseball, instead of waiting for his sister's boyfriend to do it.

"What's a natural?" Henry asked.

"It means you're good at something without too much effort," Greta said. "You just naturally know how to handle a baseball. Some people can practice a lot and they'll never get very good, and some people are naturally good. You see? Your dad is a natural with numbers."

"I like counting," Henry said.

"And baseball," George said.

"Henry, have you had enough to eat?" Greta asked.

Henry looked down at his clean plate and nodded. "Yes, thank you, Grandma."

"You're very welcome, dear. Why don't you and Grandpa go play in the living room, and then we'll see about some ice cream."

Henry scampered off and George stood up slowly, saying, "Our little major leaguer."

Greta smiled. "I'm sure he'd love to play some catch with you, but don't start telling him he's the next Willie Mays."

"Willie Mays? That's the last guy you can remember playing baseball? You're dating yourself."

She made a face. "Let me clean up the kitchen. I'll call you when the ice cream's ready."

George went into the living room where Henry was already lining up some trucks in a caravan. He sank down onto the couch and watched the boy mound up the blanket into a hill and start moving the vehicles over it one at a time. Once he'd accomplished that, he looked at George and said, "Grandpa? You know Santa?"

"Santa?" George said. "Great guy. Known him for years." He thought Henry was a little young to be doubting the existence of Santa Claus, and he sure wasn't going to be the one to tell him the truth.

"And the chimneys?"

"Yup."

"And the Easter Bunny?"

George wondered what Henry was talking about. "What do you want to know, buddy?"

"About how Santa brings the babies to the Easter Bunny, and the Tooth Fairy brings the baby teeth? I don't understand."

Henry was looking at George so sincerely, so expectantly, as if George could sort everything out for him. All George could think was, what the hell is he talking about? The poor kid was definitely mixed up, and George wasn't sure what to say. He could handle the confusion about Santa and the Easter Bunny, but how babies get here? No way. His mind raced as he stared at Henry, and Henry patiently stared back. Finally George said, “It sounds like you’re pretty confused about things, huh?”

“Yes,” Henry said. “And Aunt Emmy didn’t know, and Mommy and Daddy explained, but I really don’t understand.”

George nodded slowly, trying to look wise. If only Greta were here. He cleared his throat. “I think you might be too young for this talk, Henry. I don’t think you’re ready for it.” And I’m certainly not, he thought.

“I have to be older? And then it will make sense?”

“That’s it,” George said, relieved.

Henry didn’t say anything for a minute, and then he asked, “Why doesn’t Aunt Emmy understand, then? She’s old enough, isn’t she?”

“Yes, she is,” George said. “I’ll talk to her about it, okay?” As he said it, he realized maybe a conversation with Emily would sort this whole thing out. She must have some idea what Henry was talking about, and with any luck he could put this whole thing onto her. He’d see what Greta thought. Anyone but himself.

“Thanks, Grandpa,” Henry said. “Aunt Emmy would like to know. And I’ll wait until I’m older.” He seemed satisfied with the conversation, much to George’s relief.

***

That night George lay in bed next to Greta, both of them reading. He sighed and put his book face down on his chest, removing his reading glasses and waiting for Greta to stop reading. She did so almost immediately and asked, "What's on your mind?"

"I had a mighty strange conversation with Henry today. About where babies come from."

"And did you tell him?" Greta asked.

He ignored her and continued, "He thinks they come from Santa or the Tooth Fairy or some such nonsense."

"Well, that's ridiculous."

"I know. I told him he was too young to understand. But he said something about both Emily and Alan and Isabel trying to explain it to him, so you should talk to them. You should probably start with Isabel since she's the mother. The birds and the bees conversation is a mother's job."

"We're in the twenty-first century, George," Greta said. "And I'd rather not talk to Isabel about this. I have trouble talking to her about tea, for goodness' sake." She paused, tapping her forefinger on her book. "I'm sure this all came up because of the goats Henry saw being born. You haven't seen Emily in a while. Why don't you go visit her tomorrow, and you can ask her what's going on."

"Yeah, okay," George said, picking up his glasses.

"Speaking of Henry," Greta said.

George put his glasses back down.

"Henry knows we love him to pieces."

George waited.

"But he's getting older now." Greta paused. "More active."

"We've still got the energy to handle him," George said, worried about where this was going.

"Yes. But he's at an age where he should be doing things like riding a bike, running around with a dog, exploring the out-of-doors. Somewhere he doesn't have to worry about traffic, where the adults can keep up with him."

"I can keep up with him," George said defiantly. "And our kids did just fine in this neighborhood."

"Yes, but the area has changed. There's a lot more traffic, and you don't run as fast as you used to. I think he would benefit from time spent somewhere with a lot of room and fresh air."

"Emily's place," George said, and Greta nodded. "Good place to learn baseball," he mused. "Nice of Carl to get him started, but why'd Henry have to wait for his aunt's boyfriend to do it? What about his own father?"

"Alan is very busy, and he never liked sports anyway. But some years from now they'll probably be doing calculus together," Greta said. "And it's more likely Henry will get a job using math than earn a place in the major leagues."

George grunted. Alan wasn't very athletic but he could certainly teach a five-year-old how to throw a ball.

Greta smiled. "Emily mentioned she'd like to have Henry over more often. Weekends, if Alan and Isabel agree. We both think it would be good for them to have some time together as a couple."

Now George realized this had already been decided, and Greta was really just informing him, however politely she did it.

"We could always visit Henry there or take him out for a meal or two." She squeezed his hand and let it go, returned her glasses to her face, and opened her book again. George stared at the ceiling for a moment, knowing Greta was doing the right thing for the family, even if deep down it wasn't what she wanted.

***

Emily stole a look at her father as they walked the perimeter of her farm. Not only was he steady on his feet but he looked more fit. The sun glinted off a new patch of grey at his temple, and his crow's feet had deepened, but his eyes were alert as he scanned the countryside. She knew he wasn't admiring the newly leafing trees or the many grasses beginning to grow in the fields. She imagined him as a lion guarding his cub, on the lookout for predators, ever the protector. She smiled to herself as her father turned to look at her, and their eyes met.

"What's so funny?" he said.

"Nothing. I was thinking how great you look. Not tired at all. And have you lost weight?"

George grunted. "Your mother's on a health kick."

"Well, it suits you. She told me she thought you were more handsome now than before the surgery." Emily knew that comment would please her father, although he'd never admit it.

He looked away for a moment and said, "The physical therapy's paying off. I feel pretty good walking around."

Emily could hear the feeling of pride and relief in her father's voice. They walked in silence for a bit, and she enjoyed the warm breeze on her forearms, finally in a t-shirt after months in long sleeves. Underneath her feet she could feel the give in the soil, soft after months of hardening to the cold. Spring was truly a gift for people in northern climates. She inhaled deeply, content to be circling her piece of earth with her father.

"So, Dad," Emily started. "Mom said she talked to you about my having Henry over here more often?"

"Yup."

"Because he's getting older and needs more room? It has nothing to do with you or Mom, you know."

George nodded.

"And Carl loves playing with him," Emily said. "He's like a big kid with Henry."

"I heard they were playing baseball," her father said, and she could hear the satisfaction in his voice.

"Yes, they had a great time. So that's a benefit. And it might help me get along better with Alan, and I think he and Isabel could use some more time alone, don't you?"

George didn't respond and Emily didn't really expect an answer. But she and her mother had talked about it at length, and they'd both decided something was going on with Alan and Isabel, and that having Henry visit Emily more often would give them a chance to work out whatever was going on.

Emily knew that her parents would greatly miss seeing Henry, so she continued, "Just the same, there'll be times when I'm busy and Henry won't have much to do. Maybe you and and Mom could take him to your place for a meal or something when he visits?"

"That would be great, Em. I can't go cold turkey seeing Henry. He's like medicine for me. Keeps me young." He nodded to himself. "Kids keep you young." Looking at Emily, he said, "I have to ask you something. Henry told me he saw those baby goats being born."

"Yes, lucky boy, the timing was right. He loved

it."

"Well," he hesitated, "ah, he seems to be a little confused about the process."

Emily laughed. "He asked me where babies come from and I told him to ask his parents. He thinks I don't know! Pretty good, right?"

"I don't know what they said, but now he thinks it has something to do with Santa and the Tooth Fairy."

"What?"

"Probably just got mixed up. But maybe you could talk to Isabel. You're the one who got him asking in the first place."

"They knew he might be seeing a live birth. They should have been prepared for a question or two. What could they possibly have said that got him mixed up?"

"I don't know, Em. I'm asking you to find out. And leave your mother out of it, okay? She doesn't like confrontation with Isabel."

"Yeah, okay, I'll talk to her." Emily shook her head. Normally she wouldn't bother, but Henry had seen something out of the ordinary for a five-year-old, and she wanted to make sure it hadn't scarred him for life. But what on earth could Isabel have said to him?

***

Late that evening Emily and Carl were curled up on the couch together, talking by the fire they'd built to ward off the spring evening's chill. Emily mentioned that she'd be having Henry over more often.

"That's great," Carl said. "I can get his throwing arm in shape in no time."

"In shape for what?" Emily asked. "I think he's a little young for the majors."

"You're never too young to start playing baseball."

"I didn't realize my childhood was so deficient," Emily said. "Maybe you better teach me too."

"You want to?" Carl asked. "Then the three of us could play. We'd have a pitcher, a batter, and an outfielder. That'd be … oh, was that sarcasm?"

Emily smiled. "You're so cute. It was sarcasm, but I can't say no to that kind of enthusiasm. Plus Henry would probably love it."

"I'll get you a glove. Baseball, not softball. Get it ready. And a cap, you need a cap."

"I'll pick up that stuff next time I'm in town," Emily said.

"No worries, I'll get it."

"I'm perfectly capable of picking out these things," she said.

"Actually, you're not, you'd probably get a leftie glove and a fashion cap."

"Look, I've made it through many years making

decisions for myself without your help, and I don't need it now. In fact I won't use any glove you bring. And I don't even know what a fashion cap is. So if you think—hey!"

Carl had started tickling her, and she wrestled away from him, laughing.

"You're bristly like a porcupine," he said, "but that's why I love you."

Her breath caught for a moment and she stopped squirming and looked at him, still smiling from her laughter.

"I do," he said, his voice soft. "I love you."

"Me too," Emily said. "I love you too."

They were quiet for a moment and then Carl said, "So are you going to be less of a pain in the ass now?"

She burst into laughter and reached for an especially ticklish spot on his side, saying, "Never!"

She didn't have him on the defensive very long before he'd pinned her down on the couch and started kissing her. She broke away and said, "You just reminded me of Henry."

"Well, that's awkward," Carl said, pulling away.

"Don't be gross," she said, punching him lightly in the arm. "Not the kissing, the idea of sex. Not that I was thinking of sex." She caught Carl's look and said, "Okay, I was, but that's not it. See, after Henry saw the goats being born—"

"Fifi and Foofoo?"

“Yes. I told you that he thinks I don’t know where babies come from, so he asked his parents, and now he thinks they come from Santa and the Tooth Fairy.”

“That makes no sense.”

“I know!” Emily agreed. “My dad said the kid is totally confused, so now I’ve been elected to talk to Isabel about it because I’m the one who started it. Can you believe that?”

Carl looked at her, not saying anything.

“You’re right, I did start it. But they knew he might be seeing something like that.”

Carl nibbled her ear.

“Okay, I’ll talk to Isabel tomorrow.” Carl moved down her neck. “Oh,” she sighed, “keep doing that.”

***

Isabel was supposed to be deeply engrossed in her notes for her next fundraiser, but her mind was wandering. She was determined to think of a hobby or activity that she and Alan could participate in together besides drinking and having sex. They weren’t teenagers, after all, and their behavior lately had been uncharacteristic, to say the least. She had a vague sense that she wanted to change the track of their lives. She thought of and immediately rejected golf, knowing how time-consuming it was. Art wasn’t really an interest of Alan’s. In fact, when she first met him they mostly enjoyed eating out and going to movies, but that wasn't really a hobby, and it meant spending time out of the house, away from Henry. Jigsaw puzzles? She fiddled with the items on her desk, lining everything up perfectly parallel to each other. She wanted to get back to work but solving this issue was becoming equally important. When the phone rang it startled her and she picked it up quickly.

"Isabel? It's Emily."

"Oh! Hi, Emily. What's up?" Isabel had never gotten a call out of the blue from Emily before, and was curious but also pleased.

"Well, I wanted to ask you about a few things if you have a minute."

"Sure." Maybe Emily would ask her over again, or out to lunch.

"First, I was wondering if I could have Henry over to visit more often. We had such a good time. I know I'd be taking him away from you and Alan, but I thought you two might like some time alone together. You guys have seemed kind of, I don't know, stressed lately."

Isabel was surprised that Emily had picked up on it, as she thought they both tried to mask it around the family. Maybe this would give them a chance to find something they liked to do together, something they could talk to other people about, anyway. "I think Henry would love that," she said. "And Alan and I could use some time together. I guess we are a little stressed out."

They discussed some dates for a possible visit, and then Emily said, "So, the other thing I'm calling about is a little weird."

I'm not getting an invitation to lunch, Isabel thought.

"You know how Henry saw the goats being born? And he wanted to know where they came from, or rather, where they came out of? And I told him to ask you guys?"

"Yes. He never did, though."

"No?" Emily sounded very surprised.

"No. He was so tired that night he fell asleep getting his pajamas on, and he never brought it up again."

"Okay, that's even stranger, because apparently Henry thinks babies have something to do with Santa Claus and the Tooth Fairy. "

"Santa Claus?" Isabel felt a pull in her stomach.

"And the Tooth Fairy. And some other mythical creatures, I guess. My dad says he's totally confused."

Slowly an image came into focus in Isabel's mind, of her and Alan rolling with laughter on the couch, making up outlandish stories to poor little Henry. She felt sick to her stomach.

"Isabel?"

"I … I'm getting another call, Emily. Can I call

you back in five minutes?"

"Sure, I'll be home."

Isabel hung up the phone and immediately dialed Alan's cell phone.

"What's up, babe? I've got a meeting in five."

"Alan," she whispered, still nauseous. "Oh my God."

"What's the matter?" he said, sharp concern in his voice.

"Emily just called me."

"Is it my dad? What's wrong?"

"No, everyone's fine. But—"

"Jesus, Isabel, you had me freaking out. Everyone's okay?"

Isabel took a deep breath. "Yes, but Emily called me and said that Henry thinks babies come from Santa Claus and the Tooth Fairy. Does that ring any bells with you?"

There was silence on Alan's end of the line. Then he said, "Oh. Shit."

"We are a couple of class A idiots, Alan."

"No. No. We were just joking around."

"Well now your father and your sister are in on the joke, but I get the impression they don't think it's very funny. What am I supposed to say to Emily? That we were so drunk we not only made up a bunch of crap but completely forgot about it?"

She could hear Alan drumming his fingers on his desk as he thought. Finally he said, "Just tell her it was late and we were half asleep. It was like a dream."

"Like a dream? I guess. But I think we need to talk when you get home."

"Yeah, okay. Listen, I have to go. I'll see you tonight," he said, hanging up the phone.

She sighed and dialed Emily's number.

"Hi Emily, sorry about that. Now what were you saying about Santa Claus?"

"That Henry thinks babies come from Santa Claus? And I have no idea where he's getting this information. Are there any new adults in his life? You have to be so careful these days—"

"You know, Emily, I have a vague recollection of Henry waking up me and Alan that night, saying something about the goats. Alan and I started joking about Santa Claus, I think. We were really half asleep."

"Why would you start joking about Santa Claus?"

"I don't know." Isabel winced at how lame her explanation sounded, but she didn't know what else to say.

There was silence on the other end, and then Emily said, "Well, I guess if he woke you up out of a sound sleep. Maybe you were only half awake?"

"Maybe. Yes. Anyway I didn't remember it at all until you started talking about it. So silly, but no wonder poor Henry is confused. I'll have to sort it all out with him."

"Great," Emily said, sounding relieved. "I'll let my dad know not to worry. He didn't even tell my mom, it sounded so weird."

Isabel paused, and then said, "Emily? Do you think you might like to have lunch together sometime?"

"Lunch? Um, sure! When?"

They picked a date for lunch the following week and then Isabel hung up the phone, staring at her desk for a full five minutes before finally going back to her work. Later, after she brought Henry home from his yoga class, she had an age-appropriate discussion with him about sex, gleaned from among the many childrearing books she'd purchased before he was born. Afterwards he said, "I'm glad Santa doesn't bring the babies. He's busy with all those presents anyway." She smiled and ruffled the soft hair on his head, glad the drama was over.

***

Emily watched as the waiter refilled their wine glasses and settled the bottle back into its chiller. After he left, she looked at Carl, who regarded her silently.

"Waiters always come at the most awkward moments, don't they?" she said, attempting a smile.

"Why does it have to be awkward?"

"Because we're arguing."

"You love to argue," he said.

"Not when it's you and me."

"But this is important, Emily. I don't think I'm off base here. I really think Alan might have a problem."

"He's just a little stressed, for God's sake. He has a job, a kid, an active social life." She was ticking off her statements on her hand and paused with three fingers up in the air. "We just had dinner with them, and they were fine." She added a fourth finger and then noticed that the waiter was headed back their way, thinking she was waving at him. She quickly put her hand down and shook her head, mouthing the word 'sorry' at him. "You might be stressed too if you had any of those things." She heard the sarcasm in her voice but couldn't help herself. "But I wouldn't call you an alcoholic if you had a few glasses of wine with dinner. You're not exactly a teetotaler yourself."

Carl sighed, his face serious, and asked softly, "Have you ever heard of a functional alcoholic?"

"A what?"

"There are people who drink excessively, who can't stop, but who can still maintain basic life skills. Not all alcoholics are sitting on a sidewalk drinking out of a paper bag."

"Oh, come on, Carl. Seriously? Alan is not an alcoholic," Emily said, slapping her palm on the table.

Carl looked at her steadily for a moment and then said, “For the longest time, I didn’t want to admit my father was either.”

“Your father?” Emily asked. “He was a drunk?”

“It’s not like he staggered around the house in front of my friends or embarrassed us in public. But he drove drunk—even lost his driver’s license a few times—he passed out on the couch a lot, missed days of work or went in late. He and my mom acted like things were completely normal. Their friends never seemed to notice he had a problem. When I was older I read a few books on alcoholism and tried talking to them about it but they laughed at me, said I was making a big deal out of nothing. Now he’s got a lot of health problems but he still drinks and they still won’t talk about it.” He shook his head. “He’s a functional alcoholic and has been his whole life.”

Emily frowned. “Carl, it’s terrible that you had to grow up with that. And I’m glad you shared it with me. But are you saying that you think Alan acts like that? Because he doesn’t. He’s never had any of those problems.” She hesitated, then reached her hand across the table and put it on his. “Isn’t it possible that because of your own upbringing, you’re seeing something that isn’t there?”

Carl took her hand in his. “I don’t think so. Maybe I’m more open to seeing it, but something’s going on with him.”

Emily shook her head and pulled her hand away. "Okay, give me one example of his behavior that says 'drunk' to you."

Carl exhaled loudly. "When your dad was brought to the hospital he was agitated, remember? Don't roll your eyes, I'm not finished. He said he was going to take a walk. I thought that was strange because he'd just arrived to see his father in the hospital."

"He was upset. He needed to calm down."

"Sure. Maybe. But when he left the room, I went out to get snacks, remember? And I followed him. He ducked into a bathroom and stayed in there for a long time."

Emily laughed. "Ignoring the obvious answer to why he was in there, maybe he just needed a good cry."

"No," Carl said, "there was no crying. There were other noises, though. This might come as a shock, but—"

"Were you eavesdropping on my brother outside a bathroom door?" Emily interrupted, angry now. "Now that is crazy behavior!" She folded her arms across her chest and glared at him.

"Please, Emily, I'm trying to tell you something important. Listen to me. The reason I followed him is because I saw signs of drug use."

"Oh good, we've gone from alcoholism to drug use!" she said, voice raised, leaning forward and slamming her palms on the table. "What next? Is he a serial killer too? What do you have against him?"

"Nothing!" He grabbed her hands with his own and held them tightly, leaning forward as well. Dropping his voice, he said, "He was edgy, he wiped at his nose a lot, and I think he was snorting coke in that bathroom." His grip on her hands tightened to the point of discomfort. "And I recognize a coke addict because I was one." Abruptly he let her hands go and sat back, shoulders sagging.

Emily didn't move. She was speechless. They sat that way for what felt like minutes, Emily staring at Carl, Carl staring at the table, until the waiter appeared with their main course. They barely glanced at him, muttering a thank-you as he hurriedly left. Finally Carl looked at Emily and said, "What are you thinking?"

"I … I don't know. I don't know what to say."

"Are you going to dump me?" he asked quietly.

"No. What? No! Why would I do that? You did use the past tense. It's not like you quit using coke yesterday. Right?"

Carl shook his head. "It was years ago. My friends liked to party, but I was afraid to drink, of course. One of them turned me on to cocaine. It never occurred to me that addiction is addiction, no matter what the substance. I finally joined Narcotics Anonymous. Coke is a tough habit to break. And it's a great way to cover up a drinking problem. Which I did not have. But I think your brother might. He might have both."

Emily leaned back, shaking her head. Carl's confession explained his far-fetched theories about her brother, but she still didn't see Alan as an alcoholic or a drug abuser.

Carl put his palms flat on the table and said, "I've been an addict and I've sponsored ones who are trying to get clean, and I honestly think Alan has some kind of addiction. Look, I'll admit I'm more sensitive to the amounts of alcohol people consume, but I'm also more aware of whether they're overindulging, and it seems to me that Alan and Isabel overindulge a lot. Only Alan never appears to be drunk, have you noticed that? Isabel's always way more inebriated than he is."

"Women get drunker than men," Emily said, still not believing what Carl was telling her. "We're smaller."

"Alan disappears a lot. Slips out of the room. Comes back sober and full of energy. Have you noticed?"

Emily shook her head. "He's always been full of energy. He was born that way."

Carl sighed. "You think I'm being paranoid. But I'm right."

"I'm not saying you're right or wrong," Emily said, although she did think he was completely off base. "I need to think about this. Maybe talk to

Isabel. Again, maybe your own history is coloring your judgment here. I'll make my own decision about whether or not my family has a problem. But I do appreciate your concern, and I'm glad you were honest with me about your own past."

Carl snorted. "You sound like a politician."

Emily frowned. "I just want some time to think about what you've said."

"Okay, but think about it fast. Because my main concern here is Henry. I know what it's like growing up with addiction."

Emily's heart sank. Was there even a chance that Carl was right? Could Henry be in danger? She really doubted it; she may not be best friends with her brother but she knew him well all the same. But she saw that look on Carl's face and knew he wouldn't be letting this go. "You're so bossy sometimes," she said.

"Thanks."

"It wasn't a compliment."

They ate in silence for a few minutes until Carl stretched his hand, palm up, across the table and said, "Are you okay?"

She sighed and put her hand in his. "Yeah." He squeezed her hand and she added, "I'm meeting Isabel for lunch next week. After I see her, we can talk more about your outlandish theories."

Carl smiled. "It's good you're taking my concerns so seriously," he said.

"Goats are so much easier than people," Emily replied. They spent the rest of the meal pointedly discussing safe topics, but in the back of her mind, Emily was wondering how to get Carl to ease up on Alan. Maybe if he knew Alan better?

***

Isabel opened her laptop and sat forward, hands poised on the keyboard. She was determined to find an activity that she and Alan could do together, something besides the drunk sex they'd been having lately, that would help them to connect. Not that she minded the sex, but it seemed like they were only getting closer in a very physical sense, and she missed the emotional connection they used to have. She typed "activities for couples" into the search bar and started reading. Clear out the garage, she read. She skimmed further down. Shopping, art galleries, extreme sports, picnics. She didn't know where to start. She wanted something new, something neither of them had tried before, and she wanted to be fairly sure Alan would like it before she suggested it. Horseback riding, she saw. She'd never been on a horse and she didn't think Alan had either. It would be a new experience for both of them.

She searched for horseback riding in the area and found a place that offered "trail rides." That sounds like the Wild West, she thought. It would be an adventure. She called and spoke to a nice young woman who told her, to Isabel's surprise, that they didn't need any experience being on a horse, and that they had space available the following weekend. Isabel booked a trail ride and hung up, pleased. Worst case, they would have something to laugh about. She was almost certain Alan had no plans that weekend, but she headed for Alan's office to check his calendar just in case.

Sitting down at his desk, she wiggled the mouse to wake up the computer. She clicked and crossed her legs as she waited for the calendar to appear, dangling her right pump off her toes and bouncing it on her foot. As she thought, his Saturday was free. She pushed back from the desk and her right shoe fell, bouncing off the spike heel and landing far under the desk. She got onto her knees to reach it, pleased to see that the housekeeper was vacuuming under there. As she picked up her shoe she noticed a glint of silver where the desk met the carpet. She slid the shoe back onto her foot and reached for what she expected to be a quarter. She was surprised when her fingers grasped something thicker wedged between the carpet and the desk. She pulled hard and retrieved a small object. Scurrying back out from under the desk, she examined it in the light. It was about three inches long, shiny, with two etched bands around the wider bottom half and an indentation at the tapered top. It looked like a bullet, she thought, mystified.

What on earth was a bullet doing in her house? Frightened, she picked up the phone and called Alan's cell phone, but it went right to voice mail.

"Alan, it's Isabel," she said. "I just found something really weird under your desk. This is going to sound crazy but it looks like a bullet. What on earth would a bullet be doing in our house?" She paused, trying to form her thoughts. "Look, I don't know what it is, but I can't imagine it's yours, so … call me back." She hung up the phone and left, hoping he would call soon.

Returning to her own office, she opened her laptop, wanting to put a name to what she'd found. The pictures she looked at online didn't help. "Bullet-shaped object" gave her many links to UFO stories. "Silver bullet" brought up vibrators, movies, and firearms. She tried a few more descriptors but got nowhere. Glancing at her watch she realized she'd spent too much time on the computer and would have to hurry to pick up Henry on time. She slipped the mysterious silver object into her purse and left.

***

Twenty minutes later Isabel was driving Henry home, only half-listening to him chatter about his day. As they turned onto the main street leading to their neighborhood, Isabel realized they would be passing the police station on their way home. Why not stop in and show them what she'd found? Certainly they'd be able to tell her what it was. She wasn't even sure if it was a bullet, and she knew they didn't spontaneously explode, but she'd feel better having someone look at it. "Henry," she interrupted, "how would you like to stop by the police station?"

"Right now?" he asked excitedly. "Will they do the siren again?"

Isabel had taken Henry to an identity program for children at the police station recently, where the kids got to see a police car and all its working parts in addition to getting their picture taken.

"No, I don't think so. I want to ask them a question. But you can come inside and I'm sure you'll see an officer." Henry was in awe of police officers.

"How many will there be?" Henry asked as she pulled into the station's parking lot.

"I don't know," Isabel said.

"Ten?"

"I don't think that many."

"One?" he asked as they walked up the steps.

"Why don't you count them when we get inside?" she said, holding the door open for Henry.

They entered into a foyer with a key-padded door and a bank of windows, behind one of which was an officer. "Can I help you?" he asked.

"One!" said Henry.

Isabel approached the window, which was much

like a bank teller's, and said, "Yes, I have an object I found, I have no idea what it is. I'm sure it sounds silly but," she leaned forward and lowered her voice, not wanting Henry to hear, "it sort of looks like a bullet."

"Just a moment." He turned and said something Isabel couldn't quite hear. Then he turned back to her and said, "Someone will be with you shortly." Looking down at Henry, he said, "How you doing, buddy?"

"Fine thank you," Henry said.

"You staying out of trouble?" he asked, winking at Isabel.

Henry reached up for Isabel's hand and said, quite seriously, "Yes."

"Good man," the officer said as the door to the foyer opened and another officer stepped out to greet them.

"Hi," she said. "I'm Officer Johnston. How can I help you?"

"Two!" said Henry.

"Hi," Isabel said, ignoring Officer Johnston's curious look at Henry. "I'm sorry to waste your time, but I found something that kind of looks like a … like ammunition," she used a word Henry didn't know, "and I want to make sure it's not real." She opened her purse and started to reach into it.

"Ma'am? If it's possible you have live ammunition, maybe you'd like to come inside?" The officer gestured to the door that had just swung closed.

Isabel said, “Of course,” the officer punched in a code to open the door, and they went through. They walked a short distance down the hall into a small room where Officer Johnston observed Henry thoughtfully for a moment. He was looking at her with a solemn expression on his face. “What’s your name, young man?”

“Henry.”

“Henry, would you like a tour of the police station?” she asked.

“Yes, please!”

After getting Isabel’s permission, she called another officer, “Three!” for Henry, and they went off, Henry clearly excited to see the rest of the station. Then she turned to Isabel. “All right, ma’am, let’s see what you’ve got.”

Isabel dug the thing out of her purse and handed it to Officer Johnston, who took one look at it and started shaking her head. “What is it?” Isabel asked. “Is it a bullet?”

“Where did you find this, ma’am?” the officer asked, a very serious expression on her face.

“In … my house,” Isabel said. “Is it a bullet?” She was frightened by the officer’s sudden change in demeanor and tone.

“It’s called a bullet for obvious reasons,” was the reply, “but it’s drug paraphernalia.”

Isabel stood mutely staring at the officer, an uncomfortable silence between them. Finally she repeated, “Drug paraphernalia?”

“Yes.” She grasped the top and bottom of the metal contraption and twisted until a hole appeared. Then she twisted again to expose a hollow chamber. “The drugs go in here, and they’re snorted through the hole. Easy to use, easy to hide.” The look on the officer’s face made Isabel feel like a criminal. “You found this in your house?”

“Yes. Not inside my house. In my yard.” Isabel cringed inwardly at her lie.

“I thought you said you found it in your house.”

“Yes, but I meant at my house. In the yard. Just … in the grass. Near the dogwood. It was shiny and I noticed it.” Isabel knew she sounded like an idiot but she didn’t care. She was shaken and only wanted to get out of the station as quickly as possible.

The officer nodded. “Do you use a landscaping company?”

“Yes. Oh, but no, I’m sure it’s not from them,” Isabel said, not wanting to shift blame. “Him. It’s just one man, he’s older, really, I can’t imagine him using drugs. He’s a grandfather.” She couldn’t believe how much and how easily she was lying.

“You’d be surprised what kind of people do drugs. This particular device is often used to hold cocaine. Cocaine in powdered form is a popular drug among your wealthier citizens.”

Isabel struggled to keep her face calm. “That’s terrible,” she said. “I’ve certainly never seen anything like that. Well, I’m just glad that’s not a real bullet,” she continued, zipping up her purse. “You can keep it, of course. I really should get going; it’s almost dinner time.”

“Your son’s not quite done with his tour,” Officer Johnston said, “and I need to take down some information before I can let you go. I’ll be back in a minute.” She left and Isabel waited for two minutes that felt like twenty until the officer returned and took Isabel’s statement. “We have to file a lot of paperwork these days,” she said. As she finished filling out the form, the door opened and Henry stepped in, escorted by a young man in uniform.

“Here’s Henry,” he said, smiling and putting his hand on Henry’s shoulder. “He got up to ‘Six,’” he said to Isabel, and added to his colleague, “He’s counting officers today.”

“Thanks,” Officer Johnston said. “Would you mind walking them out? Ma’am, you’re free to go. We’ll call you if we have any questions.”

Isabel nodded and grabbed her son’s hand, saying, “Come on, Henry, we’ve got to get home and make dinner.” They left, Henry smiling and waving to all the officers he saw as they left, Isabel holding his hand tightly, trying to smile calmly and not run out of the place. She barely listened on the way home as he described the station and all the nice people he'd met there. There was only one word on her mind, and it was drugs. She would try Alan again the minute she got home. He had to know immediately that a business associate was using drugs. She hoped it was a client and not a colleague.

Isabel didn't have to wait long; her cell phone rang in the car on the way home. She saw it was Alan and answered right away, "Hi, I'm in the car with Henry," so she wouldn't have to say anything inappropriate in front of him.

"Isabel, what's going on? You found a bullet? Is everything okay?"

"We're fine. We just had a fun trip to the police station, didn't we, Henry?" She raised her voice a little and smiled, looking at Henry in the rear view mirror. "As I said, Henry and I are on the way home. Why don't I call you when I get there?"

"I can't, I stepped out of a meeting to check your message. Why did you go to the police station?"

Alan sounded so concerned, she wanted to reassure him that they were fine, but without Henry understanding a word she said. "It's conceivable that when an item resembles ammunition one would … hasten to the … constabulary. They informed me that said item was not … incendiary but rather a form of paraphernalia." She glanced in the rear view again; Henry was staring out the window.

Alan exhaled loudly. "Paraphernalia? You mean

drugs? You found drug paraphernalia in my office? What did the police say?" His voice had risen.

"They were very nice. I'll tell you all about it when you get home tonight. Okay?"

"Yeah, okay, all right." Alan sounded somewhat less upset. "I have to go. I'll try to get out early. Christ."

They said goodbye and Isabel hung up, glancing again at Henry, who seemed oblivious to the entire conversation. Not that she'd said much, really. She really wanted to tell Alan the whole story, but not in front of Henry. Or anyone else, for that matter.

***

That night after Henry was asleep, Alan and Isabel took a bottle of wine and two glasses into his office and shut the door. They settled into the two dark brown leather chairs opposite his desk and Alan poured them each a glass of wine. Isabel rested her head against the firmness of the chair back and started talking. With great relief she explained how she'd found the drug paraphernalia, how she'd impulsively decided to stop at the police station, about the conversation she'd had with Officer Johnston, and how kind the police had been to Henry. Isabel even demonstrated how her shoe had fallen off her foot and under Alan's desk.

"My biggest concern," she concluded, "is that

someone you know is using drugs."

Alan stared at her for a moment and then said, "Someone I know?"

"A client or a colleague. I can't imagine where else it would have come from."

"Did the police say they'd check for fingerprints?" he asked.

"No. They kept it but I don't think they'll do anything with it. They made me so nervous I lied and told them I found it in the yard. But if you have an idea who brought that into our house, get them some help. The police were very serious when they saw what it was."

"I can imagine." Slowly Alan rotated his wine glass in his hand. "Wow. I don't know whose it could be." He was silent for a moment, staring at his desk, frowning. "Maybe it was someone from that big client dinner I had last summer."

"I suppose it could have been," she reasoned. "It was pretty well wedged between the carpet and the back of your desk, so it could have been there for ages. But who would have been sitting at your desk?"

Alan was silent for a moment, then ventured, "The waitstaff used my office to settle the bill."

"That's right," Isabel said. "You think it could have been one of them? They all seemed perfectly fine that night."

Alan nodded thoughtfully. "I guess you just can't tell."

Isabel was relieved. Perhaps it wasn't anyone they knew after all. "Let's hope it's not someone at work who's having problems. You don't want to be associated with anyone like that. You could lose your job."

Alan smiled. "I'm not worried about it. By the way, why were you at my desk?"

"What?"

"You said you were at my desk when your shoe fell off." Alan looked at her curiously. "Were you looking for something?"

"Oh! Yes, I was checking your work calendar. I was going to surprise you, but I guess I can tell you now. I signed us up for horseback riding."

"Is Henry doing that now too?"

"No, not for Henry, for you and me. The two of us."

"Why?"

Isabel looked away briefly and then said, "I wanted to do something together, just the two of us."

"We do things together," Alan said defensively.

"No, I know, I just felt, I've been feeling disconnected lately, somehow," Isabel trailed off, not sure she wanted to get into this discussion now.

"Disconnected? From me? We spend almost every night together." Alan looked concerned and a little upset.

"We do, but it's always at home, and we're usually drinking wine and watching a movie, or having sex. I feel like there's an emotional distance between us."

"I don't feel that way. At all." Alan frowned, taking a big gulp of wine. "But if you do, and riding a horse will make you feel better, I'll do it."

Isabel sighed. "I don't want to force you to do anything."

"It's fine," Alan said, taking another gulp and putting his wine glass firmly on his desk. "I've never ridden a horse. Might as well try something new."

"Great," she said, relieved. "It's a week from Saturday. I'll ask Emily to watch Henry. I really think we'll have fun."

Alan reached over and took her hand, pulling her into his lap. "You have your idea of fun, I have mine."

***

Isabel knew she was overdressed for her lunch with Emily, but she didn't mind. Better that than underdressed. Had she given it any thought, she would have realized that when Emily said the restaurant had "the most amazing food" it didn't necessarily mean it had the ambiance to match. No matter. As Emily checked in with the hostess, Isabel took in Conga Burger's dining room with goofy drawings, irreverent signs, and silly objects strewn about, battle-scarred wooden booths and tables, and strings of colored lights hanging from the ceiling, and thought that it matched Emily perfectly. They were seated in a corner booth where a colorful pot attached high on the wall spilled forth an ivy.

Isabel put her purse next to her, crossed her hands, and smiled as their waiter, dressed in a pair of beat-up jeans, a Hawaiian shirt, and brown sandals, handed them each a menu and took their drink order.

"You'll love this place," Emily said as he left. "It's a new favorite for me and Carl. And they happen to use my goat cheese," she added.

"Is that why we're here? Are you doing business research?" Isabel was impressed.

"No, although that's how we discovered it. I like to check out the places that sell my product. But now we come here because of the burgers."

Isabel nodded slowly as she perused the menu. "There certainly are a lot of those," she said. "Normally I have salads for lunch."

"If you're worried about the cholesterol they have vegan burgers, absolutely delicious."

Isabel wasn't worried about the cholesterol so much as the calories, but vegan burgers had to be better for you than beef. She looked up as the waiter approached the table with their drinks.

"Iced tea and a Diet Coke," he said, putting them down. "Do you know what you want yet?"

"I do, but she's undecided," Emily said.

"How are the salads?" Isabel asked.

"Everything here is great," he said, "but you won't find burgers like these anywhere else."

"Yes, I hear they're amazing," Isabel said. "All right. Emily, pick out your favorite vegan burger and I'll have one too."

"Two vegan mushroom burgers with goat cheese and caramelized onions. And sweet potato fries."

"Not for me," Isabel said.

"Yes, for you," Emily replied. "Live a little. That's it," she said to the waiter, adding after he left, "if it makes you feel any better, the fries are baked."

"I'll do extra time on the treadmill tomorrow," Isabel shrugged, although she suspected it would have to be an extra hour or two. "I haven't had fries in ages."

"More of a kid thing, huh?"

Isabel smiled. "Henry adores fries, but we almost never let him eat them. They're really quite bad for you. Not if they're baked, though. And he would love it here."

Emily looked around the restaurant. "We could get a great game of I Spy going in here. How is Henry?" she asked.

"He's fine," Isabel said. "We straightened out the whole … birds and the bees business, by the way. He understands Santa has nothing to do with babies, and that's as far as we got."

"I'm glad, Isabel. That was bizarre, him thinking those things. Really weird."

Isabel colored a little, glad she had on makeup to mask it. She would never tell Emily the real story, but in the end she was glad Emily had said something. “Yes, very strange. But I’m glad you spoke up, otherwise who knows how long he would have labored under that delusion.”

Emily nodded. “I was worried that I’d be causing problems, butting in.”

“No, I really do appreciate it.” Isabel twirled her straw in her soda, hesitating. She was the one who had initiated this lunch and now she was nervous, but nerves had never stopped her before. “Actually, it’s why I asked you to lunch.”

“Because I butted in?”

“Yes, sort of. I wanted to see you because I need someone to talk to, and I really don’t have anyone. Most of my friends are work colleagues and I don’t like to mix my personal life with business.”

“Is it about something specific?” Emily asked.

“Not really. I don’t know. Maybe.” Isabel knew she sounded incredibly vague. “I need a sounding board. To try to make sense of what I’m feeling, because I can’t.”

Emily smiled at her. “Okay. Spill.”

Isabel sighed and said, “I don’t know. It’s nothing big, really. It’s just that … I feel like Alan and I are drifting apart a little bit. But we’ve been married for a while, and we have a child now, so I guess that’s not unusual.”

Emily nodded. "I've heard kids can put a strain on a marriage. Has it helped having Henry stay with me?"

"Yes, of course. We really appreciate it. It's just that we don't seem to … do stuff anymore."

"Stuff?" Emily asked. "Are you talking about intimate stuff? Or out-on-the-town stuff?" She looked a little uncomfortable.

"God, no," Isabel said, looking down at the table. "I'm sorry, Emily, I should have realized you won't want to discuss this, since it's about your brother."

Emily was quiet for a moment, then she said, "No, it's fine. I know you need someone to talk to. I'll just ignore the fact that he's my brother."

Isabel nodded, relieved. "Thanks. Well, like I was saying, we don't do things anymore. I mean, we do, um, intimate stuff, but nothing else. And it seems like the intimate stuff is all we do anymore, like it's the only way we connect." She paused and looked at Emily, whose face was neutral. "I'd like to have something else we could do together. A hobby. I thought we could try horseback riding."

Emily made a noise that sounded suspiciously like a snort, then coughed, but to her credit, all she said was, "Horseback riding? Interesting."

Isabel nodded eagerly. "Yes! I wanted something different, something to pull us out of ourselves, if you know what I mean."

Emily nodded, an odd, almost relieved smile on

her face.

"It's something neither of us has ever done, so it would be a new challenge and hopefully a lot of fun."

"I think it's a great idea, Isabel. I really do. Do you know where you're going yet? One of the farms near mine has horses."

"Thanks, but I've already booked us an appointment for a week from Saturday," Isabel said. "Which means I have to ask you a favor. Would you mind if we dropped Henry off with you? It would only be a few hours."

Emily said, "Of course, I'd love to have him," as the waiter approached, setting down their plates along with a ramekin of homemade ketchup.

He left as Isabel tried the burger. "Oh my God," she said behind her freshly manicured hand, her mouth still full. The combination of goat cheese and caramelized onions alone was worth the bite, but the vegan burger had a nutty earthy flavor that put it over the top. "It's absolutely delicious!"

Emily grinned, taking a huge bite of her own burger and nodding.

Isabel tried a sweet potato fry and once again was impressed. It was light and crisp, and perfect dipped in the homemade ketchup. This place was worth the calories, and she'd love to bring Alan and Henry here sometime.

"I'm glad you asked me to lunch," Emily said. "What you were saying before, about needing a sounding board … most of my friends are still climbing the corporate ladder, too busy to get together, and my schedule is so weird. I wouldn't mind getting together with you on a more regular basis." She dunked a thick fry into her ketchup and bit it, looking at Isabel expectantly.

"I would love that," Isabel said. "Can I tag along on your next business research trip?"

"Sure," Emily said. "But you can pick the next restaurant, as long as it's not too expensive." She dipped another fry in ketchup but didn't eat it, just kept dipping it. "So, with you and Alan, your relationship, it sounds like maybe he's kind of stressed out?"

Isabel nodded. "After that promotion last year he's had a lot more work, and he brings it home with him. He tries to spend time with Henry, of course, but it's hard for him."

"Right," Emily said. "More work responsibilities, family demands. Who wouldn't be stressed, right? Carl is stressed sometimes and he has none of the above."

"Yes, that's true," Isabel said, sipping her soda. "And I don't see any of it easing up for Alan, which probably makes it all the worse. The better he does, the more work he gets."

"So a few glasses of wine every night is perfectly understandable," Emily said, almost to herself.

Isabel looked at Emily, surprised she'd brought up wine. She thought they were talking about her marital woes. "What?"

Emily's face reddened. "This is awkward. But Carl said he noticed that Alan drinks quite a bit, and of course I said he was being ridiculous, but I promised I'd talk to you about it." She trailed off, staring at the table.

"He drinks quite a bit?" Isabel repeated. Of course they both enjoyed a bottle of wine lately, but 'quite a bit'? That was a little much. Except for that one night when they'd told Henry those awful things, and that night she'd been as smashed as he was. Did that mean she had a drinking problem? Of course not. Her mind was racing but she didn't say anything, only looking at Emily with what must have been a stunned look on her face.

"I'm sorry," Emily said. "You look shocked. But I had to ask. Carl and I—it doesn't matter. Obviously the answer is that Alan doesn't have a drinking problem."

Now Isabel was getting angry. "Of course not. Why would you say that?"

"Well, he does seem to consume a lot whenever I see him."

"You only see him on special occasions," Isabel said defensively. "Holidays, parties."

"You're right," Emily said. "But … "

"Yes?" Isabel demanded.

"Well, um," Emily hesitated, shifting in her seat, "he never seems that drunk. He always seems fine. Like he hasn't been drinking at all."

It was exactly what Isabel had been thinking in the back of her mind for weeks. How did Alan manage to drink all that wine and remain apparently sober? But how did that equal a drinking problem? "I'm confused," she said. "You're saying he has a problem because he's not acting drunk? Maybe he's one of those people who can hold his liquor."

"Okay, I'm just going to say it," Emily said. "Carl thinks Alan may have a drug problem that masks his drinking."

"A drug problem?" Isabel said, alarmed. It was as if Emily knew about that cocaine bullet Isabel had found, but that was impossible.

"Specifically cocaine," Emily said. "And full disclosure here, Carl used to have a cocaine addiction, and he says he sees what could be signs of it in Alan."

Isabel's mind was reeling with Emily's accusations. She thought about Alan, a loving husband, a solid dependable man, a good father. He was not a drunk or a drug addict. What Emily was saying was ridiculous.

"I'm sorry," Emily said. "I can tell this is freaking you out. Look, I promised I'd bring it up, and I have. Does any of this sound possible to you, or is Carl completely off the mark?"

Isabel shook her head slowly. “Sometimes I think Alan’s drinking a little bit more than he should. But no,” she said, more certain as she thought about it, “I haven’t seen any odd behavior. No.” That thing she found in Alan’s office had been there for ages; it was from waitstaff at a party. Alan could never have lied to her face about it.

“I didn’t think so,” Emily said. “I know my brother, and I can’t see Alan having problems like that. Carl had me all worked up. It must be his own past coloring his judgment.”

Isabel nodded. Carl was a former addict. She didn’t hold it against him, but he was pushy, and probably overreacting to nothing. He just didn’t know Alan that well. It was all a simple misunderstanding.

“I hope we can be honest with each other about anything, even if it’s hard to talk about,” Emily said.

Isabel saw the look on Emily’s face and realized suddenly that Emily was worried she’d upset Isabel. She smiled briefly. “Of course. I understand why you had to say something, and I’m glad you felt you could ask. And now we both know there’s nothing to worry about.”

“Exactly,” Emily said, her face brightening. “Now, I hope you have some extra time for your treadmill tomorrow because the desserts here are amazing.”

Chapter 9

"THIS ISN'T BAD," Emily said. She was sitting in the cockpit of Carl's plane, looking out the window. The enclosed space was very small, not the place for someone with mild claustrophobia.

"Enjoying the view?" he asked, and she could hear the smile in his voice.

"The tarmac is lovely this time of year," she said, looking at the asphalt six feet down.

"It looks even better from the air."

"One step at a time. You know I don't like flying, and this is a very small plane." She looked at the dashboard directly in front of her knees, covered in instrument panels and digital displays, then over at Carl, to her left. She felt like she was in a Volkswagen Beetle.

"Okay," Carl sighed, putting his hand on her knee. "Maybe someday we can taxi to the other end of the airport." He must have seen alarm on her face because he added, "We'll be going slower than a car on a highway. And much less chance of an accident."

Emily grimaced. "Talking about accidents doesn't increase my comfort level."

"Sorry." He cleared his throat. "So you were going to tell me about your lunch with Isabel?"

"Yes, and I'm happy to say we have nothing to worry about."

"You asked her if her husband had a substance abuse problem?"

"I did. And he doesn't."

"Could you be a little more specific? How exactly did the conversation go?"

"I asked her if it was possible that Alan had a drinking problem, and she said no." She saw Carl open his mouth and said, "Wait, I'm not finished. Then I pointed out that he seems to drink a lot but never appear drunk, and I told her that it was possible he had a drug problem that was masking the effects of the alcohol."

Carl nodded. "Good."

"I also told her why we thought that," she added quietly.

"You mean because I had a drug problem myself?"

"Yes. I hope that was okay."

He shrugged. "I'm not embarrassed about it, especially not if it helps someone. So how did she respond to all this?"

"She said that we're only seeing him on special occasions, that he holds his liquor well, that maybe occasionally he drinks a little more than he should, and that she had seen no other signs of odd behavior."

"Humph."

"That sounded like a skeptical grunt."

"I should have gone with you. I'd like to have

seen her face."

"She looked shocked, Carl, like none of this had occurred to her before. Really surprised. I don't think she could have faked her reaction. I'm convinced all is well. I'm not worried about Henry at all, except that his parents need to put some romance back into their marriage. They're having some marital difficulties, which is where the extra drinking is coming from, I'm sure of it."

"'Marital difficulties'? What does that mean?"

"We discussed their marriage as a whole. She mentioned their sex life, but that wasn't a big part of it. The big problem was that they don't spend a lot of time alone together anymore."

"Did you mention our sex life?" Carl asked, alarm in his voice.

"Why? Our sex life is fine. My point is, they need to remember why they got married in the first place."

"You mean if our sex life was bad, you'd be talking about it?"

"Carl, focus. Isabel says she's feeling disconnected lately, and Alan's been working a lot, and she thinks they need to find some new way to connect. So get this: they're going to try horseback riding."

Carl laughed. "Somehow I can't picture your brother on a horse."

"Me neither, but I wasn't going to tell her that.

She seemed really hopeful that this could be a turning point for them. Meanwhile, I'm watching Henry the Saturday morning they're going. You're welcome to join us."

"Sure. It's fun having a kid around. Especially when he's on his best behavior and you can give him back to his parents later."

Emily hesitated. She wanted children someday, and she couldn't have a long-term relationship with a man who didn't. But she didn't want to sound presumptuous, nor did she want him to think she wanted children this instant. Finally she said, "You mean you like them in theory but maybe not in your own future?"

Carl looked at her, his eyes wide, then looked straight ahead out the windshield. His mouth was open a little. He looked like a man in shock.

Damn, she thought. Why did I bring up children? That was Chapter 1 in How to Break Up a Relationship. She gave him a few seconds, then said, "I think I just had a major brain cramp. Let's pretend I never asked that question."

He nodded, then looked at her again. "Okay."

Emily met his gaze and held it, looking into his deep brown eyes, wondering if their color would be inherited by his hypothetical children. She wondered what his silence meant. Was he afraid to have kids based on his own past? Did he want them someday, but not anytime soon? Or did he want them sooner rather than later, but maybe not with her?

They were both quiet for a long moment, regarding each other, then Carl shifted his gaze to a speck of dust on the instrument panel, brushing at it with his finger, and saying, "So you think all of Alan's behavior is because he's not getting enough from his wife?"

Emily made a face. "He's getting plenty, actually. More than enough. It's probably just job stress, something you may not remember."

"So back off?" He smiled. "Got it. But I'm still going to keep an eye on things. Now tell me," he said, putting his hand on her knee, "how much is 'more than enough'?"

"What are you talking about?"

"You said Alan was getting 'more than enough' sex. I'm just wondering what that amount is. I wouldn't want to be suffering a deficiency."

"I'll make sure that never happens," she laughed. "But maybe we should get out of this airplane first."

Emily stood next to Carl as he and Henry, wearing a new Red Sox cap his grandfather had given him, tossed a baseball back and forth. They were keeping up a constant stream of chatter. Sometimes Carl commented on Henry's form as he threw and caught the ball, but mostly he just prompted Henry with a few questions and then listened until Henry had exhausted the subject.

Henry was currently relating the entire plot of The Sound Of Music. “And at the end they get married,” he finished proudly.

“Married?” Carl asked. “What about the Nazis?”

“What are those?” Henry asked.

“Carl!” Emily said under her breath. She knew Isabel never played the end of the movie for Henry.

Carl looked at her quizzically as he said to Henry, “You know, the bad guys.”

“There are no bad guys in the movie!” Henry said, as if Carl were making a joke.

“Sure there are—”

“Carl! Don’t be so silly!” Emily interrupted. He opened his mouth to say something and she said under her breath, “Isabel doesn’t let him watch that part.”

He swore under his breath and said to Henry, “You know what, buddy, I’m thinking of a different movie. Sorry about that!” Then quietly to Emily he said, “That’s ridiculous.”

“I agree, but she says right now she wants him to think the world is a happy place.”

Carl shrugged and they tossed the ball a few more times before Henry said, “The police catch bad guys.”

“Yes, they do,” Emily said, “but there are no bad guys around here. Just some naughty goats.”

Henry smiled and then frowned. “There are some bad guys,” he said. “One of them left a bad thing in our yard."

"What bad thing?" Emily asked.

Henry bent to pick up the ball he'd missed. "I don't know, but Mommy had to bring it to the police station."

"You don't know what it was?" Emily asked.

Henry shook his head and threw the ball to Carl.

She continued, "What did it look like?"

Henry shrugged but didn't answer.

"Was it big or small?" she asked.

"Small. In a plastic bag. It looked like," he stared off for a moment, "maybe, the fancy saltshaker Grandma uses at Christmas?" Henry shrugged his little shoulders. "It didn't look bad."

Carl tossed the ball to Henry just over his head, so Henry had to turn and run after it, then asked Emily, "What does your mother's saltshaker look like?"

"Like a saltshaker," she said, teasing, but the look on his face was serious.

"Tall? Short? Thin? Fat? Plastic? Metal?"

"Silver. Tapered. Holes at the top. Your basic saltshaker. I have no idea what he's talking about, by the way." Emily looked at Carl, his brows drawn together, concern on his face. "What is it?"

He shook his head and said, "I'm not sure," as Henry ran up to them and threw the ball to Carl.

"Isabel would have told me if she found anything important, especially after our conversation at lunch.

It was probably nothing. I'll ask her about it next time I see her. In fact, we're getting together with them this weekend, remember?"

"Yup. Your place this time, right? And I'll be grilling?"

"Portabello mushrooms. You promised to try one."

"On the condition that there would also be steaks." He called to Henry, "Here comes a pop fly," and tossed the ball high in the air. "I could teach Henry to grill a steak," he said.

"He can't see over the top of the grill," Emily laughed. "And Isabel's a good cook if you can get her in the kitchen, so let's leave that lesson to her, okay?" For someone who wasn't ready for kids, she thought, Carl was certainly enjoying having one around.

***

A few days later Carl stopped by just as Emily was finishing the morning milking. She took a quick shower and joined him at the kitchen table, where he'd poured them each a cup of freshly brewed coffee and put out some scones he'd picked up on the way.

"What's the occasion?" she asked, sliding into a chair and taking a sip of coffee.

"Can't I bring my girlfriend breakfast without it being an occasion?" He looked at her and sipped his coffee. He had an odd expression on his face.

She ran her foot up the inside of his shin and said, "Are you thinking of something besides breakfast?"

He grinned but pulled his leg away and said, "Okay, I might have had an ulterior motive."

"What?" she said, smiling. "To get me into bed?"

He ran a hand through his hair and exhaled through pursed lips. "You know I'd like nothing better. But I need to talk to you about something."

"Uh-oh," she said, trying to sound casual, "this sounds serious." She leaned back in her chair and waited. He'd just called her his girlfriend so she hoped this wasn't a relationship conversation, but that meant he was going to talk about her business, which often resulted in a heated discussion. She was feeling too relaxed for one of those.

Carl squared his shoulders and said, "It's about that thing Henry said Isabel brought to the police station."

"What about it?" Emily asked.

"It's possible it was a bullet. Not a real one, that goes in a gun, although it might as well be. It's a small container people use for cocaine. You can carry it in your pocket and you can snort from the top just by giving it a twist."

"You got all that from Henry saying it looked like a salt shaker? It could have been anything. Like a salt shaker." Carl's distrust of her family was starting to get on Emily's nerves.

"Why would Isabel bring a common household object to the police station? It had to be something she wasn't familiar with, something that scared her enough to bring it there. And these things can look like large bullets, hence the name. I'm guessing she found it at home, was worried enough to bring it to the station, and found out what it was. Which means that it's not hers, which means it's Alan's," he finished, an I-told-you-so look on his face.

"Jesus, Carl, can't you just let this go? I had a face-to-face conversation with Isabel, and she assured me everything's fine. I don't know what she found or why she went to the police station, but if it was that bad, she would have told me. I trust my family. Maybe you don't have that same trust, growing up the way you did, but don't assume we're all like you."

Carl slumped back in his seat. "Like I was," he said. "Look, you're angry, and I understand that. It's not an uncommon reaction."

"Stop analyzing me and my family," she said, her voice louder than she wanted it to be. "I've known them a hell of a lot longer than you have. I'm telling you you're wrong, and I'm asking you to drop it, for my sake, and for the sake of our relationship." She sat up straight and folded her arms over her chest, taking a deep breath, trying to contain a full-blown outburst.

Carl looked down at the table. He had broken his scone into pieces, which he was halfheartedly moving around the plate. Finally he sighed and said, "Fine. But I reserve the right to bring it up again if necessary."

Emily put her hands on the table. "I'd rather you didn't, actually. From this point on, unless you have concrete evidence of something, leave Alan and Isabel alone. Got it?"

The expression on his face was unhappy, but he nodded. "Got it."

***

Greta placed two mugs of hot tea on Emily's freshly cleaned kitchen table. The evening's chill was a stark contrast to the warm spring day she'd just enjoyed, and she hadn't brought a sweater. She'd spent a pleasant afternoon with her daughter, taking a long walk around the property and going to a farmers' market nearby, and she'd cooked dinner while Emily milked the goats. They'd cleaned up together and now they were settling in for a few games of Scrabble.

Emily appeared from the other room bearing the board game, paper and pencil. "Are you ready to lose?" she asked as she set up the game. "After all the times you've beat me lately, I'm due for a win."

Greta smiled. "You've just had some bad luck.

But I'm not going to go easy on you."

"You never do, Mom." Emily handed her mother the bag full of letters.

Greta took a tile out of the bag and handed it to Emily, who did the same. Her E beat Emily's R, so Greta was going first. They put the letters back, and as Greta rummaged in the bag for seven tiles, Emily said, "I had a nice lunch with Isabel."

"Yes, you told me about the restaurant. You said I should bring Dad there."

"Right. We had an interesting conversation at lunch. About Isabel, and Alan, and their relationship."

"Oh?" Greta was looking at the letters on her rack, but she could hear the seriousness in Emily's voice.

Emily nodded, one hand tapping on the handle of her tea mug. "She said she wanted to find some hobby that she and Alan could do together."

"That's a nice idea," Greta said, placing a word on the board. "Every couple needs to have some mutual interests. Ten points."

Emily wrote down the score and turned the board to face her. "They're going horseback riding."

Greta could see the smirk on Emily's face, but she ignored it and said, "It doesn't matter what it is, as long as they're happy. And I see that eye roll, young lady."

"Can you really picture Alan happily sitting on a

horse?"

Greta smiled to herself. She couldn't, not really, but she wanted the family to support each other. "When you told us you were quitting your job to become a goat farmer, did we roll our eyes at you?"

Emily sighed and put some tiles on the board. "No. Twenty-four points." She recorded the score as Greta turned the board again, and then added, "She says she and Alan are unhappy."

"Did she use that word?" Greta asked. She had noticed worrisome signs in their household for the past year, signs that their marriage was strained. Alan brought work home many nights, Isabel was often out at dinnertime, and they had Henry in so many activities that it was a rarity when the three of them ate together.

"No, she said 'disconnected'."

"And now they're finding some activities to do together. I'm glad."

"Mom," Emily said. "You used to spend a lot of time over there. Did you ever notice anything strange?"

Greta looked up from her letters to Emily's face, puzzled. Her daughter's expression was one of concern. "How do you mean, 'strange'?"

"I mean," Emily paused, waving her hand vaguely in the air, "weird. Out of the ordinary."

"Could you give me an example?" Greta asked. Emily exhaled and ran her fingers through her hair, a sure sign she was frustrated, but Greta couldn't imagine why. The girl was making no sense. "I just don't understand what you're asking, dear."

"Okay, fine. Have you noticed Alan drinking excessively?"

"No!" Greta was shocked at the question. "Have you?"

"Yes, but it's always when they're entertaining. Like at Thanksgiving."

"For heaven's sake, Emily, Alan wasn't drunk at Thanksgiving."

"Well, that's the thing," Emily said, clearing her throat. "He consumes a lot but he never seems that drunk."

"I didn't notice him having anything but wine, and he certainly didn't seem to be overindulging." Greta shook her head. "Why the sudden worry? Did Isabel say something to you?"

"No. She said he was stressed out from work and they were disconnected. That's it."

"Then why the concern about drinking?"

"Carl thought, maybe, there was reason for concern. Based on his observations. And his experience."

Greta looked at Emily, thinking for a moment. "Carl's experience?"

Emily nodded. "His father was, still is, an alcoholic. Carl grew up with it and he thought he saw some of the same behavior in Alan."

Now it was all clear to Greta. Carl was overly sensitive to those who drank. Alan clearly didn't have a drinking problem, but Emily was blinded by love. "Well, you can stop worrying, Emily. I know Alan doesn't have a drinking problem. I can understand why Carl might see it that way, but he's just wrong. You see how your brother is: holding down a job, entertaining family, working on his marriage. That's not a man with a drinking problem."

"But Carl said—"

Greta interrupted her. "Emily," she said firmly, "I'm sure Carl says a lot of things, and I won't discount his past, but I know my family, and I won't have him making unfounded accusations about Alan, or anyone else."

Emily took a sip of her tea but didn't respond.

Greta looked at her rack again, set aside five tiles, and said, "I'm swapping," turning the board back to Emily. She waited to see if Emily was going to continue their conversation, but she merely recorded a zero for Greta's score and started moving letters around on her rack. Greta saw Emily's mouth twitching and knew she was thinking hard, but she doubted Emily was thinking about the letters. No matter. At some point she would realize Greta was right.

***

"I have to admit, Emily, those mushrooms were very satisfying." Isabel lifted her glass toward Emily and took a sip of wine.

"Yes, as an appetizer," said Carl.

Alan laughed. "The steak is what hit the spot for me. Well-grilled, by the way. Is there any more wine?" he asked, holding up his empty glass.

Isabel looked at the two empty bottles sitting on the table. "Looks like it's all gone," she said.

"The night is young," Alan said. "You're not kicking us out before dessert, are you?" he asked Emily.

Emily looked at Carl, who shrugged, said, "I'll get a bottle," and went into the house.

"Do you have a dessert?" Isabel asked. "Not that I need it."

"S'mores," Emily said. "Why do you think I have the fire pit going?"

Isabel loved everything about the fire, the smell of the smoke, the vibrant oranges and yellows, the crackles and sparks. She thought Emily had lit it for pure ambiance. She could sit outside staring at the flames, sipping wine, and chatting with this group all night. She was so glad she and Emily were becoming friendlier. Maybe this foursome would help her and Alan out of their marriage funk. Alan certainly seemed to be enjoying their company. Perhaps he needed a friend, too, someone besides his wife, to confide in or whatever it was men did when they spent time together.

Carl returned with an opened bottle of wine and refilled Alan's glass, topping off everyone else's while he was at it. They sat talking idly about a variety of subjects for a long while. Isabel was feeling very relaxed when Emily stood up and said she was going in to get the S'mores ready.

"Any more wine in there?" Alan asked. "Think I'd rather have another glass than a marshmallow."

Carl exchanged a long look with Emily and then said, "I'll go with you, babe, and get the wine."

After they walked away Isabel said, "You really want another glass of wine? We'll be driving home soon, won't we?"

"We've got all night, remember? Henry's at your parents' house, and these guys don't have kids. Except the goat kind, of course," he laughed. "I think I'll use the bathroom, though. Back in a sec."

"Okay," Isabel said, content to sit by the fire.

She hadn't been alone more than a minute when Alan returned, picked up his jacket, and said in a hard voice, "Let's go."

"Where?" she asked. "Are we having dessert inside?"

"We're leaving."

Isabel sat up and turned to look at Alan. His face was twisted in anger but she had no idea why. "What happened?"

"I'll tell you on the way home," he said. "Come

on." He reached down and pulled her up, handed her her purse, and took her hand, walking toward the car.

"We at least have to say goodbye, Alan! What's the matter? Are you sick?"

Carl and Emily came out of the house and starting walking toward them, Carl carrying a bottle of wine and Emily's arms filled with graham crackers, marshmallows, and chocolate. As they neared the fire Isabel could see they were angry too, although they seemed to be angry at each other. They looked surprised when they saw the look on Alan's face.

"Where are you going?" Emily asked. "What about the S'mores?"

"Fuck the S'mores," Alan said. "And fuck you. And especially fuck you," he added, pointing at Carl.

"Alan!" Isabel cried. "What's going on? Emily?"

Emily looked ashamed and angry and confused. Carl's face was a stone she couldn't read.

"Now," Alan said, jerking her arm, pulling her toward the car.

"I don't understand," Isabel said, not wanting to leave, but not wanting to fight him either. She'd never seen Alan so upset. "Emily, I'm sorry," she called.

"I'm not," Alan growled. He got into the driver's seat as Isabel hurried in next to him, then started the car and sped off down the driveway, bits of gravel flying up from the tires.

"Please, Alan, slow down."

"I want to get as far away from here as possible."

"Okay, fine, we're away, but pull over up there, see that dirt patch? Please? You're scaring me!"

Alan exhaled loudly and his shoulders slumped a little, although he retained a white-knuckled grip on the steering wheel. "Yeah, okay." He pulled into the small unpaved area and squealed to a stop, looked at Isabel, and said, "Sorry. I didn't mean to frighten you."

Isabel could see his face clearly in the moonlight. "Can you tell me what's happened? I've never seen you so upset."

He shook his head and didn't say anything for a moment. Then he said, "I overheard my sister and her asshole boyfriend talking about me. About me having a drinking problem. About me using drugs! Like I'm some fucking loser! And behind my back, not even having the balls to talk to me to my face. What the fuck?!" He banged his fist on the steering wheel.

Isabel didn't know what to say. Why had Emily brought up all these ridiculous ideas, especially after their recent conversation at lunch? Hadn't that settled it? Or was it Carl, being his usual pushy self, who was refusing to let it go? She put her hand on Alan's arm. "I don't know why they were talking about that, but you have every right to be angry."

"Damn right I do!" He sighed loudly. "I'm sitting there having a great time thinking I could definitely see those guys more, and then, bam!—" he pounded the steering wheel again—"I find out they think I'm a fuck-up. Me!"

"They don't think that, Alan. They're just worried about you. But they handled it all wrong."

"Worried about me," Alan sneered. "If they were worried they could have—wait, what do you mean—did you already know this? Did you know they thought this about me?"

"Yes, but—"

Alan flung open the car door and got out, slamming it behind him, and started walking down the road.

Isabel hurried out her side and started off after him, calling, "Alan, wait!"

"That's just perfect, honey, just perfect," he yelled, not slowing at all. His shoes crunched down hard on the gravelly surface.

"Alan, Emily brought it up to me and I told her she was wrong!"

"Yeah, well, thanks for telling me about it, partner. My wife."

Isabel was struggling to keep up with Alan. "I told her she was being ridiculous! So ridiculous I didn't even want to tell you! Alan, please! I've got wedges on!"

Alan stopped, turned to look at her, and yelled, "What?!"

"I told her she was being ridiculous!" Isabel said,

hurrying to catch up to him.

“I thought you said you had a wedgie,” he said loudly.

She stopped, a few feet away from him now, breathing hard, and said, “A wedgie?” She giggled. Wrong time, wrong reaction, but she couldn’t help it.

Alan stared at her for a moment, then laughed. “No wedgie?” he asked.

“Wedges,” she said, pointing to her shoes.

They both started giggling and before she knew it they were crying with laughter, holding each other up, until finally they settled into each other’s arms. Alan started caressing her hair and she looked up at him. His face was no longer pinched and hard, but he looked worried. “Alan,” she said quietly, “I know you’re not an alcoholic or a drug addict. You’re a good man. And Emily knows that too. Carl is pushing all this on her because he’s a former drug addict himself. He’s seeing something where there’s nothing. That’s why I didn’t even tell you. It’s silly. Please don’t be mad.”

“Carl was a drug addict?”

“That’s what Emily said. She thinks he’s just overreacting because of his own past.”

Alan nodded. “So Emily was on my side?”

“Absolutely. She had to ask me because Carl was bothering her about it, but I could tell she thought he was wrong.”

“Okay. That makes me feel better. I guess I owe

her an apology. That Carl is a pain in the ass, though."

"He's a buttinsky, that's for sure."

"A 'buttinsky'?" Alan laughed. "Hold on there, young lady, I won't have any cussing."

"And a know-it-all. And a busybody."

"Silence, woman, before someone hears you!"

"And a—" Isabel started, but Alan stopped her with a kiss.

***

Emily stood watching helplessly as Alan and Isabel got into their car and drove away. She waited until the sound of tires rumbling over dirt and stones faded away, her back to Carl, unable to face him for fear she would hit him. He had the common sense to keep his mouth shut, because he wasn't saying a word. Finally she said, without turning to face him, "Get out."

"Me?"

He sounded genuinely surprised, which made her all the angrier. She whirled around, her voice rising as she said, "Yes, you! Christ! This was all going so well, and you—you—asshole, Alan is right, you just ruined it! We talked about this! What is your fucking problem? You think you know everything, do you? Well, you don't know my family, and you certainly don't know me. So get the hell out. Now!" She turned on her heel and headed for her house.

"Emily!" Carl called.

She didn't stop walking, just yelled "Go!" over her shoulder.

"Emily, we need to talk about this," he called.

She stopped and turned. "We're done talking," she screamed. "Go and don't come back!" She could feel traitorous tears filling her eyes and turned and ran to her house, flinging open the door and slamming it behind her. She ran into the bathroom, grabbing a tissue and viciously wiping her eyes. She would not cry over this man, this arrogant man who had come into her life and tried to control her, who thought he could fit into her family, who was dead wrong about everything. She heard Carl knocking on her front door and calling her name, but she remained where she was, trying to control her breathing, knowing she would never open the door to that man again.

Several minutes passed before she heard Carl yell, "I'll call you tomorrow! We need to work this out!" And finally she heard his old Porsche roaring down her driveway.

Even now he thinks he can tell me what to do, she thought. Good riddance.

Tomorrow she would visit Alan and apologize. She'd never seen him that angry.

The next morning Emily arrived on Alan's

doorstep with a bag of warm bagels and two kinds of cream cheese. She'd already arranged to take the morning off from milking the goats and sleep in, so she wasn't radically early. Hopefully Alan would be in a better mood today. Through a sidelight she caught a glimpse of Isabel in the kitchen, still in her pajamas.

Isabel heard her knock and opened the door quietly. "Hi."

"Hi," Emily said. "Can I come in?"

"Sure. Alan's upstairs. He's feeling much better now."

"I just wanted to apologize in person, to both of you. I'm really sorry about last night."

"You don't need to apologize to me," Isabel said. "I know it was all Carl's doing."

"Still, it wasn't the greatest dinner party," Emily said, smiling. "Peace offering?" She held up the bagels.

"Thanks! I'm starving," Isabel said, taking the box and heading into the kitchen. "I was just making coffee. Want some?"

"Yes, please." Emily followed her into the kitchen. "So how was Alan after you left? He was ballistic last night."

"He scared me, he was so angry. I asked him to pull over because I was worried about him driving. But we talked, and I explained about Carl, and his past, and that you and I had talked, and I think he understood. But he's not a fan of Carl," Isabel said as she started the coffee machine.

"Neither am I," Emily said. "I broke up with him last night."

"Oh, Emily," Isabel said. "Are you sure? You seemed happy together."

"Except for his thinking Alan is an alcoholic," Emily said.

"Yes, that's bad," Isabel smiled. "But I do think it came from him caring for you."

"It may have started out that way," Emily agreed, "but he didn't trust my instincts. That's been a problem for us all along. Last night made it clear to me."

"Made what clear to you?" A sleepy Alan walked into the kitchen, still in his pajamas, rubbing his eyes and yawning.

"Alan, I'm here to apologize," Emily said. "And I brought bagels."

"You think I can be bought for a bagel?" Alan asked, reaching into the bag for one. "Besides, Isabel explained everything to me last night. And it's your boyfriend who owes me the apology, not you."

"Ex-boyfriend," Emily said.

"Ex? Since when?"

"I dumped him right after you left last night."

Alan looked at her, then turned to get three coffee mugs from the cabinet. "You did that for me?"

"No, for me," Emily said. "I was just telling

Isabel. We've struggled all along with him not listening to me, and last night it became clear to me that he doesn't respect my opinion. And he messed with my family. So I told him to go."

Alan was silent, looking at Emily and then at Isabel. Finally he looked back at Emily and she could hear emotion in his voice. "I know you liked him. But you stuck up for me."

"You are my brother."

"Yeah. Well … thanks."

"Sure." They fell into an awkward silence, which Isabel filled by pouring everyone coffee and asking if Emily wanted cream or sugar. She set out plates, knives, and napkins, and they all took a seat at the counter. Then she quietly sang "We Are Family," bumping her shoulder gently against Alan's.

He laughed and said, "I've had enough touchy-feely talk lately."

"Me too," Emily said. She pulled out a stool and sat, taking out a bagel and spreading cream cheese on it. Half listening as Isabel told them about Henry's latest audition, Emily thought about how much she was enjoying her own family. She felt closer to Alan now than she had in years, since they were very little. And Isabel was becoming a good friend. She could finally see why her mother had insisted on them getting together all the time, urged them not to fight. As she got older, and thought about having children, Emily realized she wanted a strong family circle around her. Carl didn't have that, so he couldn't understand how important it was. He couldn't be a long-term prospect, no matter how much she liked him.

***

Isabel sat in the kitchen, staring out the window. A bright red male cardinal was flitting around the birdfeeder outside. The drab brown female darted over from a rhododendron occasionally, but he was bolder. She wasn't really focused on the birds, though. Her mind kept wandering back to a bad dream she'd had the night before. In it she'd lost Henry. She was running all through the house looking for him. She could hear him calling for her but she couldn't find him. That was bad enough, but Alan was chasing her, shooting at her with a gun. She'd awakened in the middle of the night, heart pounding, so angry at Alan that she wanted to hit him. Relief that it was a dream came instantly, but sleep did not, and now she was on her third cup of coffee and still feeling tired. She could not get that dream out of her head. Luckily Henry had a busy day of activities, because she was going to need all her energy to focus on her work.

She topped off her coffee and stood, heading to her office, but once she reached the hallway she stopped, turned, and walked to Alan's office instead.

She stood in the doorway, looked around briefly, then went and sat in his chair. It was very comfortable, a cushioned leather chair that tipped back easily. Kicking off her heels and putting her feet on the desk, she put her head back and sighed. The tray ceiling was painted cream, although they'd flirted briefly with a faux finish. She remembered how much fun they'd had coming up with paint colors, picking out furniture and carpets, lamps and drapes. They had the same taste so it was easy, and they always made a night of it, going out to dinner and then hitting the stores. What had happened to them? It wasn't easy any more. Alan had become so tightly wound, he would never enjoy decorating a room now.

Work was definitely a stressor for Alan. The more successful he became, the less fun he seemed to be having. Having a child had seemingly doubled his stress. But Isabel worked, too. Her workload had almost doubled and she loved it. And having Henry hadn't been a stress for her, although she had to admit she couldn't have handled it without all the help from Greta. So why had Alan changed? If she could figure that out she could change him back. She remembered last Thanksgiving when they'd had a quickie in the wine cellar. That was the impulsive, exciting Alan she'd married. As her mind wandered back to the wine cellar, she thought about those wine bottles she'd noticed, the ones that had seemed to dwindle in number overnight. How many bottles were they going through? Should she start counting them? Alan kept meticulous track of their finances, so surely he recorded his wine purchases. Maybe she should take a look at those records.

She pulled her feet off the desk and reached down for a heel, then slid the chair back and stared under the desk, thinking about the drug paraphernalia she'd found there. She was shocked that people had brought drugs into her own home, maybe even used them there. And right at her husband's desk, although it made sense; his office was one of the most private rooms in the house. Still, who would use such a thing, and then not even notice they'd dropped it? Weren't drug users obsessive and paranoid? Wouldn't they have searched high and low for it? Before she thought about what she was doing, Isabel had pulled open the top drawer to Alan's desk. She flipped through papers and business cards, pens and pencils, various office supplies. Then she opened another drawer, not finding anything besides cords, plugs, and computer accessories. Finally she pulled open the file drawer. She looked unsuccessfully for a file labeled "Wine," but even though she looked inside some of the unmarked files, she found nothing of interest. What was she looking for, anyway? A gun? That dream had rattled her more than she realized. She slipped on her shoes and went back to her office, plowing into her work.

Much later that night, after they'd tucked Henry into bed and Alan had started in on phone calls and paperwork in his office, Isabel curled up on the couch with some of her own work. She made some notes but her mind kept wandering. Restless, she stood and went into the kitchen. Was she hungry? Not really. Maybe a glass of wine? Then she thought about the wine cellar, and decided to go down there and really count those bottles. As she pulled open its door, she thought about how they would have to get at lock for it when Henry was tall and strong enough to open it himself. Right now even she had to tug on it. She turned on the lights and looked around. There weren't exactly the same number of bottles in each rack, but she thought she could do a fair approximation by counting the racks and multiplying by five. She ended up with 90. Then she decided to count them all one by one, and ended up with 98. All right. She would come down and check again in a month, and she would keep track of any wine that Alan brought home as well.

Her counting done, she stood immobile, looking at the dark wood and the crystal glasses, the burgundy and golden hues of the wines, the soft lighting. This was Alan's domain, his private oasis. She walked over to the racks, looking at each one carefully. Covering every inch of the room, she examined under the racks, inside the slots, and even slid open the drawer where Alan kept a collection of antique wine openers. He wanted to display them but had never gotten around to it. She pulled them toward the front of the drawer and reached into the back, feeling nothing but empty space. The click of the door made her jump so badly she hurt the top of her hand pulling it out of the drawer. Whirling, she turned to see Alan standing there, a quizzical look on his face.

"What are you doing?" he asked.

She rubbed the top of her right hand with her left palm as she thought, What am I doing? "I'm, um, I hurt my hand," she said, holding it out for him to see. There was a red mark on it.

"Looks like it'll be okay," he said, coming a step closer. "How did you hurt it?"

The drawer was still open behind her. "I was looking at the wine openers."

"Why? You know we can't use them." He looked at her, frowning.

"I know," she said, looking away.

He crossed his arms over his chest. "You've been down here a while. I was looking for you earlier, then I got a phone call. What have you been doing?"

"Admiring the wine cellar," she said, pulling her shoulders back. She was not going to admit she'd been snooping.

"Did Carl ask you to admire it for him?" he asked, a hard edge to his voice.

"What's that supposed to mean?"

"You're spying on me, is what it means," he said, agitated. He took another step towards her.

She backed up slightly and hit the open drawer. She turned to shut it and then turned back, walking around him and moving towards the door. "I'm not going to talk to you if you're going to make ridiculous accusations."

He followed her out of the wine cellar, slamming the door behind him. She heard the crystal glassware rattle as she headed up the stairs into the kitchen. Alan joined her there and said, "We need to talk. Now."

"Keep your voice down; Henry's sleeping."

"Fine," he said quietly, teeth clenched, "let's go into the living room."

Isabel sat down on the couch and Alan took an armchair. He wasn't even going to sit next to her. "What would you like to talk about?" she asked.

"You know exactly what I want to talk about. What were you doing down there?" He held up his hand as she opened her mouth to speak. "I know, you were admiring the wine cellar. Please. You've never done that, ever. Now one person, one person, thinks I have a problem and suddenly you're down there snooping around."

"I was not snooping! I was just lost in thought, daydreaming—"

"You were snooping down there, because you

couldn't find anything in my office," he hissed.

"What?" Isabel was startled.

"I know you went through my desk. Are you going to lie and tell me you didn't?"

Isabel didn't know what to say. How could he possibly know she went through his desk? Did he have cameras in there?

"It's not what you think," she said.

"I think you don't trust me!" he yelled.

"Please don't wake up Henry," Isabel said. "He shouldn't hear us fighting."

"I'm not fighting," Alan said, lowering his voice again. "I'm trying to find out why my wife doesn't trust me."

"I do trust you. I do! I admit I went through your desk, but it was because I had a bad dream—don't make that face, it's true—and it scared me, and I was so unsettled, and I found myself in your office—"

"Magically?" he asked.

Ignoring him, she went on, "—and was going through your drawers without really thinking about what I was doing, and then I suddenly realized I was behaving irrationally and I left. That is the absolute truth."

Alan had a skeptical look on his face but he didn't speak right away. After a moment he asked, "And the wine cellar?"

She shrugged. "I was feeling restless and wanted a glass of wine, so I went down to get a bottle, and then I was lost in thought, just sort of poking around. I don't know why."

Alan frowned, silently staring at her.

"My imagination was running wild, what with everything that's been going on." As soon as she said it, she wished she hadn't.

"Like what?" he asked, his voice going up again. "Like Carl accusing me of being an alcoholic?" He yelled the last word, waving his arms out to the sides. "A drug user? Or is there something else I'm missing?"

"Alan! Henry's sleeping!" Isabel said urgently, but too late. She could hear the thump of Henry's feet coming down the stairs. The look on Alan's face told her he had heard it too. They sat silently until moments later Henry appeared in the doorway, his face bleary with sleep.

"What are you doing out of bed, buddy?" Alan asked.

"You guys are being loud," he said. "It woke me up."

"Sorry, sweetie," Isabel said. "We'll keep it down."

"Daddy," Henry said, "are you mad at Mommy?"

Alan shot Isabel a look and then smiled at Henry. "No way! We were just talking, that's all. Let's get you back into bed, okay?" He looked at Isabel again and said, "I'll be right back," scooping Henry up against him.

Isabel watched as they left, Henry's tousled hair against Alan's, his arms around his neck. Henry peeped over Alan's shoulder and said, "'Night, Mommy."

"Goodnight, Henry," she said, smiling. Alan had a good relationship with Henry. He had always tried to make that a priority. Good husband, good father, good, good, good. What was her problem? Something had made her poke around. What? She thought about that day she'd wondered if bottles of wine were missing from the cellar. The day she'd brought that bullet-shaped item to the police station. The fact that she and Alan drank a lot more than they used to. As she was mulling these facts over in her mind, Alan returned, this time sitting next to her on the couch. She shifted so she was facing him.

"He'll be asleep in a minute," Alan said. "He was pretty tired. I promise not to raise my voice, but we need to finish this conversation."

Isabel nodded. "I was thinking about what's been bothering me. It's nothing Carl said. I don't believe you're a bad guy, you must know that. But a few little things have been bothering me for a while now, and maybe if we could talk about them calmly, then I could let them go."

Alan looked skeptical but said, "Okay. Go ahead."

"Well, first of all, sometimes it seems like our

wine is disappearing faster than we're drinking it. Like it seems we should have more bottles in our cellar than we do."

"Anything else?"

"There was that bullet thing I found."

Alan nodded slowly, watching her, his own face neutral.

"And we drink more than we used to. Both of us. Maybe more than we should." She leaned back and crossed her arms, relieved to have gotten everything off her chest.

"Okay. First, wine is not 'disappearing' from the cellar. I would know if it was. Second, we already discussed that weird drug thing and the police weren't very worried about it anyway, so I'm not either. And third, I don't think we drink too much." He looked at her, his face angry again. "Anything else?"

She wasn't going to let him bully her. "Are you sure no one could be stealing the wine? Do you keep track of it?"

He rolled his eyes. "I'm a finance guy. Of course I keep track of it. I have spreadsheets on our wine cellar. Some of those bottles are an investment."

"And you're not worried about the drug paraphernalia?"

"I would be if it was yours. Is it yours?"

"Of course not!"

"Then I'm not worried. The next big party we

have we'll lock my office, and keep an eye on the hired help."

Isabel leaned toward him. "You really don't think we drink too much?"

"No, babe, I don't. Do we drink more than we used to? Yes. We also listen to more children's music than we used to. We have a kid. Things have changed. But are we falling down drunk every night? No way. Okay?" He picked up her right hand in his and stroked the top of it gently with his thumb. "How's the bump feel? It's still a little red." He lifted her hand to his lips and kissed it, then looked at her, keeping her hand near his mouth.

She shrugged. "It's okay."

"And are we okay?" he murmured, his lips barely touching her hand.

She could feel his warm breath on her skin. His thumb was caressing the inside of her wrist. "Yes." Damn him. Someday she was going to make sure they didn't end every disagreement with sex.

***

Children were sweet. Baby goats, too. Put them together and you had the definition of adorable. Emily smiled as Henry lay on the ground, squealing as Fifi and Foofoo nibbled on his t-shirt. Those two would nibble on anything, but she thought the maple syrup Henry had dripped on his shirt during breakfast might be what was so intriguing. And since he'd dripped it on his belly, that's where the goats were nosing around. The babies' mother, Francie, was looking on, chewing at some tall grass. Emily was standing next to her, feeling the sun on her face and the warmth of the air on her skin. Henry was spending the afternoon with her while Isabel went to the salon.

"We must have our nails done for horseback riding, huh, Francie?" she said aloud, smirking as she scratched the top of the goat's head. She'd like to tell Carl that one, she thought, then immediately corrected herself. No, not Carl, but someone like him. A boyfriend. Someone she could talk to besides the goats. Maybe she should get out more, like her mother had been saying for years. After all, how many men were going to drop to her farm from the sky? Just the one. Too bad he'd turned out to be such a controlling bastard. She scowled and kicked at a stone in the dirt, to which Francie butted her gently in the hip. Her mother had asked her repeatedly what had happened between her and Carl, but Emily didn't want to talk about it with anyone. Honestly, it was too painful. She hated to admit it, but she'd felt really good about Carl, like maybe they had a future together. What an idiot. Carl had called her repeatedly, sent her many bouquets of flowers, and even shown up at her house once, but she'd ignored him, even stooping so low as to hide and pretend she wasn't home while he banged on her front door. He'd known she was home—her schedule wasn't a big secret—but she didn't want to see him again. It was too hard. Goats really were easier than people.

"Aunt Emmy! Look!"

Emily looked up to see Henry sitting, each side of his t-shirt stuffed into a baby goat's mouth. She laughed. "They're going to eat you up!" she said, walking over and pulling the cloth out of their mouths. She shooed them away and they trotted over to their mother, who was unconcernedly grazing by the fence.

Henry stood up and pulled at the bottom of his t-shirt, stretching it out in front of him. It was wrinkled, wet, and dirty. He looked up at her, concern on his face.

"If that had been a grown-up goat, you might have holes there, but lucky for you, it'll look good as new after a wash. Do you want a different shirt to wear?"

Relieved, Henry said, "No. I just don't want Mommy yelling."

"Would she yell at you for a dirty shirt?" Emily asked. Isabel might be a bit of a neatnik, but yelling wasn't her style.

Henry shook his head. Then he bit his lip and said, "Maybe Daddy would."

Emily looked down at Henry. He was worried about something, she could see it on his face. She plopped down cross-legged in the grass and said, “Sit down, Henry.” He sat next to her and picked a large blade of grass, flattening it between his fingers. A few of the goats noticed and began to amble over, curious as always. “What’s going on, kiddo? I can see something’s bothering you.”

“Mommy and Daddy had a fight.” He folded the blade in half lengthwise, and held it between his thumbs. “Is it like this?”

“What?”

“How Uncle Carl said to make the grass whistle?”

“Oh.” Crap. Uncle Carl. She hadn’t really thought about how much Henry and Carl liked each other. No way she was telling Henry that Uncle Carl wasn’t going to be around anymore. “I don’t know. Henry, you said your mom and dad had a fight?”

He nodded, blowing into the blade of grass. No whistle. “Daddy was yelling. It woke me up.”

“Did you hear what he was yelling?” Emily felt guilty pumping Henry for information, but not guilty enough to stop herself.

“No. I didn’t hear the words. He said he wasn’t mad and they were just talking. Then he brought me back to bed.”

“Where were they when they were talking?” They’d probably been in the kitchen and their voices carried up the stairs.

“In the living room.” Henry had adjusted his

blade of grass and was blowing again, still to no avail.

The living room. Not good. That was the farthest point from Henry's room. Alan really must have been yelling to wake up Henry, who was quite the sound sleeper. She would have to ask Isabel about this. "Sometimes grown-ups argue, and they raise their voices, even though they're not supposed to. It's nothing to be scared of, okay?"

Henry nodded. "Why doesn't it work?"

"Well, sometimes two people have a different idea about things, and they each think the other one is wrong, and they don't want to change their minds." Emily hoped that explanation would do.

Henry looked at her, squinting in the sun. The breeze lifted his hair from his forehead momentarily. "The whistle." He held up his blade of grass. "Why doesn't it work?"

"Oh. I really don't know, Henry. I never learned how to do that."

"Can we ask Uncle Carl?"

He looked so hopeful, she just couldn't let him down. "Sure. Only Uncle Carl had to go away for his work. We might not see him for a while. But as soon as he gets back, I'll ask him, okay?"

Henry nodded. "Okay. Can we go to the pond? I want to look for frogs."

Emily agreed and they set off for the pond. She fervently hoped that Henry would forget all about the whistling blade of grass, and maybe all about Carl as well. Although she had to admit, she was having trouble doing that herself.

Later that day, when Isabel stopped by to pick up Henry, Emily invited her in for a cup of coffee. Henry went off happily to play with Jake in the other room. Emily had attached some pieces of yarn to one end of some fishing line, and the other end to a long and flexible twig, and Jake absolutely loved chasing that bit of fluff. Isabel had given Henry a quick hug and, to Emily's relief, had kept her mouth shut about his clothing, muddy pants legs having been added to the wet and sticky shirt.

"Aren't you worried that bright red color is going to scare the horses?" Emily said, noting Isabel's new nail polish as she wrapped her hands around the coffee mug.

"Would it?" Isabel said, looking alarmed.

Emily shook her head. "Kidding. So Alan's excited about your big horse adventure this weekend?"

Isabel smiled. "The best I can say is he's willing. But he's being a good sport about it."

"And you?"

"I really am excited. I've never been on a horse but they're such beautiful animals, and these horses are supposed to be very tame. But mostly I want this for Alan and me, to help us get out of our rut."

Emily nodded. "Speaking of which, I have to ask you about something, about you and Alan. Henry mentioned today that you two had a fight. Loud enough to wake him up. He was a little worried about it, I think."

Isabel's face fell. "He hasn't said a word to me about it. What did he say, exactly?"

"Just that Alan's yelling woke him up. Is everything okay?"

"Yes," Isabel said. "We were fighting about—" she stopped, pausing for a moment to listen for Henry, then lowered her voice. "I'm embarrassed to say Alan caught me snooping around."

Emily glanced at Isabel's nails again as they tapped on the coffee mug. No wonder they'd been arguing. "Looking for what, exactly?"

"I don't know, Emily. I'm not sure what I was doing. I went through some drawers in Alan's desk and then I looked around the wine cellar. Honestly, I don't know what I thought I'd find. I just wanted to make sure there would be nothing there. And I was right. There wasn't. But Alan caught me and he was very upset."

"I can see why," Emily said.

"I know. It was wrong, snooping on my own husband. Really bad. I know it sounds pathetic, but it all started because of a dream I had. Alan was chasing me with a gun and I woke up panicked in the middle of the night. I couldn't get back to sleep and I couldn't get it out of my head the whole next day. And before I knew it I was looking through drawers in his office. Then that night I was in the wine cellar, and that's when he found me."

Emily didn't know what to say. This did not sound like the calm, competent Isabel she knew. She must be really stressed out, Emily decided. Stress could make a person do strange things. "But you and Alan resolved everything? You're not fighting anymore?"

Isabel shook her head. "We both felt terrible when we woke up Henry. I didn't think he even remembered it."

"I don't think he's that worried, he just didn't like hearing Alan yell. And I explained to him that adults argue sometimes, but it's nothing to be afraid of."

Isabel nodded. "It's funny, Alan and I almost never fight. I think that's the first time Henry's heard either one of us raise our voice."

"Nothing wrong with a good argument every once in a while. Carl and I—" Emily stopped. "Never mind."

"Do you miss him?" Isabel asked softly.

"I do, but only a little. And the negatives outweighed the positives. But it made me realize I wouldn't mind having a boyfriend again. I'm finally getting my head above water with my business. Trouble is, I don't meet many eligible men farming."

"I think I could help you out," Isabel said. "I organize so many fundraisers, and there are always eligible men in attendance. I'll put you on the invitation list to some of the more promising ones."

"I can't just show up at a fundraiser by myself. I wouldn't know anyone there."

"You'd know me. I'd take you around and introduce you. But you'd have to be dolled up, cocktail dress and heels, makeup, hair done."

Emily groaned. "I'll think about it." She had no desire to go through all that on the off chance she'd meet someone. Maybe it would be easier to wait for a man to drop out of the sky.

"It's a bit early yet," Isabel said. "You just broke up with Carl, after all."

Emily let Isabel think that's why she wanted to wait. They finished their coffee and Isabel took Henry home. Emily sat down to read and Jake promptly appropriated her lap, barely waking when she moved him aside to do the evening milking. Another Friday night alone, she thought. She wondered if the consignment shop in town had cocktail dresses.

***

Isabel rummaged in the large wooden crate for a riding helmet that would fit her. They looked like oversized bicycle helmets, definitely not attractive on anyone. She would get hat head for sure. She looked at Alan, who had already found a helmet that fit and was buckling it under his chin. He had a delighted expression on his face.

"What a beautiful day," he said, spreading his arms wide. "Look at this. Warm, sunny, light breeze. Perfect! And smell the fresh air," he added, inhaling deeply.

All Isabel could smell was horse and a hint of manure but she agreed, thinking more of Alan's happiness than anything else, "It's beautiful, all right." The fourth helmet she tried finally fit well enough to buckle snugly under her chin. She looked around. Sarah, the woman who'd sent them to get helmets, was leading two horses over, one brown, the other white. They both seemed as big as elephants to Isabel. No wonder they needed helmets.

Sarah led the animals over to a wooden structure that looked like a boat dock, looping each set of reins over a different post alongside the flat part. The horses moved of their own accord, leaning their left sides against the platform.

"Let's get saddled," Sarah said. Alan moved to the right of the brown horse and she added, "From the other side, cowboy."

Alan looked at her, disappointment on his face, and walked over to the platform, climbing the few steps up and walking over to the horse. From there all he had to do was throw his leg over the horse and lower himself on.

"That's Thunder you're sitting on," Sarah said. "You get Snowflake," she said to Isabel.

Snowflake. That didn't sound scary. Isabel followed Alan's lead and got into Snowflake's saddle. She was sitting on a huge creature many feet up in the air with no idea how to control it. Scenes of runaway horses flashed through her mind.

"Don't be nervous," Sarah said. "These horses are old and gentle. Always use 'em for first-timers. They know the way; they don't need any steering. Just keep your balance, hold onto the reins, and enjoy the ride." She flipped the reins off each post and handed them to Alan and Isabel, then walked up ahead to an even bigger black horse and swung into the saddle. "Blackie," she said, as if they'd asked, then started off away from the barn and toward the woods.

Thunder and Snowflake immediately started off after her, startling Isabel. Her horse had a mind of its own! She didn't tell it to go, and it had gone anyway, so how would she ever get it to stop?

As she pondered that question, Alan turned his head and grinned. "This is awesome, isn't it?"

"Uh-huh," Isabel said, but it's not what she was thinking. The saddle was hard and it creaked as the horse walked, shifting slightly under Isabel's thighs. There were a few flies buzzing around Snowflake's ears, which kept twitching when the flies landed. The tail kept swishing, too. Her calves were stretched to accommodate the stirrups, and she had to concentrate to stay upright and avoid moving with the horse. She gripped the reins tensely and suddenly her horse stopped. Great. Sarah and Alan were rapidly moving away from her.

"Go," she whispered, but it didn't move. "Go!" she said again, louder. Nothing. Finally she swung her legs out and into the horse's side like she'd seen in movies, holding the reins tightly to brace herself for the horse's flight. Still nothing. "Um, hello?" she called, as Alan's horse was now several lengths ahead of her.

She saw Sarah turn her head and stop Blackie. Thunder immediately stopped as well, and Alan turned to look at her. "What's the matter, babe?"

"The horse won't move."

"Let go of the reins," Sarah said.

Isabel dropped them and Snowflake bent its neck down to nibble on some grass.

Sarah turned Blackie around and trotted over to Isabel. "No," Sarah said, "don't drop 'em, pick 'em up again. Just hold 'em loosely. You must've pulled on 'em, which told her to stop. Just relax."

Isabel picked up the reins again and tried to loosen her shoulders.

Sarah looked her over and said, "Move with the horse. Snowflake wants to feel like you're with her, not fighting her. Let your body follow hers. Got it?"

Isabel nodded, although she had no idea what Sarah was talking about. But she was embarrassed and wanted nothing more than for Sarah to go back to the front of the line and get them going again.

Sarah made a clicking noise and Snowflake started walking. Sarah trotted off, slowing Blackie to a walk as she reached Alan, and then they were moving again.

This time Isabel decided to do some deep breathing and try to relax her whole body. She let her arms and shoulders drop, loosened her grip on the reins, and let herself sway from side to side with the horse. No way was she releasing the tension in her legs, though. No matter how big and sturdy this saddle was, she wanted a grip on the only thing keeping her from falling several feet. Still, her adjustments worked. She felt much better as they continued into the woods along a dirt path.

Birds sang in the trees, the horses snorted occasionally, and their hooves thumped quietly on the earth. The flies had disappeared. The smell of horse was still there but pine had replaced the manure. Sarah wasn't talking, and neither was Alan. Isabel was concentrating so much on staying on Snowflake that her mind was completely empty of anything else. They passed a stand of birches and a small creek, skirted a pond, went through a field, up and down a hill, and back into some woods. Isabel didn't know how much time had passed when she saw the beginnings of civilization again, but she was surprised to find herself disappointed. She recognized the outbuildings from when they'd approached the farm in their car, and realized they must have taken the horses in a large loop through the countryside.

Thunder and Snowflake sidled right up to the platform again and stopped. Isabel and Alan waited for Sarah, then handed her the reins, thanking her and climbing off the horses and the platform, back onto the ground.

"Enjoy yourselves?" Sarah asked.

Isabel nodded, "Yes."

"One hundred percent," Alan said. "Great day. Thanks so much."

"Pleasure. Leave the helmets where you found 'em. Come on back." She lifted a corner of her mouth in what Isabel assumed was a smile and walked off with Snowflake and Thunder, leaving Blackie tied to a post next to a water trough.

Isabel watched the horses as they left, thinking again how big they were, and how she'd actually been riding one.

Alan wrapped his arm around her shoulder and pulled her close. "That was amazing. Really cool. I loved it. Thank you so much." He squeezed her shoulder and let go to remove his helmet.

She followed suit and they left the helmets in the bin, Isabel wondering briefly whether they were ever cleaned and then deciding not to think about it.

As they walked back to the car Alan held her hand, playfully swinging it back and forth. He was more lighthearted than he'd been in months.

"So are you going to become a horse guy?" Isabel asked.

Alan laughed and shook his head.

"No? I thought you loved it!"

"I did, but it wasn't the horses that did it for me, it was the woods. I loved being out there. It was so quiet and peaceful, so relaxing. No demands. I feel great."

Isabel nodded. "My mind is empty right now. Like I don't have a care in the world."

"That's it exactly," Alan said. "I was thinking while we were out there, we should take up hiking."

"You mean like up mountains with backpacks?"

"I didn't say in the Alps," he teased, "but yes, sturdy shoes, water bottles, snacks. And Henry, of course. It's something we could all do."

Isabel's heart filled. This was exactly what she'd hoped for, Alan inspired to do something new, something that made him happy and brought them closer together. "I love it," she said.

"You do?"

"Of course," she said. "Why wouldn't I?"

"Well, when we were dating you told me you didn't like camping because of the bugs. There are bugs in the outdoors. So I figured you didn't like the outdoors."

"Now that I've changed poopy diapers, bugs don't seem so bad."

"Amen," Alan laughed. "Speaking of which, should we go get our son who is thankfully out of diapers?"

They hopped into the car and chatted happily all the way to Emily's, discussing what they'd need to get for their first hiking trip, and where they'd go.

***

The next day Alan was eager to take Henry out for some ice cream. Isabel wanted to stay home and catch up on some work, but she also thought it would be nice for Alan to spend some time with Henry alone. They'd spent the afternoon at Emily's farm yesterday. Emily and Henry had lunch prepared for them when they arrived after horseback riding, then Henry had asked to go to the frog pond, and they'd ended up talking and walking for so long that Emily invited them to stay for dinner. Then Henry had begged them to see how Emily milked the goats. It had been the first time that Alan and Emily had spent a day together without bickering. Isabel felt like she understood Emily a lot more now and she hoped Alan felt the same way.

Isabel finished her filing and made a few calls, then decided to clean the kitchen and figure out what to make for dinner. She could get Alan to stop and pick up a few groceries if necessary. After a quick assessment of the fridge, she saw she would only need lettuce and a few tomatoes, which he could get at the farm stand near the ice cream place. Henry loved to visit the farm stand because they had chickens running around. She called Alan's cell but he didn't pick up. She left him a message and tackled the kitchen dishes.

She was washing the frying pan from breakfast when the phone rang. Hurriedly drying her hands, she picked up the phone on the last ring before it went to voicemail, saying, "Alan? Don't hang up!"

"Mrs. Lambert?"

"Oh, sorry. Yes?"

"This is Officer Walsh with the Cranston Police. Your husband has been in an accident."

Isabel's brain seemed to stop working. She could hear the words, spoken in a deep matter-of-fact voice, but she wasn't processing what they meant.

Unable to speak, she listened as the officer paused and then continued, "No severe injuries but the EMT's have taken him to Mercy Hospital for observation."

Husband. Accident. Hospital. These words flew around Isabel's brain as her head started to spin.

"Mrs. Lambert? Do you understand what I'm saying to you?"

"My son. Henry," she said, her voice cracking. "He was in the car."

“Yes, ma’am. He’s pretty banged up from the air bag. Children his size shouldn’t be riding in the front seat. He’s also been taken to Mercy.”

Isabel felt tears dropping on her cheeks and tried to keep her voice steady. “Oh my God. Is he okay?”

“There didn’t appear to be any critical injuries, ma’am. He’ll be in the emergency room at Mercy, along with your husband.”

Isabel sobbed out loud at the thought of the two most important people in her life in an emergency room.

The officer cleared his throat. “Mrs. Lambert?”

“Yes?”

“Do you have someone you can call?”

The question jolted Isabel back to reality. She had to call Emily and then she would head to the hospital. “Yes. Thank you,” she said, hanging up. She phoned Emily, hurriedly explained what had happened, asked her to call Greta, and left.

***

With a great deal of satisfaction Greta filled in the last word of her crossword puzzle. It had been a tough one, but she’d finally cracked it. She pushed it away and leaned back in her kitchen chair. The house was quiet. George had gone to visit that hardware store he was in love with. The dishes were done, the counters were clean, and through the open window she could hear the soft murmur of a suburban summer afternoon. One by one she mused on her family members, doing a mental check on each one's welfare. She should call Isabel and Alan, invite Henry over for a visit. Emily she'd seen recently, but she wouldn't mind another afternoon of Scrabble. If only George liked to play, she thought. He'd recovered well from his illness, but it would take a personality transplant for him to start playing Scrabble, she thought with a smile. Her mind wandered back to Emily's conversation with her about Alan. She shook her head. Alan had always been quiet, responsible, and hardworking. Carl was imagining things. She really should give Emily a call. It was her job to keep her family running smoothly. What other job did she have, if not watching over her family? You couldn't retire from that, and she wasn't going to drop the ball again like she had when George was getting sick, letting him pretend everything was fine. From now on she planned to be vigilant.

The phone ringing startled her. She had barely gotten out a hello when Emily cut her off.

"Mom? Everything's okay, but I have some bad news. Alan and Henry have been in an accident. They're both all right, but I guess Henry got pretty banged up." Emily's voice caught a little at the end.

"What happened?" Greta asked, sinking into a chair.

"I'm not sure exactly, but Alan was driving and got into an accident. Henry was in the front seat and the air bag deployed, which is why he's hurt. Isabel said Alan's fine, just shaken up. She's on her way to Mercy Hospital. Do you and Dad want to meet me there?"

"Of course," Greta said. "Your father's at the hardware store. I'll let him know to meet us there. I'll leave in a few minutes."

"Okay," Emily said. "I'm leaving now. I'll see you in the emergency room."

Greta hung up the phone and sat for a moment, absorbing what Emily had just told her. She knew it was dangerous if a child was hit with an airbag, so she was praying that Henry only had cuts and bruises and nothing worse. But surely Isabel would have said if he were in danger. And it sounded like Alan was all right. She called George's cell phone. It went to voice mail. She knew it was because the hardware store had spotty service, but he would get the message soon. She briefly explained what had happened, said she was going straight to the hospital, and that he should meet her there. Then she hung up and hurried to the front hall closet for her purse and keys. She was trying not to think about little Henry hurt in a hospital bed. She would be there soon enough, and then she would find out what was going on and how they could fix it.

George wandered out of the closet improvement section, his head full of ideas. Greta had been complaining about their bathroom linen closet for years, saying it was too cramped with not enough shelf space. This Christmas she was going to get her dream closet. He figured he could enlarge the space a foot. He'd put in whatever shelves, hooks, or other hardware Greta wanted. He'd love to do the work ahead of time, put a big bow on the door, but that was impossible, so he'd ask Emily to make a nice card with a picture instead. As he moseyed over to the electrical supplies his phone buzzed. It was a missed call from Greta and she'd left a voice message. The only bad thing he could say about the store was that the cell reception was terrible. He wandered outside, punched in his voice mail code and listened. In thirty seconds he was maneuvering out of the parking lot.

As he drove to the hospital he wondered why Alan had Henry in the front seat. Even George knew better than that, after the lecture he'd gotten from Isabel the first time he and Greta took Henry in his booster seat. Still, if Henry had been properly seat-belted, George didn't think he'd get too hurt. Alan's car was fairly new, and air bag standards had come a long way. When they first came out he'd read that small women could get injured by them, so he kept up to speed on them until he was satisfied Greta was in no danger. Meanwhile he'd made her sit so far back from the wheel that she had to point her toe to floor it, but she wasn't that kind of driver anyway. Greta, of course, had sounded worried in the phone message. He could only imagine how Isabel was doing. Alan might be lucky to survive the accident, but he might not survive what that wife of his was going to do to him. Isabel was like a mother tiger around Henry.

***

When George walked into the Emergency Room he didn't see anyone from his family in the waiting area. The nurse at the desk commented that Henry was developing quite an audience, and directed George through the doors to the third room on the left.

Walking down the hall he could faintly hear Emily's voice. He stepped quietly into the room. Henry was lying on the bed, eyes closed, looking pretty good for a guy who'd been in an accident. He had a big bandage over his nose and one on a shaved patch on his temple. There was a splint on the pointer and middle fingers on his right hand. Isabel was holding his left hand, facing Emily over the bed.

"Dad," said Emily, coming over and giving him a hug. "We just got here too. Henry's okay."

"A broken nose and a few broken fingers," Isabel said quietly, giving him a weak smile. "He's sleeping. They said he's in shock."

"That's normal," George said. "Poor little guy. So what happened?"

"I don't know exactly. Why don't you ask Alan? I haven't talked to him yet," Isabel said in a voice that could have curdled milk. "He's just next door."

Emily gave George an unnecessary look that said, keep your mouth shut.

***

George left and went to the next room, where his son was lying on a bed looking like shit. Not banged up, just looking like a pathetic excuse for a man. The room was very warm. His shirt was off and he had heart monitors taped to his chest and a white clamp on the end of his middle finger. The heart monitor was beeping steadily. He'd obviously been crying, his eyes and nose red, his cheeks ruddy. The expression on his face was worse than anything George had ever seen. Worse than when Alan had forgotten to tie up the vacationing neighbor's dog and it had gotten hit by a car. It had survived, though, and so would Alan. But George was glad to see Alan suffering, because nothing taught you a lesson like a mistake.

"Son," George said, coming to Alan's side, "how you doing?" He put his hand on Alan's shoulder.

Alan shook his head and sniffed. "Dad," he said, but that was all he got out. His voice cracked and he rubbed his eyes with his hand. “I want to see Henry, but they won’t let me out of bed. They’re worried about my heart.” He gestured feebly at the monitors attached to his chest. “Did you see him?”

George nodded. “He’ll be fine. He’s banged up some.”

Tears leaked out the sides of Alan’s eyes and he wiped roughly under his nose. “Banged up because of me.”

George reached behind him to the counter, handed a small box of hospital tissues to Alan and asked, “What happened?”

“I don’t even know. I realized I needed a file I’d left at work, and I thought I’d bring Henry along for the ride, get him some ice cream on the way back.” Alan shook his head. “I put him in the front seat. I know I’m not supposed to, but it was a Sunday morning. I thought he’d love it. He did love it, felt like a big boy.”

George waited while Alan teared up again, took another tissue and blew his nose vigorously.

“Henry was fiddling with all the buttons on the dash, then he wanted to look inside the glove compartment, and I, I reached over, and that’s all I remember. Next thing I know we’re up on the sidewalk, a parking sign is leaning on my windshield, and I’m hearing sirens. I must have passed out for a few minutes. And Henry was just sitting there, eyes closed, bloody, and I couldn’t tell, I couldn’t tell if—

" Alan started sobbing again.

George saw the numbers on Alan's heart monitor screen go up and patted his son's shoulder. "Alan, he's okay. If you want to see him, you have to relax."

Alan nodded and took another tissue. "I haven't seen Isabel. Is she here yet? Does she hate me?"

"She just got here. She's with Henry," George said. "I think she's angry with you."

"She should be." Alan started crying again. "But I want to see her. Can you ask her to come see me?"

George nodded. "I'll let her know." He put his hand on Alan's head for a moment, then turned and left.

***

George headed back into Henry's room. He could hear an ambulance in the distance, and he thought how every day was a stressful day at a hospital. Henry was still out.

Isabel looked at George and said, "Well?"

George cleared his throat. "Alan wants to see you."

She straightened her shoulders, crossed her arms, and took a deep breath. "What did he say happened?"

"He let Henry sit up front and that distracted him. Sounds like he jumped the sidewalk and hit a sign. He's pretty shook up. Can you talk to him?"

Isabel sighed, dropping her arms to her sides.

"Of course I can." She patted Henry's hand softly, then left the room.

"Dad," Emily said, "is Alan okay? Physically? I saw he's attached to monitors."

"He says they're worried about his heart. I think his blood pressure's sky high, but no surprise there. He—" George's phone started to ring. "Shit. I get more service calls on a Sunday." He glanced at the incoming call, ready to send it straight to voice mail. The little screen said "Police." What, they were calling to tell him his son and grandson were in the hospital? Yeah, thanks a lot.

"Hello?"

"This is Officer Brandt of the Danforth Police. Is this George Lambert?"

"Yes?" George said. "Is this about Alan?"

"No, sir. Do you live at 907 Cypress Lane?"

"Yes?" Now what, George wondered. Had there been a break-in?

"Are you related to Greta Lambert?"

"She's my wife. What's going on?" George's voice had gotten louder.

"Your wife has been in a car accident, sir. She's been taken to Mercy Hospital."

"What? No, it was my son, Alan. I'm at the hospital now. He's already here."

"No, sir. A Mrs. Greta Lambert was taken to Mercy Hospital."

"What the hell are you talking about?" George

was trying to keep his voice down. Emily was staring at him wide-eyed.

"There was a car accident, sir. Mrs. Lambert is at Mercy Hospital. I would suggest you go there now."

"I'm already here!" he said, confused as hell. He hung up and stood staring at his phone.

"Dad?" Emily was looking at him, concern on her face.

"The police say your mother's here at the hospital," George said.

"What?"

"They said she was in an accident."

"Are they mixing her up with Alan?"

"Damned if I know." George shook his head, strode to the door and stepped out into the hallway, looking left and right until he saw a nurse. "Did a woman just come here in an ambulance? From a car accident?"

"No," the nurse said, "but if it was a serious accident she'd be in the Trauma Center. Would you like me to find out?"

"Where is it?" George barked.

"Through those doors, left down the hall," she said. He started moving and she said, "But, sir, it's a Trauma Center, you won't get very far."

George called over his shoulder, "Emily, I'm going to find out what's going on. I'll be back," and hurried through the heavy swinging doors.

Chapter 10

A FUNERAL ON a bright summer day wasn't right. Great black clouds should be overhead, pouring rain on his misery. Instead George was looking at a profusion of flowers, colorful against lush green grass and the dark exposed soil of his wife's empty grave. Men mopped their brows with handkerchiefs and women fanned themselves with tired hands as they began to gather to lay Greta to rest. Emily, Alan, Isabel and Henry had all ridden in the limo with him, and while George had been talking to the minister, they had formed a row across from him near the grave, and stood looking at the flowers. Isabel was trying to keep it together, he guessed for poor little Henry's sake, who was holding his mother's hand despite his two broken fingers. Alan was holding Henry's other hand. Alan had been withdrawn but focused since his mother's death. He had taken care of everything, funeral arrangements, insurance paperwork, police reports, the lawyer. He was even taking care of Emily, arranging her farm help and restaurant orders. Emily was a wreck, going from crying to angry in the time it took to hand her a tissue, and then she'd be back to crying again.

George watched as Alan put his other arm around Emily. She leaned her head on his arm and George saw a tissue wandering up to her face.

Glancing past them, George saw a young man in a dark suit walking slowly across the grass, looking around. George squinted. He was pretty sure it was Carl. That was a decent thing to do, coming to Greta's funeral. He continued to watch as Carl spotted Emily and stopped for a moment. He clearly didn't want to intrude, and instead continued walking around the crowd. George's eyes wandered away, and he fished in his pocket for a handkerchief. He needed to wipe his forehead; it was too damn hot.

"Mr. Lambert?"

Carl had materialized next to him. His eyes were red, his face tense.

"I'm so sorry, sir. Your wife was a fine woman." Carl extended his hand.

George reached out and shook Carl's hand. "Thank you. It's good of you to come."

"I couldn't have stayed away."

Carl glanced over at Emily, and George did the same.

As they watched, Emily raised her head, looked his way, and then she registered Carl. George saw the look on her face and he knew right then that his daughter still had feelings for Carl, no matter what she said. She flushed but didn't stop staring for a long moment until finally Alan said something to her and she turned her head, then brought another tissue to her face.

Carl exhaled but didn't move.

The last few mourners arrived and George went to take his place with his children, leaving Carl behind. The minister started talking. George didn't listen. The religious mumbo-jumbo was for Greta's sake, not his. He didn't feel comforted by the thought that she was somewhere better. She'd been just fine keeping him company here.

***

Later at the house George did his duty, thanking everyone for coming, offering them food and drink, and accepting their condolences. Couples he hadn't seen since the kids were little came in with sorrowful looks on their faces, expressing their regret at how long it had been since they'd gotten together. Many of his long-term clients stopped by. Small groups of Greta's friends came in together, lips pursed and heads shaking, carrying casserole dishes and plates of food. Some ladies he recognized from Greta's volunteer work when the kids were young; some he knew not at all. Seemed they all knew him though.

Men, George included, had taken off their suit coats and rolled up their shirt sleeves, and women had left their summer jackets draped over the backs of chairs. Bouquets and vases of flowers were everywhere, dotting the tables and lining the front hall. They were pungent in the heat. Alan had set up a few fans around the house, but it wasn't doing much with all the people inside.

Alan was a busy man today, George reflected. He spoke to every person there, shaking hands, kissing cheeks, somber and unsmiling. He hung up a stray coat or jacket when he could, directed people to the food and beverages, graciously accepted the full plates and dishes that were offered and brought them into the kitchen. Sometimes he would check in briefly with Isabel and Henry, who were in the corner of the living room, huddled together in George's armchair. Henry had some crayons and paper with him, but he was right-handed so his drawings weren't much to look at. He was looking at a book about volcanoes, one with lots of pictures, occasionally asking his mother a question. Isabel looked strained. George was sure she and Alan were having problems; every time he saw them they were arguing, although always out of Henry's earshot.

And then there was Henry. Poor little guy. George wasn't sure how much Henry understood about what was going on. Earlier Henry had come up to him, looking serious in his little dress pants and button-down shirt. The splints on his fingers and the bandages on his face only made him look more so.

"Grandpa?" he'd asked. "Why are there so many flowers?" He'd gestured around the house, and George realized it looked like a florist's. He'd finally answered, "People send flowers to cheer you up." Henry hadn't looked particularly satisfied by the answer. He'd only said, "Oh," and walked away. And George wondered, did Henry really understand why the flowers were there? Did he understand that his grandma was gone, that he'd never see her again? Could he even grasp the concept at his age? Did kids understand forever?

George stifled a sigh and put a smile on his face as yet another neighbor came over to give her regards. They'd been on a friendly-wave basis for years, but he couldn't remember the last time they'd spoken. He knew she'd chatted occasionally with Greta though. Her husband had passed away a few years ago. He hoped her name would come to him.

"George, I'm so sorry for your loss. It came as such a shock."

Her name popped into his head just in time. "Thanks, Mary."

"Is there any word on the accident?"

"Blood alcohol levels through the roof. Not his first offense. The lawyer says he's gotten off before. Three times."

Mary shook her head. "Terrible. He should never drive again."

"I agree. But I'm not sure what I can do about it." And whatever I do, thought George, it isn't bringing Greta back.

"But you have a lawyer?"

George nodded. "My son's."

"I think you should pursue it, George. Greta

would want you to get this guy off the road. What if he does it again?"

"That's what the other three people thought, taking this guy to court. Then how bad did they feel when he walked?" He shook his head.

"We regret the things we don't do, George, not the things we do." She patted him on the arm and walked away.

George stared after her, thinking that was pretty philosophical for a lady who spends most of her time pampering her poodles. But he took what she said to heart. What kind of person would he be if he let his wife's killer off the hook? And that's what the guy was, pure and simple: a killer. Alan had been pushing George to sue, and now George had made up his mind. He made a mental note to call the lawyer tomorrow.

As George watched Mary disappear into the crowd, he saw Carl enter the house. They made eye contact and Carl started walking over to George. He was halfway there when out of nowhere, Henry flung himself into Carl's side. Carl scooped him up and hugged him, then set him down and patted his head, pointing at the bandage on his nose and saying something. Henry beamed, showed him the gauze on his temple and the splints on his fingers, and laughed shyly at something Carl said. Then Carl asked him something, Henry nodded eagerly, and they high-fived and parted. Henry snuck a handful of cookies into his pocket before he went back to his mother. Carl's smile lasted until he reached George.

He extended his hand and they shook. "I hope it's all right that I'm here, Mr. Lambert," Carl said.

"Of course it is. I don't know what went on with you and Emily but you knew my wife and you have every right to pay your respects."

"Thanks. Henry seems to be doing okay."

George agreed. "But I'm not sure if he really gets what's going on."

"I miss the little guy," Carl said sadly.

"Sure," George said. "Well, you never know what the future holds."

"The future?" Carl looked cautiously hopeful.

George shrugged. "You never know." He wasn't about to get into specifics, but he'd seen that look on Emily's face and figured the guy deserved a tiny bit of encouragement.

The tiniest bit was all he needed, because Carl asked and George told him where Emily was. Next thing, Carl was slipping into the kitchen, where Emily had been for the better part of the afternoon.

George circulated for another half hour before he spied Carl exiting the kitchen. It had to be a good sign for Carl that he wasn't kicked out in the first thirty seconds. George noticed Carl talking to Alan for quite some time, and then to Isabel, again for a while. He wondered what they were discussing. Probably Emily, he figured. The poor girl was devastated; she was even taking pills to calm herself down. Unfortunately not pills that stopped her from crying.

His thoughts were interrupted once again by Carl. “Mr. Lambert, I’m very sorry, for everything,” he said, extending his hand. “I’m heading out now but if there’s anything I can do, please call me. I mean it.” He handed George his business card. His face was more relaxed than it had been at the funeral, so George guessed things had gone well with Emily.

“Thanks,” George said, pocketing the card. “You could do me one thing right now.”

“Sir?”

“Call me George.”

“All right, George.” Carl smiled and turned to go.

George watched as Carl left. He thought he’d check in on Emily. The crowd had thinned and he doubted she was doing much in the kitchen. He went in and came to a stop. There were plates, cups, saucers, glasses, spoons, forks, and napkins everywhere. Emily was leaning against the counter, her arms hanging loosely at her sides. The dishwasher hummed and a large plastic garbage bag bulged in the corner. The counter was dotted with casserole dishes, plastic-covered platters, and cellophane-wrapped baskets.

“Christ, what a mess,” George blurted out.

“Me or the kitchen?” Emily asked with a wan

smile.

Her eyes were red, her hair curling from the humidity and wet around her forehead, but she looked a little less sad. Maybe it was true what everyone had been telling him, that ceremony helps you move on. Or maybe it was Carl.

"You're a beautiful girl," he said gruffly. "But this kitchen is a disaster. What happened?"

"We just fed a lot of people. It takes a while to clean up with only one dishwasher and one staff person." She raised an eyebrow and looked at him.

"I didn't think you'd be … usually you're … " he looked around helplessly, not knowing what to say.

Emily handed him a dishtowel and pointed at the rack full of clean wet dishes. "How about you help me dry?"

He nodded and took the towel. They dried quietly together for a while and then George said, "Carl came to pay his respects."

Emily didn't say anything.

"I thought that was a decent thing to do."

"It was," Emily said quietly, her voice choking, and then she started to cry.

George put his arm around her and she wept into his shirt for a while, then dried her face on the dishtowel and said she was going to freshen up. Now he had a wet shirt, a bunch of people in the next room, and no help in the kitchen. He sighed, gave up on the dishes, and went back out. The mess would have to wait.

***

Isabel watched as Alan hung up the phone, finishing one of the unending number of calls he'd made since his mother's accident. His hand shook slightly as he crossed off an item on a lengthy checklist he'd taken to carrying around with him. Isabel had never seen him like this. Since his mother's death, he hadn't rested for a moment. He called doctors, lawyers, the funeral home, the insurance company. He took care of every last detail, leaving the rest of his family with nothing to do but grieve. At first, Isabel thought Alan was motivated by concern over his father, but now the funeral was over and Alan couldn't seem to stop. He was pushing his father to sue the drunk driver, calling the lawyer repeatedly with questions about their potential case, and harassing the insurance company to process the life insurance claim quickly.

When he was on the phone or at his computer, he was driven. As soon as he stopped talking or typing, he seemed to collapse in on himself. On the rare occasions when he sat with them for a meal, he didn't speak much to her or to Henry. Dark circles had appeared under his eyes and his face was gaunt. When she tried to engage him in conversation he made only minimal effort, and his eyes strayed restlessly from hers. A few times she'd encouraged Henry to ask Alan to read him a book, but Alan had read with such monotone and disinterest that finally Henry had shook his head, saying, "I don't want Daddy. He can't read any more."

It was Henry's refusal to ask his father for a story that finally broke Isabel. She needed to get through to Alan somehow, so she waited until Henry was asleep and then approached Alan in his office. She had to knock on the door twice before she heard him grunt an acknowledgement. Stepping inside, she saw Alan hunched over his desk, pen in hand, reading what looked like legal papers. A spreadsheet was on his computer screen.

"Alan?"

"Yeah," he said, not moving his eyes from the paper on his desk.

"I need to talk to you."

"Can it wait?"

"No."

He nodded his head slightly but did not look up.

"Alan," she said again, louder. When he didn't respond, she walked over to his desk and put her palm down firmly on the paper he was reading, obscuring his view.

He looked up at her, irritated. "What are you doing?"

"I need to talk to you. Now. It can't wait." She

left her hand where it was.

He leaned away from his desk and turned his body towards her, the chair creaking slightly. “Is it an emergency? Because I’m really busy here.”

She lifted her hand off the desk and crossed her arms over her chest. “An emergency? I don’t know. Does losing Henry count?”

She heard him inhale quickly, then he said, “Are you leaving me?”

“My God, Alan, no! Why would you think that?”

He pinched between his eyes with thumb and forefinger, and sighed, asking, “You said I was losing Henry.”

“I’m talking about how Henry doesn’t even want you to read him a story any more. He says you’re too tired. But I feel like it’s more than that.”

“I’m just busy. There’s a lot of stuff to do when you lose someone. When they die.” His voice strangled on the last word. His eyes wandered back to the papers on his desk.

Isabel reached her hand out. She’d had enough. “Come with me.”

“Do you see all this work on my desk?” he asked, turning toward it.

“Now.” She said it in the tone of voice she used on Henry when he was delaying his bedtime.

Alan blew out a sigh and stood up, ignoring her hand. She turned and went into the living room, sadly surprised that he was following her, pointed to the couch, and said, "Sit."

He sank heavily into the cushion, hands on his thighs, eyes staring up at the ceiling.

She sat on his left, turned to face him, and took his left hand in both of hers. "Alan?"

"Yes," he said impatiently, shifting his gaze to the carpet.

"Look at me," she said.

He finally raised his head and met her eyes. Along with the grief in his eyes was something else she couldn't identify, something that scared her. "What's wrong?" she blurted out.

With alarm she saw tears in his eyes, gathering on his lashes.

"Alan, you have to talk to me. You can't shut out your wife and child." She reached up and gently curled her forefinger under his eyes, wiping away some tears. He jerked his head away violently, removing his hand from hers and swiping at his face. She heard him sniff harshly; he was working hard to control himself.

"I think you should speak with a grief counselor," she said.

He shook his head and wiped angrily at his face again. "I'm fine," he said gruffly. "Christ, Isabel, my mother just died. Can't you give me a fucking break?"

Isabel was quiet for a moment, sensing Alan's anger, not sure how to proceed. "I'm not saying you shouldn't be sad, Alan. But Emily lost her mother; your father lost his wife. They're not suffering like you are, Alan. It's hit you harder. It's nothing to be ashamed of. A counselor would really help."

Finally he said, quietly, wretchedly, "I don't need a grief counselor. I need a jail cell."

"What are you talking about?" Isabel asked with alarm.

"I killed my mother."

Had he lost his mind? Is this what people meant when they said someone was crazy with grief? "Alan," she said, "you're not making any sense. A drunk driver killed your mother."

"Because of me," Alan said, his voice rough. "I'm a horrible person." He swiped at his eyes again. Isabel reached behind her to grab the box of tissues on the end table. Not meeting her eyes, he took a tissue and blew his nose, then took another one and wiped his face. It didn't stem the flow, though, and he sat, weeping silently, hands clenched in his lap.

Isabel didn't know what to do. She wanted to calm him down, to make him stop talking like a crazy man. She put her hand tentatively on his shoulder. "Alan, the stress is getting to you, that's all. Stress can do things to your mind. You're imagining things. You need a rest, a break from all this. Maybe we should take Henry and go somewhere quiet. A cabin in the woods."

"Shit, Isabel, I don't need a cabin." He twisted

his body on the couch so he was facing her. His eyes were hard. "You want me to talk to you? You want the truth? Because you're not going to like it."

Isabel was frightened by the anger in his voice, but she merely nodded and whispered, "I do."

"Fine. Fine." His tone was hard as he nodded, rubbing a sleeve over his face. He inhaled, and said, "I can't stop drinking." He exhaled and paused. "Fuck," he said under his breath, looking away from her. "I snort coke to mask it." Another pause. "Shit." He took another tissue and blew his nose again. "I've been doing it for months. Fucking Carl was right. I used to keep a lot of junk in the goddamn glove compartment. When Henry went to open it, I freaked out and pushed his hand away. I couldn't remember if I'd left anything in there. And that accident was the reason my mother was on the road, so without me, my mother never would have gotten hit and killed. So like I said," he glared at her, ticking off each item on his fingers, "I'm a horrible person, I killed my mother, and I belong in a jail cell. Is that enough truth for you?"

Isabel looked away, reeling from his confession. Alan an alcoholic? Snorting coke? And now he thinks he killed his mother? Could the drugs be affecting his mind?

She sat silently for what felt like hours, trying to fight her way through a fog of feeling, to arrive at some coherent thought. She thought she knew Alan intimately, yet he seemed like a stranger to her now. Was he still the man she thought she knew? The man she'd married? Or had she made a terrible mistake? And what about Henry? Could Alan be a good father to him? But she had married Alan, for better or worse. She thought about their wedding, the two of them facing each other in front of friends and family, vowing to be together forever. What did those vows mean to her now? Could she walk away from him? Was what he'd done unforgiveable?

Finally Alan spoke. "Are you going to leave me?" he demanded. He was staring at her, his body tense, his eyes wild. "You should."

She shook her head, finally able to respond. "No, Alan, I won't leave you. But you have to get some help if you want me to stay. You have to get healthy for all of us, especially for Henry."

"Oh, Henry," Alan groaned, and he put his face in his hands, elbows on his thighs, hunched over himself.

Isabel sat while Alan rocked himself back and forth, wondering what the future held. Finally she put her arm over his back and pulled him toward her. He resisted briefly and then wrapped his arms around her neck and wept into her shoulder for a long time, until finally he heaved a sigh and pulled away slightly.

"I'm sorry. Sorry for everything," he said quietly.

"I know," Isabel said.

"I feel awful all the time."

"I understand why, Alan. But I want you to know that you had nothing to do with your mother's accident. Nothing. Only the drunk driver behind the wheel is responsible for that. And the rest of your problems, we can fix together."

He didn't look convinced but at least he was calm.

She looked at him carefully. "Are you still drinking or using cocaine?"

"No. I haven't touched anything since the hospital. But I think about it every day. Every day." He shook his head. "Pathetic."

"Call your doctor tomorrow and explain the situation. He can refer you to someone."

He didn't respond.

"Alan," she said firmly. "I'll call your doctor tomorrow. I'll get everything sorted. I'm also going to call your office and say you'll be out another week."

He nodded, still silent. He looked depleted, like a balloon running out of air, his face blotchy and his hair disheveled. At least he'd stopped crying. She wondered what her life would be like going forward. Alan would have to tell his sister and father what he'd told her. How would they react? Isabel did not like her life disorganized, but now that she had figured out what to do, she felt better. She couldn't say the same for Alan.

Isabel drove down the narrow road leading to Emily's farm, the air conditioning running full blast. Her jacket lay next to her on the seat and she'd swapped her heels for sandals. She sighed deeply. She wasn't sure how she'd gotten to this place in her life, but it seemed to be the only way forward. She hoped she was doing the right thing.

As she pulled her car over next to George's, Henry came running over from the side of the barn at top speed, dressed in shorts and nothing else. She scooted out of the car quickly, barely having time to stand before he flung himself into her outstretched arms. Holding him tightly as he chattered away, his legs wrapped around her waist and his arms around her neck, she smelled grass and dirt and fresh air and hay and clasped his body to her like a life vest, and thought this, this was the hardest thing she'd ever done. Missing Henry this much was killing her, but she didn't know what else to do.

He pulled back and looked at her, putting a hand on either cheek. "Mommy? Are you listening to me?"

"I'm sorry, sweetie. I was thinking about how much I miss you all week."

"Me too, Mommy." He put his head on her shoulder and hugged her, then leaned back again. "Want to see my party table?"

She put him down and let him pull her past the small line of trees that hid most of Emily's property from her driveway. The picnic table was festooned with a bright yellow tablecloth, plates and glasses in a rainbow of colors, multiple vases of wildflowers, and balloons on ribbons absolutely everywhere.

"Did you help decorate?" Isabel asked, smiling.

"I picked all the flowers. Uncle Carl did the balloons. Grandpa set the table. Aunt Emmy is making the cake. She says we should be party planners."

"You all should be, honey. It looks wonderful. Where is Aunt Emily?"

"In the house frosting the cake. She won't let me see it until it's done. Me and Uncle Carl are playing catch with Grandpa over there."

He pointed and in the distance she could see Carl and George sitting in the grass, casual in cotton shorts and t-shirts, their profiles etched in the sun behind them. They waved and she waved back. "I'm going to see Aunt Emily. You can go back to playing catch. Tell them I'll be over to say hello soon."

Henry raced off and Isabel watched him run. His bandages were off and his fingers out of splints. You'd never know he'd been in an accident except that he hated getting into a car. She had to drive extremely slowly, eyes straight ahead, while he watched her carefully from the back. He swore he would never get in the front seat again. Isabel sighed and turned, letting herself into Emily's house with a knock and a "Hello!"

Emily was at the counter holding a pastry bag over Henry's birthday cake. She was wearing shorts and a tank top, most of which was hidden by an apron that said "Hot Stuff." Her hair was in a haphazard ponytail, and she looked tired. She put down the bag, wiped off her hands, and came to give Isabel a hug. Then she pulled back and said, "Whoops. I think I got some frosting on your skirt."

Isabel shrugged. She had bigger things to worry about than a dirty skirt. "It's headed for the dry cleaner anyway."

"All the same, you look too nice for a blob of green frosting. Let's get off what we can." She dragged Isabel over to the sink, lifted the skirt up, and started picking at it.

"Is everything okay?" Isabel asked. "I hope Henry's not running you ragged."

Emily shrugged. "Just a little insomnia. Nothing to do with Henry." She looked up and said, "I know you want to worry about it, Is, but don't. I'm fine."

Isabel smiled. "Henry showed me the picnic table. It's spectacular. He's so proud. Thank you so much for doing this, Emily. All of it."

"We can't very well skip his birthday, can we?"

"I mean for everything. The whole summer. I don't know what I would have done without you."

Emily wet the spot where the frosting had been. "It's really not a hardship, Isabel. You know that. I think it's much worse for you than it is for me." She took a dishtowel and started blotting Isabel's skirt.

Isabel didn't say anything for fear she'd start to cry. She was in full makeup and that would be a disaster. Everything she was doing was for her family, to make her family whole again. Finally she asked, "How's it going with Carl?"

"Nice change of subject," Emily said, stepping back and pronouncing the skirt as clean as it was going to get.

"I assume he's been around? Not just here for Henry's birthday party?"

Emily nodded and stifled a yawn, picking up the frosting bag and resuming her work. "We've had some pretty heated arguments, but I think we're at a place where we both feel respected."

"I'm glad. Talking it out works, huh?"

"That and he's apologized about a million times."

"Is that all? Alan's up to two million."

"A joke about rehab? Things must be getting better," Emily said.

"It's such hard work, Em. For him and for me. But we're both getting a lot out of the counseling. And he's really trying to change, I can see that. His accident was a big wake-up call." She paused, adding, "And your mother's." Isabel was worried bringing up Greta's accident. No one talked about it in front of Emily, but the rehab counselor had said it was important to address.

Emily stopped frosting the cake for a moment. "Isabel … "

"I'm sorry, Emily, but we can't avoid the subject forever. Alan's counselor says it's bad to stifle things."

Emily nodded, putting down the pastry bag and wiping at her eyes. "I know. But Henry's party isn't the time."

"It's okay to cry about it," Isabel said. "Alan and I cry about her all the time."

Emily's face crumpled and she said through her tears, "I just get so weepy about it, and I hate crying, and so I'd rather not talk about it. Now look at me. I'll be red-eyed and ugly for Henry's party."

She sobbed and Isabel pulled her into a hug, patting her back softly until Emily had stopped. Finally Isabel looked over at the counter and said, "Uh-oh. We can tell them you were crying about the cake. I think they'd believe it."

Emily stepped back and looked over at the counter.

The cake evidently had been lopsided, and the frosting had softened in the heat, bits and pieces of it sliding off in clumps or dripping down one side. The flowers and petals that Emily had so painstakingly applied to the top were flattening and sinking into themselves. At least it was all brightly colored, Isabel thought. It would match the party decor.

"Oh no!" Emily said. "Let's get it into the

fridge!" She picked it up carefully while Isabel opened the refrigerator door and cleared some space, and they settled it in and closed the door.

"Do you think it'll be okay?" Emily asked.

"It'll be fine. No one's going to remember the cake, but we'll remember the party."

"I never thought our own Martha Stewart would be saying that to me," Emily teased.

"Speaking of domestic goddesses, did you bake that cake yourself?"

"I did," Emily said proudly. "I had to buy a bunch of kitchen supplies and ingredients, but I made the whole thing from scratch, including the frosting. I'm pretty sure you're not supposed to make it in two-hundred-degree weather, so that might explain why it's melting. Henry helped with the batter, and Carl helped me figure out how to use the pastry bag. Don't tell Henry, but the whole thing was a giant pain in the butt. Carl figures we spent fifty dollars and four hours of our time. He says we could have gotten ten bakery cakes for that price."

"But the togetherness? Priceless."

Emily smiled. "Listen, I've got to clean up. Why don't you go on out and visit with Carl and George? I know they're both looking forward to seeing you."

"Are you sure you don't need help?" Isabel asked.

"How many hours did you put in this week? Fifty? Sixty?"

"Something like that," Isabel admitted. "But I've added a lot of for-profit clients and my commissions should really pick up. None of which I could have done without you."

"Isabel, for the last time, I love having Henry with me during the week. He's great company, and I think he's having a ball. It's like camp for him. And he gets to spend every weekend with you."

"I couldn't do this if I didn't see him on weekends," Isabel said. "I live for those."

"I've heard about your crazy weekends," Emily said. "Breakfast for dinner, camping in the living room, hide-and-go-seek marathons. Does Alan know about the hell breaking loose at home?"

Isabel smiled. "He suggested a few of his own ideas, but I think a permanent chocolate fountain is going too far."

Emily laughed. "Don't tell Henry about that one, or they'll gang up on you. Tell the boys to fire up the grill in about half an hour, okay?"

Isabel nodded and left, pausing on the porch to take a deep breath. The air was hot, although thankfully not humid. The goats that she could see were lying down, and the tall grass barely moved in the slight breeze. Glad she'd put on a sleeveless blouse this morning, she stepped down into the yard and headed over to the boys.

George walked over to meet her. "It's good to see you, Isabel. How are you?"

"Fine, now that I'm here. I miss Henry so much during the week." She stopped and watched Henry playing with Carl.

George nodded. "He misses you too. But you shouldn't worry, he's having a pretty great time here."

"I can tell." She sighed. "Alan and I are working very hard to get the three of us back together again."

George stared off at the trees and asked, "How's Alan doing?"

"Working hard. Seeing a counselor, both alone and with me. And soon, with you. The counselor thinks it would be helpful."

She watched George's mouth twist a little, but all he said was, "Any time he wants."

They stood together for a few moments, Isabel quietly enjoying the late summer afternoon and the sight of her son rolling around in the grass giggling while Carl advanced on him like a cartoon lion stalking its silly prey.

George asked, "How did Emily seem to you?"

Isabel shrugged. "The same, I guess. Still crying a lot."

George nodded.

"I brought up the accident. Greta's."

George looked surprised. "Why?"

"The counselor said it would be a good idea. That we shouldn't avoid the subject. It's not good for any of us."

Frowning, George asked, "How did she react?"

"She cried. You'd think she'd run out of tears at some point. I wish she'd talk to someone."

"Me too. It sure helped me, and I'm the last guy I ever thought would need someone to talk to."

Isabel smiled. "We all need someone to talk to," she said gently. "And now maybe we've all got each other?"

"Let's not go crazy," George smiled back.

They stood and watched Henry and Carl for a few minutes, then George asked, "Did she say anything about Carl?"

"She says they're back together. Hasn't she mentioned it to you?"

"That was more the kind of thing she'd talk to her mother about. I wouldn't know how to go about it."

"You just ask, like you did with me. You'll get the hang of it. Our counselor says … okay, I saw that eye roll. I suppose you know what he says?"

"He probably says I've got to talk to my daughter more, and everyone else too, right?"

Isabel laughed. "You have a future in counseling, George."

He smiled and they made their way over to where Carl and Henry were now practicing whistling through a blade of grass. At some point this evening Isabel would tell Carl how much Henry talked about him, and how much she appreciated the time he spent with her son. Carl had been very open and direct at the funeral reception, but he'd said some hard things as well. At first she'd been quietly stunned, then angry, but now after everything that had happened she thought she understood Carl's point of view. Certainly she and Alan were both changed, and she believed Carl was as well. She had every hope that someday they would all be good friends again.

***

Emily trundled up the front steps to Isabel and Alan's house. A light breeze lifted her hair off her shoulders. It was uncharacteristically warm for November, not that she minded a reprieve from winter coats and gloves. A few stray brown leaves blew around the porch, where a plastic ride-on toy sat at one end along with a whiffle ball and bat.

"Glad to see Henry's still practicing his swing," Carl said, grinning.

"You have him thinking he's going to be a major league player," Emily said. She shifted her canvas bag from one hand to the other.

"Do you want help with that?"

"I'm fine," she said, irritated.

"Emily," Carl said softly, stopping and putting his hand on her shoulder, "are you going to be okay?"

"I'm not going to cry anymore, if that's what you're worried about." She couldn't help the sarcasm in her voice.

"Emily."

"Sorry. I'm so tired of crying, Carl. I just want to get through this."

They'd barely reached the top step when the door flung open to reveal Alan, looking very casual in a pair of jeans and a flannel button-down shirt.

"Hey guys!" he said. "You're a little later than I expected."

"We had a goat emergency," Emily said.

Alan laughed. "Carl told me all about the goat emergencies you two have."

Damn it, Emily thought, feeling a blush creep into her cheeks. Carl and Alan were getting awfully close. That could only mean major teasing for the rest of her life.

Bruiser was a flash of black banging against Carl's leg as he streaked past them into the yard. "Bruiser!" Alan called, laughing. The dog came racing back, his hind quarters wriggling madly. He turned back and forth from Alan to Emily a few times, barked once, and skidded into the kitchen. They heard him scrabbling on the tile and then thumping up the stairs.

"Sorry, Dad's got him all riled up," Alan said. "He gave him a turkey squeaky toy and I'm pretty sure he's been slipping him cheese. That guy's the worst babysitter ever. Don't say I didn't warn you."

Emily inhaled the tantalizing smells of turkey,

sweet potatoes, and baking bread, handed Carl the canvas bag, and hugged Alan. “Too late. He’s already made it perfectly clear he expects one night a week with the baby.” She rubbed her round stomach. “And to think I was worried he’d be mad because we weren’t married.”

“And the latest marriage plans are what exactly?” Alan asked, closing the door behind them.

“Well, I couldn’t talk her into a justice of the peace up in my plane,” Carl said, giving Alan a hug and a few manly thumps on the back.

Alan laughed and said to Emily with mock surprise, “Why not?”

She rolled her eyes and said, “The current plan is to get married next summer, when the baby’s sleeping through the night. At my house.”

Carl cleared his throat loudly.

“My house that Carl is living in,” Emily said, giving Carl a grin. He elbowed her and she said, “Our house. Saying that takes some getting used to.”

“Wait’ll you’re trying to remember your last name is Strand,” Carl said.

“I never said I’d take your last name,” Emily said, surprised. Was he serious?

“I never thought you wouldn’t,” Carl said, and he seemed genuinely surprised as well.

“Uh-oh,” Alan said. “Can we put off this conversation until later? Please?”

Emily smiled and agreed. She heard the sound of

cartoons coming from the living room. "I'm going to say hi to Henry," she said.

"I'll be in in a sec," Carl said, "right after I put these pies in the fridge. But we will be discussing this later," he added quietly, before he followed Alan into the kitchen.

Yes we will, Emily thought. She couldn't believe yet another argument was looming on the horizon. Her pregnancy had bound them together abruptly, and so far their new relationship had been exciting but also upsetting at times. The fact that they were going to be parents soon was thrilling, but it also gave every decision they made huge import. She hoped that after the baby was born they would fall into some sort of equilibrium. The last time she'd mentioned that hope to Isabel, Isabel had laughed for a solid five minutes.

Emily walked into the living room and saw Henry on his stomach on the floor, surrounded by crayons and paper. He was wearing jeans, a bright green turtleneck, and yellow socks. "Meep-meep" was coming from the TV. She snuck up behind Henry, planning to grab his feet and tickle him, but found she couldn't bend over far enough. By the time she'd lowered herself to her knees, Henry had heard her. He rolled over and sat up, saying, "Hi Aunt Emmy! Look!" He thrust a sheet of paper at her, his hand outlined on it. "We learned how to draw a turkey in school. See?"

“Very impressive,” Emily said.

“And Daddy gave me some feathers to glue on after.”

Feathers and glue in Isabel’s living room, Emily thought. Would wonders never cease?

Henry put his little hand on her belly and asked, “How’s Fafa?”

Emily frowned and waggled her finger at Henry. “For the last time, young man, we are not naming our baby ‘Fafa.’ It’s not a goat!” She reached out to tickle him and he shrieked and fell backward, giggling.

“What’s going on in here?” Carl said, coming in and standing next to Henry. “Someone need tickling?” He bent over and scooped Henry up into his arms, throwing him over his shoulder and spinning around a few times.

“Put me down!” Henry laughed.

Carl pulled Henry back into his arms for a hug and plopped him down on the couch. Then he reached down for Emily’s hands and pulled her back onto her feet.

“Thanks,” she said. “Soon I’m going to need a crane.” She straightened the waistband of her leggings up over her belly and tugged down one of Carl’s oversized sports shirts. Isabel had offered to lend her maternity clothes, but she wasn’t ready for that yet. She was feeling decidedly unattractive as it was.

“You look beautiful,” Carl said.

Emily smiled. She couldn't ask for a more supportive boyfriend. She hadn't even been sure of his response back when she'd told him she was pregnant, but he whooped, hugged her, and then started dancing. She'd forgotten just how much he wanted a family, and he'd already made it perfectly clear that he wanted their child to grow up with siblings.

"Hi Em, Carl," Isabel greeted them as she walked in, giving them each a hug. She had on a black skirt, a low-cut cream blouse, black tights and high-heeled boots. "And how am I supposed to get any work done with all this noise?" she asked Henry, sitting next to him on the couch and pulling him into her lap.

"Mommy, it's Thanksgiving! Do you have to work today?" His little face fell.

"No, I'm joking, sweetie. Grandpa and I were watching some football upstairs." She looked at Emily and said, "Well, I was watching and he was nodding off, as usual. Good game, though."

Emily looked at Carl, who was trying not to look like he was dying to get up there. "Go ahead, babe."

Carl kissed the top of her head and hurried out of the room.

"Are you still working a million hours a week?" Emily asked, sitting down in one of the armchairs opposite the couch.

"Not even close," Isabel said. "I've got enough

clients to make a living on a reasonable forty hours a week. I never could have done it without your help, and Henry's." She squeezed him again and kissed his head as Alan walked into the room. "I missed you so much last summer," she said to Henry.

"Me too," Alan said, walking over and sitting on Henry's other side. "Both of you." He put his arm along the couch around them.

"It's good to see you all in one place," Emily said. She, Carl, Alan and Isabel had become really close over the months she'd been taking care of Henry. They'd all worked hard and it had paid off. "How do you like the stay-at-home dad thing?" she asked Alan.

"Now that Henry's in school, I have all day to putter. Mostly I just watch TV with my feet up, eating chocolates and flipping through the sports channels."

Henry's eyes got wide and he said, "Daddy! You eat chocolates all day?!"

"I was just joking around, Henry. Of course not. And I don't watch TV either. Actually," he said, looking shyly at Emily, "I'm thinking of doing a little financial planning."

"Really?" she asked, surprised. "Back to your stressful job? Are you sure that's a good idea?"

Alan looked at Isabel, who was smiling, and then back at Emily. "The stress came from the workload. But if I'm on my own, I can pick and choose my clients, and limit my hours. I'm going to be my own boss. I'll only work while Henry's at school." He ruffled the hair on Henry's head.

"Are we eating soon?" asked Henry. "I'm hungry."

"Soon," Alan said. "Run up and tell Grandpa and Uncle Carl that they should be down in twenty minutes. My guess is at least one of them will be asleep on the couch, so make sure to sneak up on them and yell 'Boo!'"

Henry jumped down and rushed out of the room, a boy on a mission.

"So what do you think about the financial planning?" Alan asked.

Emily glanced at Isabel, who raised her eyebrows and nodded slightly.

"I guess it sounds like a good idea, on a smaller scale," Emily said.

He leaned forward, forearms on his thighs, looking intently at Emily. "Since I'm starting from scratch, I've been thinking about what kind of clients I'd like. I don't want to work for wealthy elderly people anymore. It's not very interesting, and that was part of the problem. I want to be a little more creative."

Emily smiled. "Creative financial planning? That sounds like what people do when they cheat on their taxes."

Alan laughed. "I want to do financial planning

for people who don't necessarily have a lot of finances. Small business owners, for instance. Maybe they've just started, put a few years in, and they haven't given the future a lot of thought, because they're just struggling to make a profit."

He paused and looked at her, and Emily nodded. She could see where that would be more interesting than working for some rich old farts.

Alan continued, "Maybe they're wholesalers who've started selling their products retail. Maybe in high-end gourmet shops."

He paused again and looked at her, as if she should be saying something. Emily looked back at him, confused.

He sighed and said meaningfully, "It could even be a small business owner who suddenly finds herself pregnant and unable to take a hint."

Emily blinked for a moment and then laughed. "Oh, I get it! Me!"

"Yes," he said. "I'd like to have you as my first client. I'd do the work gratis, and then I'd use you as a reference. I'm hoping eventually I could get a lot of your contacts signed up."

"That's an excellent idea, Alan. Especially because I get free financial planning."

"I partially have Carl to thank for the idea. He told me to forget about all the constraints and just imagine what I'd like to do most, and then see if I could make it happen. So I did."

"That man has potential," Isabel said. "Hang on to him, Em."

"I don't think there's any risk there," Emily said. "I've never seen a man so excited about having a baby."

"If only he could carry it to term," Isabel said.

"Uh-oh," Alan groaned. "I better get out of here before the male-bashing starts."

"Do you need help in the kitchen?" Emily asked.

"Not right now. Ten minutes?"

The two women agreed and he kissed Isabel before he got up and left.

"He seems so much better," Emily said.

Isabel nodded. "He worked really hard to get where he is."

"So did you."

"I had to."

They were silent for a moment, Emily thinking about how she would feel if anyone in her family were threatened. She would do whatever it took to protect them.

Finally she asked, "How's Henry doing?"

"School has been great for him. As for everything else, Alan and I took a hard look at how we were spending time as a family. Too much driving, too little relaxing. It wasn't good for anyone. And you know where that got us."

Emily forced back the tears that suddenly threatened to well up in her eyes. Her midwife had assured her the mood swings would go away, but any day now would be fine with her. "Do you think Henry misses show business?"

"Maybe a little," Isabel said. "But he understands that school comes first. We think we might make it a summer thing. We'll see. He's really happy spending time with Alan right now. They've been learning to cook together."

"Are they any good?"

"They made a stuffed acorn squash for you. I haven't tasted it but it looks good. And Alan brined the turkey himself. Plus he's making a homemade cranberry sauce."

"Geez. Where can I get one of these guys?"

"Alan is going to ask George over because he needs to learn to cook too. Maybe Carl could join them. A big male-bonding experience."

"Can we go to a chick flick instead? I have no desire to watch those boys learn how to cook."

Isabel laughed. "Sounds like a plan."

"What sounds like a plan?" Alan asked, poking his head into the room.

"You teaching yourself, Henry, your father, and Carl how to cook, all at the same time."

Alan looked from one to the other, eyebrows raised. "I don't suppose either of you will be there to help us?"

"Nope," Isabel said. "We'll be off learning how to watch chick flicks together."

"Okay, but we'll be eating the fruits of our labors. Think of that while you're eating your movie popcorn. Now, I could use your help in the kitchen." He walked over and stood between them, offering one hand to Isabel and one to Emily.

Emily was impressed with the disaster she saw in the kitchen. She wasn't really surprised, because Alan had made a lot of dishes from scratch today, but she'd never seen their kitchen like this before. Dirty bowls and utensils competed for sink space with cutting boards and knives. At least four wadded-up dishcloths dotted the counter. Flour dusted spots here and there, and a massive stack of sweet potato peels topped the pull-out garbage can, now too stuffed to close. Above the fray sat Alan's turkey, magnificent and brown, on a huge wooden cutting board. The roasting pan was simmering over two burners. Emily glanced at Isabel, who had taken a deep breath when they first walked in. Now she was looking around wide-eyed, but she didn't say anything. Finally she asked, "What can we do?"

"Can you take care of the gravy?" Alan asked, handing her the whisk. "Everything you need is right there, including the directions. I've already done through Step 4." He slipped a clean brown chef's apron over her head and tied it behind her.

"I'm going to carve here and bring the bird in on a platter," Alan said, slipping a much dirtier red apron over his head and tying it.

"What about me?" Emily asked.

Alan picked up a very long knife and fork and said, "You could grab the rolls out of the oven and put them in that basket." He waved the knife at a woven basket lined with a square of warmly colored cloth.

Emily took a potholder, removed the rolls, and transferred them carefully to the basket. These days she had to really concentrate even when she was doing the most menial tasks. Isabel said it was pregnancy brain. Her goats did not tolerate mistakes well, so she'd had to compensate by focusing like she was a surgeon. When she finally looked up, proud that none of the rolls had landed on the floor, Alan was smirking at her.

"What?"

"You take your roll gathering very seriously," Alan said.

"It's a serious job," Emily said. "You can't have Thanksgiving dinner without the rolls." Then she stuck her tongue out at him.

Grasping the basket carefully, she went into the dining room, which was warm and bright with sun. A golden yellow tablecloth lay under simple red plates, and each cream colored napkin was encircled with a little homemade beaded elastic with a turkey feather tucked into it. Small votive candles and little piles of acorns and pinecones dotted the center of the table. A large glass pitcher of ice water sat off to the side, and simple glass tumblers were at each place setting. Emily solemnly placed the rolls at one end of the table like an offering, and turned to see her father standing at the entrance to the dining room. He had a strange look on his face.

"Dad," she said, moving towards him. "Sorry I didn't come up and say hi." She gave him a hug.

He hugged her back, dragging his eyes from the table to her. "No problem, Em. You get bigger every time I see you," he said. "How's my newest grandkid?"

"Kicking up a storm. Future soccer player."

"You mean football."

"What if it's a girl?"

"You better hope it's a boy. Carl's ready for another major league baseball player. After Henry." He smiled and put his arm around her. "Table looks nice."

"I think Henry had a lot to do with it."

"I don't know. It's about the level of your brother's artistic ability."

They laughed companionably and then her father dropped his arm from her shoulder and fell into silence, staring at the table again.

"Dad? Are you going to be okay?" she asked.

"There are seven plates," he said.

She looked and realized he was right; there were seven place settings. "That's weird. Want me to clear one?"

Her dad shook his head. “Let it be. Maybe Alan did it on purpose.”

“He seems to be doing well, doesn’t he?”

“Yup. Better every day.” He looked at her. “I’ve been over quite a bit lately. Mostly scrounging dinner.”

“Dad, you need to learn to cook a little better. And hot dogs don’t count. Besides, you know you’ve got to stick to your new diet. For all of us.”

He looked at her, and a sadness came into his eyes. He nodded and sighed.

Emily knew that he was thinking of her mother, just like she was. She felt her eyes well up once again with tears, but she dug her nails into her palms and forced them away.

Isabel came in with a dish of sweet potatoes. Emily watched as Isabel placed the dish on a trivet and stepped back, admiring the table. She too paused, observed the place settings silently, then glanced at Emily with a quizzical look. Emily shrugged and Isabel didn’t say anything.

Sunlight glinted off the glass pitcher, creating a prism of color on the ceiling. Carl entered with a cauliflower casserole and, probably sensing the quiet in the room, silently put his dish down. Emily took in his sturdy frame, his fluid movements, and met his dark intelligent eyes as he came closer to her. She felt his presence next to her like she felt her mother’s absence in the room.

Alan walked in with the golden brown turkey, already carved and surrounded by roasted potatoes and onions, nestled on a bed of greens on a crisp white platter. He opened his mouth as if to speak, glanced around the room, looked quickly at the place settings, then quietly put the platter in the middle of the table and moved to stand next to Isabel. He had a confused look on his face, but Emily didn't know if it was because of the extra place setting or because no one had spoken to him. In fact, they'd been silent for so long, Emily didn't want to break the silence.

Finally Henry toddled in, dwarfed by one of Greta's scarred wooden salad bowls filled with crisp bright greens, studded with red pomegranate seeds, candied pecans, and Emily's own goat cheese. His eyes were wide, his mouth open slightly as it always was these days. He was still breathing that way although his broken nose had healed nicely. The doctor said it was habit from the break and he would stop soon. The only other result of his car accident was that all the boys in his class were extremely impressed with the scar under his bangs. Still holding the salad, Henry looked at each of the adults in turn, then at the table.

There really wasn't room for it, Emily realized. She was about to step forward and take it from him when he said, "Grandma won't mind if we put this at her seat." He walked to the table and put the bowl down on top of a plate.

“Henry,” Alan said gently, “Did you set a place for Grandma?”

“Yes, Daddy.”

“But … why?” Isabel asked.

“I miss Grandma,” Henry said simply. “Daddy says she’ll always be with us. So I put a plate down for her.”

George cleared his throat mightily, walked over to Henry and put his large age-spotted hand on Henry’s little blond head. “Thanks, Henry. Grandma appreciates it. And so do I.”

He lifted his hand to the back of the chair next to the salad bowl and said, “Let’s sit.”

Alan said, “Dad? Would you like to sit at the head of the table?”

“That’s your place, son, yours and Isabel’s. I’ll sit here next to your mother.” He smiled and ruffled Henry’s hair before pulling out the chair and sitting down.

As if a spell had been broken, they all started moving, sliding into chairs, putting napkins on laps. When they were all seated, George picked up his water glass and said, “I’d like to make a toast.”

They all lifted a glass and waited. Emily prayed she wouldn’t burst into tears and ruin everyone else’s Thanksgiving.

“To all of us. For helping each other through these last months. I don’t think any of us would have made it on our own. To this family.” He cleared his throat and drank.

They all clinked glasses. As Emily touched hers to everyone else's, she was thankful her dad had kept it short and sweet. She was so tired of crying and feeling sad and missing her mother. She'd been worried about today, about how it would feel to have a family occasion with her mother gone. Would they still feel like a family? Or would they only feel broken? Having that extra plate at the table reminded Emily that her mother's presence was still there, even if she could no longer talk to her. Her mother had only ever wanted them to be the close-knit family they'd become. And if Emily was going to be as good a mother as hers had been, she needed to face her future with an open heart and a clear mind. She let her sadness go. She let her family fill her up.

Lightning Source UK Ltd.
Milton Keynes UK
UKHW022158300519
343634UK00005B/128/P